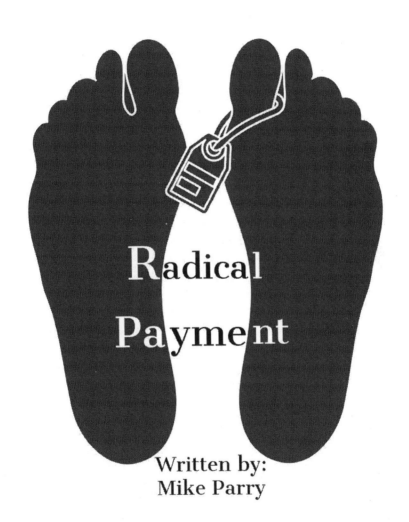

Radical Payment

Written by:
Mike Parry

Published in the United States
by The Creative Short Book Writer's Project
Wayne Drumheller, Editor and Founder
Printing Platform: Create Space
Distribution USA: amazon.com

This book was made possible, in part, by a one-time gift-in-kind sponsorship for book design, editing assistance, and writing encouragement from The Creative Short Book Writer's Project.

ISBN-13: 978-1981645787
ISBN-10: 1981645780

Hell has no fury, like a woman set on vengeance.

- Eduardo Yo

I will never give up the hunt.

- Jack Quick

Solutions always come with a price, not always with a money back guarantee.

- Toby Lipton

Ante up boys, the stakes just got higher!

- Timmy

To have the ultimate reward, you must see it through to the end.

- Archie

I will not be the one with cold feet in the city morgue...

People want to win games, but serious games could mean death!

- Angelina Gear

Mike Parry

TRACEY & DAVID –
HOPE YOU ENJOY THE BOOK!
BEWARE OF ARCHIE...
HE CAME TO PLAY

RADICAL
PAYMENT

[signature]

Mike Parry

Chapter 1

It was a beautiful glorious day, but everyone involved in the project had no clue what the weather was outside. They were inside the lab located in the wilderness, in the middle of nowhere, because they wanted it this way. They wanted to make sure no one could prove what was going on, so that the government had complete and utter deniability if they were discovered. This did not mean there was no security close by; just the opposite. Many people had given up everything for this project: their loved ones, happiness, free time, even the ability to read what they wanted. Everything was controlled by the leaders of this elusive project in the complex. Again, everything was hidden underground in vast tunnels, and the main tunnel to access the complex was heavily fortified by weapons, personnel, and electronic instruments of all kinds and styles. Most noticeably were the magnetometers that were required by the host government, though not one of the scientists understood why they were using them. Anyone carrying out any active item would be dead by the time they reached anything that looked like a small village. All the lead scientists cleared for the project knew these magnetometers would be useless in detecting any radiation if the project was completed.

One scientist, Angelina Gear, had talked in depth with several of the top government military minds to explain her concept, and to get the clearance for *her* project. She had final say in whatever happened, and her head was figuratively on the stone waiting to be beheaded if she failed. She had thought this through every day for the last year as the revenge for her family that was killed many decades ago. She hated that a country, (not her own), could send in enemy troops or teams, and get rid of people covertly and never be held responsible for their actions. This was going to change!

Many people, her military minds, her scientists, and her government told her that her project just had too many moving pieces, and could not be put in place any time in this decade, and possibly not within her lifetime. She refused to listen to the naysayers, some of them still living. She insisted that given her education, her motivation, and her handpicked staff, this seemingly impossible task could be accomplished. Her government insisted that they be kept informed about the project, but even if the project were to be successful, they could not act on her results without proof of concept.

This only proved to drive her harder, as not winning meant death to her and her staff. A partial win would mean the hatred inside her would fester into a long, never-ending battle with herself and her rage. This was not an option.

Now, on this day, the staff were still trying to finish the first part of their project making the new isotope safe. They had discovered a new isotope for a highly dangerous form of radiation that had yet to be balanced and workable. Workable in the sense that one could handle it in a lab environment without dying. All the tests thus far had shown the isotope to be highly unstable. They vowed not to use it for fear of killing their own people. Their scientists were too valuable to accidentally kill. After all, the tests were supposed to be safe for the scientific staff, right? Therefore, her government chickened out, and went with other less hazardous projects.

Angelina decided to give her people a new direction, one that was going to change this project into a workable model sooner, rather than later. She gathered her staff of 21 scientists, and explained her theory.

She had a tube of epoxy on the conference room table because she knew most of her scientists liked visual demonstrations, over white papers, anytime she could find them. She explained that in the tube were two different compounds. Each by themselves were perfectly safe, but once the two substances met, or got mixed, they would dry and set into a very tight bond within minutes.

One of her scientists seemed annoyed and

confused, and asked, "Why are you showing us glue? Did someone break your favorite beaker in the lab?"

Angelina then announced that she wanted to make two separate components that would make this new isotope completely safe and transportable until one component was contacted by the other. Several of her youngest, newest scientists smiled. One even laughed at her.

Without hesitation, Angelina withdrew a 9mm, and proceeded to fire it directly between the eyes of the laughing scientist. In front of everyone she said, "Anybody else think that this is funny?"

Again, her government did not want to waste time, and if any scientist in the project was not completely on board, they were out – *permanently*. Angelina refused to be laughed at for her lifelong dream of revenge.

She then removed a tiny tablet from her lab coat and the box that it came in. It was an appetite control suppressant used in dieting fads. Even *her* country wanted skinny people, although that sounded absurd to the other nations on the planet.

Angelina reminded her staff, "Time release tablets have a coating which will dissolve over time, little by little, to let the suppressant enter the patient's body to prevent them from being hungry. However, the isotope compounds won't have to compete with stomach acid, just air.

"This is the second part of our new task. I want the other component to be a time release activation of the new isotope. One that will be inactive for six months in air before it contacts the other component.

"From now on, we will call it isotope 625, or i625, for all our records. The coating will be a clear coating called cc625. When i625 and cc625 come in contact, the mixture will remain safe for a shelf life of six months. If i625 sits on a shelf in the lab without encountering cc625, it will remain completely safe for decades. The same is true for cc625. It will be safe for decades, even if the coating wears off. However, if i625 and the worn off cc625 contact each other in any state, lethal doses will be in effect."

They all knew the death and destruction they had seen with the new isotope. She looked around the conference room table, met each of the remaining scientists' eyes, and in turn, they saw their boss in a much different light than ever before. No longer happy and approachable, but determined, and full of vengeance.

She opened it up to questions. There were none. The staff had their orders, and now they must complete these tasks.

Chapter 2

Jack was seated at an outdoor cafe; sipping his coffee and watching a street vendor selling breakfast from a cart. He liked to watch this busy, small town, but it was small only in square miles. Jack was in Washington, DC. Every day, he had a routine. From one of 15 of his favorite cafes, he'd sit outside and watch people on their way to work.

Jack B. Quick was a veteran Secret Service agent who had worked several years in various departments. Currently, he was working on discovering high tech counterfeiters, and that was leading to several other problem areas that Homeland Security was considering as well. Homeland Security was a very large organization which was currently trying to recruit computer specialists to help combat cyber criminals who hacked large scale companies and banking institutions. Most notably: big box chains, major credit card databases, and most recently, credit scoring facilities. It was getting to the point where credit cards were no longer safe to use for any purpose. This is the reason Jack bought coffee and most anything else with cash. It just wasn't worth the risk of identity theft and dwindling bank accounts to buy his morning coffee and the occasional fruit salad. It was also his form of surveillance, since he knew most currency was passed at quick locations like cafes and small vendors who didn't want to inconvenience their patrons.

Chapter 3

After several days of having no apparent success, there seemed to be a slight improvement four days later. Angelina's staff discovered that they could mix the i625 with most any compound, and it didn't change the color of the mix. This proved to be a wondrous discovery. They had always thought they would have to add coloring of some kind to disguise the product in its final form.

Angelina called her scientists together again to discuss the project and how they thought they were progressing. Angelina Gear seemed to be more like her original self; content with minor improvements. She sounded like she understood that dictating progress wasn't as easy as simply telling her scientists to do it. Her main topic of the meeting was to encourage her staff by saying, "This isn't a failure, we just now know more ways that it doesn't work." This made the staff much more open and candid about the theories of what they were trying to do, and made everyone feel better about sharing ideas.

Amazingly, it happened as suddenly as a paper cut! One of their youngest scientists found a mixture that made the i625 non-reactive. Angelina's staff proceeded to test the mixture, and over the next week, their tests proved it to be harmless across the board. They made assorted items with the i625, and had it sitting in the open of the top-secret lab, like you'd have a notebook sitting on a desk in a classroom. Now, they just needed to design the matching pencil.

Needless to say, Angelina Gear was thrilled with her staff at this moment in time! She took a sample in a lead box out of the lab to show the military naysayers that had said it was impossible to stabilize i625.

Many of the generals requested that she take the box back to her lab immediately without opening it. At gunpoint, they put her under guard to do just that. If she hesitated, their guards would shoot her on the spot. Her generals thought this was a plan to kill them off when she opened the box to show them it worked. She was angry at herself for not thinking of this idea herself, first. But again, she still needed most of them to carry out the shipment to the United States and make her ultimate plan work.

As she returned to the lab, she found herself obsessing over the stupid, scared men who couldn't think in bigger terms, especially when she was going to hand her research, and all its effects, to them on a golden platter.

Once she was back in her lab, and the guards were gone, she began crafting her request to leave the facility. She saved it to her drafts folder on her email system, knowing that it would be too dangerous to stay in her country much longer. If the generals were thinking of killing her, a successful project would just expedite their plans.

Angelina Gear hated politics just as much as most Americans, but it too was a necessity before going to the United

States. How was she going to get to leave this facility, and carry out her plans without being assassinated by the generals first? She'd give this challenge more thought later. Maybe her college mentor could help her with ideas of escaping to the United States successfully.

Three days later, her scientists had another breakthrough. They discovered how to make the cc625 function as the catalyst it was supposed to be. They still didn't have the time release agent completed yet, but this was the easier part of the project.

Now, one of her staff, forgetting they were playing with death, set down the non-reactive i625, and it momentarily touched the cc625 on the counter.

The other two scientists saw it, and moved the components apart immediately, thinking it wasn't a big deal since they had caught it as it happened. They didn't even mention it in a report, since the two compounds were only contacting each other by a square millimeter for only milliseconds.

Within four hours, all three scientists were dead.

Angelina Gear and the remaining 17 scientists inspected the lab. Fortunately, the lab video showed that the components had touched. Angelina realized that even though the components had been immediately separated into i625 and cc625, the momentary contact was enough to kill the three of them. However, the lab and equipment showed little, or no lasting radiation values in the lab.

Angelina was smiling ear to ear, like the Cheshire Cat, knowing that she had just seen her proof of concept in the death of her scientists. Now, they just had to put some finishing touches on the project and do more testing.

Some of the data they needed tested included:

1) Up to what range was a square millimeter lethal?
2) How long did someone need to be in that range to receive a fatal dose?
3) How long would the active radiation last?
4) How much time did it take to stop radiation once the two components stopped moving, or separated?
5) Could the components be dry mixed?
6) Could the components be wet mixed?
7) Could fire/heat stop this reaction?
8) If burned would it let off toxic gases?
9) Do freezing temperatures effect it?
10) Was there an antidote?
11) Would a typical radiation suit protect against a large dose?
12) How long would the radiation last in years on metal surfaces and in the environment?

Angelina Gear knew some of these answers based on what her military minds already knew, but she had to know if changing the components made a

difference, or not.

Chapter 4

Trent Lester was a director with a major problem. Like many other people, he worked for the United States Government. In his particular case, the Bureau of Engraving and Printing. He had just gotten out of a budget meeting with his bosses. It was the seventh monthly meeting this year, and if something drastic didn't happen soon, he was going to lose a substantial part of his staff. He worked with 600 dedicated BEP people at two facilities in Washington, DC and Fort Worth, TX. These were some of the best craftsmen in the world, and you've seen their work daily anytime you bought something with cash.

Like many other businesses in this radically declining economy, the BEP was also looking for ways to cut costs, improve longevity of their product, and be kind to the environment, if at all possible. If the BEP could make a greener product, they would get a whole lot of good press from the media and activists. Good press was much better than the bad press, of which the government was currently getting way too much of these days.

Trent's department was now just five months from losing 75 percent of its staff, and none of them knew anything about it. It would devastate his department, morale, and make the currency much harder to produce.

Trent Lester decided it was time to stop stalling, and break some of this news to his department, since their heads and families were on the line, not his. He was what they called a lifer, a person so deeply entrenched in policy and political persuasion that he could destroy the BEP, and they would just call him back to rebuild it.

He knew his place and his power in the organization, but even that would not be enough to save his staff, come the end of the year. So, he called a video conference with all his employees, managers, contractors, interns, absolutely everybody.

He opened the meeting with his standard

morning greeting and safety comments, and urged everyone to continue their jobs with the utmost safety. Next, he discussed the monthly meetings, and the decline of the economy. Several people in the audience started to get the real idea of this meeting. Sensing that they were fearful, Trent reassured them there was still time to save everything. It was going to be a momentous task, but he knew they would find ways to cut costs and get greener by the end of the year. The meeting ended on a pleasant, but cautious note, and there were several new team assignments passed out to various managers and staff to evaluate innovative ideas and methods.

Trent saved his best manager, Toby Lipton, for what he thought was the best of both worlds. Toby had been with Trent through thick and thin. Trent had actually bet against him once or twice in the beginning of Toby's career, but soon learned that Toby rose to the challenge. Later that day, Toby met with Trent to discuss Trent's big project. Trent began with the fact that the expense of the BEP ink budget was the only genuine cost savings he could imagine.

Currently, Toby understood that the BEP used approximately nine tons of ink a day to produce currency at the two sites. Toby knew that this ink was very toxic in its liquid form, and he'd always thought there had to be a better way. After a brief discussion, Toby told Trent that he'd look into replacing the dangerous and environmentally unfriendly ink with an innovative ink. Trent appreciated that once again Toby didn't disappoint. Their meeting broke up, and Toby mentioned to Trent that he was still trying to get his pilot's license, but somehow work kept interfering.

Trent smiled and said, "You'll get it soon enough, and if this ink project fails, you'll have plenty of time!" Toby knew Trent was just trying to make light of a serious situation.

Chapter 5

When Toby was in high school many, many years ago, he used to be a big computer gamer. His online handle was Death_Hiding_in_Plain_Sight. However, this pastime dwindled as his days were consumed with college, then his masters, and he was now working on his PhD, not to mention getting a pilot's license. But, recently he missed playing against many of his old gaming buddies. One in particular, was Angel_of_Death. They had hit it off well online, and kept in touch somewhat over the past 20 years, and had recently found each other online again. Toby thought this was just fate giving him someone to talk with who understood him. He didn't even know truly who Angel_of_Death was, but he thought it was a female about his age.

Angel_of_Death knew who Toby was, and had followed his career closely over the past twenty years. She basically fell in love with his online name, thinking it was really cool back then. That was the only reason she had contacted him online. Now, it was just plain groovy!

Later that night when Toby Lipton got home, he threw his keys on the counter, got a cold drink, and fired up his computer. At that point, he started looking up environmentally friendly commercial inks. As he was typing, unbeknownst to him, his computer was logging all his searches into a file that Angel_of_Death would review later at her convenience.

Later, while Toby was on the computer looking up information about the environment, and searching press releases about other companies going green, he got pinged. Angel_of_Death was wondering how things were going, and if he'd completed any more tests for his pilot's license.

Toby took a drink, and began to inform his friend that his day was the typical boring day, and that if things didn't change, he might lose his job by year's end. He then proceeded to say that his piloting dreams would be put on hold until he gets a handle on his new assignment at work.

AOD suggested he just quit, and come rescue her from her country and dead-end job, too.

Toby was curious now, he'd always thought she was in America, too. He took a chance, and asked her to reveal some details. She revealed she thought he lived in Canada, and that he should come to California and rescue her. Then, she decided that they had discussed too much, and she wasn't happy about sharing that much.

He understood, reluctantly, but their whole friendship had been sketchy at best. She signed off, but first told him she was almost ready to start sharing details, just not yet.

Toby Lipton smiled to himself, and knew this was progressing slowly, but he could wait. After all, 20 years was a long relationship, and he wanted to get this one right.

Chapter 6

Now the lab in that far off distant place was buzzing with activity and testing. They had discovered that the time release substance was fairly easy to get access to, and it also didn't have a color associated with it. This meant they could produce cc625 as a clear coat, like you would for a modern car or a wooden picnic table. Only, when their clear coat wore off, it would mean death to millions of guilty people. Guilty in the sense that Angelina Gear believed all Americans knew and approved of what their government did in other countries.

Now that the cc625 was being produced, they had made several discoveries on the timing of their product. If the cc625 was dry, the wear time was dead on at six months. If the cc625 got water on it and then dried, it was much shorter of a duration, on the order of 3-4 months. If, however, the water stayed in contact with the clear coat indefinitely, then the cc625 wore off in as little as two weeks. Lastly, they tested treated water. This water could contain salt or chlorine such as found in pools, fountains, and theme parks. The cc625 did not adapt well to either. In most cases, it dissolved within a week. But, if the chlorine was high, or the pH level was off in pool water, the cc625 all but melted away instantly. This meant theme parks with water attractions could be the first to see victims of the i625.

Several of Angelina's staff were curious what application this was going to be used for in the military. Most of her staff knew the radiation was deadly, but they had all thought it was being developed for a specific military reason.

Angelina Gear was now reading more emails and computer logs of various sources, trying to figure out how best to get her i625 into America the fastest way possible. She knew there would be other deaths related to the American attack, but that couldn't be helped. Besides, those countries were not too friendly either, so no harm, no foul.

Angelina got a message from the most

senior ranking General at the facility, and was scheduled to have a face to face with him and his staff at 3pm. When she arrived, she didn't detect the hostility she witnessed two weeks ago. She wondered what had changed. The General started with an apology before starting the meeting. This shocked Angelina, and she still sensed no danger, but instantly put herself on guard. Feeling in her lab coat for her 9mm, a friend in times of anger and danger, she kept her eyes locked on the General and other eyes in the room.

The General then asked how progress was coming after the death of her three scientists. She was cautiously optimistic, and said that there still were some major hurdles to pass. Basically, she lied. Right now, she was ready to go into mass production with both the i625 and cc625, but she did not say that. She did, however, say that she and her team needed much more of the military's new isotope to continue the testing.

The General waved his hand at the staffer, and asked if three tons was enough for now.

Angelina almost fell over, but understated, "It's a start."

The General told her it would be in the lower vault within 24 hours. Angelina Gear couldn't believe what she heard. How much of this dangerous substance did they have?

The General then surprised her again by saying they had over 200 tons to dispose of safely, and soon.

Up to this point, Angelina's scientists had only used 1.5 pounds to make two tons of product. As far as she was concerned, this was an infinite supply!

America was not going to get away with murdering her family, and she would become Angel_of_Death sooner than she had planned.

Angelina contacted her comrade in California by email, and said that Phase I had been achieved, and to start preparing the California site for the project. Soon, they would be receiving i625 and cc625 to be mixed with the other new products. They would need a vast storage facility to hold dry contents of i625 and cc625, and to make sure the warehouse humidity system and sensors were in place and active. It wouldn't do to have a moist product, ever.

Chapter 7

Toby Lipton had been using the last two weeks to investigate samples of "green" inks. He and his team found out surprisingly, that going "green" was going to be exponentially more expensive than the present system of printing. Also, their tests showed that the "green" inks were nowhere near as durable as the toxic ones. Many of the ink manufacturers corrected the durability issue with a clear coat that was double the cost of the "green" ink price. Going "green" was very expensive. It would be cheaper in the long run to buy a newspaper, hire writers, and write good press about the new money, and lie. To Toby, this was an ethical point, and the boy scout that he was would never consider this tactic.

So, he finished his day, and went home early to try to solve this puzzle. While he was at home, he got pinged again by Angel_of_Death. Delighted to hear from his old friend, he quickly accepted the chat. He began explaining that he was tired of hitting brick walls, and that there had to be a better solution to his troubles at work.

AOD was happy that he was starting to confide about his work to her. She listened patiently, like a friend who knew nothing of Toby's problems. When he paused for her response, she asked, "Have you looked internationally for a solution?"

He had, but that had inherent risks, too. He typed, "If the outside nation is an ally, it's sort of doable, but probably too much red tape to get an international supply set up that's rock solid on logistics and raw materials. If the outside nation is an unfriendly government, it's definitely out of the question, because they might be able to counterfeit the currency, and we have enough threats on that front already."

Angelina knew that she would have to take this conversation slowly as to not spook him. So, she asked, "Who in the US have you been working with on the ink testing?"

Toby replied with the answer she expected. "We have dealt with all the major printer and copier manufacturers, and none of them will save the BEP any money. They will raise the current budget from $719 million to about $3 billion."

AOD typed, "So what? You work for the government. Just ask for a bigger budget."

Toby started to lose it, and started typing in all caps, "THAT'S WHAT GOT US HERE IN THE FIRST PLACE! IT'S NOT AN OPTION ON THE TABLE."

AOD said, "OK, OK. It was just a thought." Angelina smiled to herself and typed, "I have a friend in the ink business, if you'd like me to make a call. It's probably a dead end, but what do you think?"

Toby couldn't believe his eyes. He blinked, "What kind of ink business?"

AOD replied, "He's the number one refill ink provider in the US, and all his ads run in the back of the computer magazines to get people to buy refill kits which are much cheaper than buying the original manufacturer's ink cartridges. The quality in the last eight years has improved, so that he has a 200% satisfaction guarantee. If you don't like his product, he'll refund your money, and buy you an original cartridge instead."

Toby said, "Damn! ...and he's still in business?!" He continued, "It can't hurt. Please make a call, and send me the information." Toby couldn't believe his luck, and refused to get his hopes up. But if this was true, it would mean this guy would be indebted to Toby for taking his business from maybe $4 million per year to off the charts. Now, the Secret Service would be called in, but he was getting ahead of himself.

AOD made some small talk, and soon said, "Good night," and signed out.

Toby thanked her for the information and for trying to solve this problem for him. He hoped in his heart that he would meet his old friend in person someday.

Angelina Gear sat back in her lab office chair and screamed, "YESSSSS!!!!" She still had a billion items to plan, but soon the project would begin for real. A shiver went down her spine, and she started making plans to visit California with 267,000 tons of the modified i625 and cc625.

Chapter 8

Jack was sitting at his desk going through his daily emails, when he came across a new assignment. It was to follow up with a bank in Oregon about a suspicious note they found in an ATM deposit. The machine had flagged it, because there was no security thread embedded in it. This was not all that surprising, since people held on to money for years, and years, stockpiling it for emergencies, vacations, trust funds, college, a new car, house, fancy dates, prom, weddings, and anything really. There is usually a mix of old and new money. So, it was not unusual to find non-threaded styles, since there was much more out there that they hadn't yet recovered, or replaced.

The federal reserve banks had the tasks of replacing money over time, when they found worn money, or really old money that was not threaded. They caught most of it, but now the newer, more advanced ATM's pulled out the non-threaded type to a specific questionable stack for the local banks to examine.

After the operator at the bank in Oregon, most likely a teller, examined the stack, she noticed an anomaly on a hundred-dollar bill and flagged it. That bill got sent to the bank's central office branch, and they reviewed her findings, and noticed it looked like 800 others they had found in the surrounding areas. Then, that bank forwarded all their suspicious funds to the local federal reserve, which checked each bill again, and then flagged the local Secret Service branch. Their findings were forwarded to the Washington, DC offices where they got assigned to Jack for follow up.

First, Jack requested all the banks' ATM video footage be sent with each note that was deposited. He was thinking that to save time, the submission form for crimes over $50K should have a prerequisite to collect video. Local agents could start tracking these idiots faster themselves. But, this was DC, and the bureaucracy meter was off the charts here. Washington wanted to be kept informed of everything, and giving the local agents this power would be crazy to them.

Jack had grandiose ideas. Someday he would be in charge of the Secret Service, and then he could make some meaningful changes.

This video request would take several hours, so he decided to answer all other emails of the day, and then go to the racquet ball club before going home for the night. As he was walking to the club from the office, his mind couldn't release the $80K found in Oregon. It probably was a drug deal, where one side was trying to rip off the other side, and they had no idea that they had been cheated. This was the most likely scenario for sums of this kind, but why Oregon? Well, drugs were everywhere now, and counterfeiters followed the drugs faster than local police departments, or the Drug Enforcement Agency arrests.

Jack disliked working with other agencies because their bureaucracy was so much worse than his, it was hard to believe.

Also, there were usually undercover agents involved, and that complicated things even worse. Counterfeit bills were often used to trick drug dealers working with undercover agents, because playing with fake money was far easier to convince your boss to put at risk than the real thing. If something went wrong, you had one less headache than explaining to your chief that their budget needed to drastically increase to cover the missing funds.

Jack played astoundingly well for the thoughts running laps in his head. Maybe the thoughts of whacking these idiots with a racquet ball helped him place his shots. His opponents all accused him of taking lessons from a pro recently, because he was on fire tonight. At $20 a game, he was up $100 for the night! Exhausted, he just waved good night, and hit the showers.

Walking home, he decided on a nice rare steak, a baked sweet potato, and green salad with tomatoes, carrots, peas, pickled beets, and bread and butter pickles for dinner with a Dr. Pepper® to wash it down. Life was good for this Secret Service

agent.

He hoped the video would be clear and present when he got to work tomorrow morning. He hated waiting for things, like at the doctor's office, for laundry to finish, lab results, waiting for others to be on time, military deployments, and loved ones to return.

Chapter 9

Now back in the well-hidden foreign lab, Angelina Gear and her staff of scientists were developing a very efficient assembly line to modify i625 and cc625 in bulk quantities. Angelina had now requisitioned 100 tons of the deadly material, which had produced 267,000 tons of the deadly binary product with the time release cc625 in vacuum-sealed containers that prevented the countdown from beginning.

Angelina overnighted a sample containing ten pounds of i625 and cc625 to her comrade in California. She had discussed with him at length the tests that she thought the BEP would run on the samples for duration and longevity for the new inks. Finally, her plan was coming together!

Eduardo Yo, everyone just called him "Yo" for short, was a happy, take things as they come, kind of guy. It was hard to upset Yo, and even harder for him get visibly angry over details, at all. This served him well in the refill ink business, because some customers were very demanding when it came to the quality of his inks. Some had even tried to get ink for free using his 200% ink guarantee against him.

Yo loved to travel, and to prove his product was the best. He had never lost a claim yet. He was a hero salesman to his clients. If they were having any difficulties with his ink, he would hop in a car or plane, and go see their application(s). By physically being on site, he was able to show them where in their process the ink should be applied. In most cases, it was as simple as making the items dry before inking them. If the process had to be done wet, they'd need a clear coat, which he usually threw in for free to satisfy the grouchiest clients.

This *go get 'em* kind of attitude allowed for on the job training, which he kept very clear and meticulous notes on. If he ever had to revisit a site, he knew exactly where in the process it had worked before. This trait was going to prove invaluable for Angelina Gear's upcoming project. Now, if they could only convince Toby Lipton to accept their modified new "green" inks, the project would be underway!

Yo waited for the samples to arrive. Angelina had overnighted ten pounds of the i625 and cc625s, which she told him stood for sample. The truth was, cc625s was a modified cc625 without the other active ingredient, to make sure the inks never got radioactive, *ever!* She wanted the BEP to do their worst on the samples without giving them any reason to discover any problems with their inks. Once the tests were completed, she would be able to send the original product, *undetected.*

It was amazing how fast things progressed after the samples arrived. Yo had already spoken to his ink manufacturers, and discovered that ordering much larger quantities of refill inks would not be a problem at all. In fact, Yo was going to be able to make much more profit on large shipments than he could believe. He should have done this years ago in his personal business, because there were no expiration dates associated with his inks, and at these quantities they were practically giving away the base inks.

It was a lot like a mega store example. You could buy a small jar of pickles for $2.98, or you could buy the monster jar of pickles, that equaled 20 small jars, for $4.25; the only issue being, did you have enough storage space in your house to buy it?

His mobile phone rang and instantly made him focus. The caller ID read "BEP". Yo took a deep breath, and answered the call.

Chapter 10

Angel_of_Death was chatting with Toby Lipton again this evening. Earlier, she had passed Eduardo Yo's contact information to him. Toby had thanked her, saying that he hoped this would be a quick and easy solution, since none of the other ink manufacturers were interested in negotiating their contract prices with the BEP. They too, thought they could get rich off the deep pockets of the government agency.

Toby and AOD chatted online for about 30 more minutes, and then disconnected.

Angelina Gear was now deciding which five of her scientists would get to live past the end of the month. Soon, they would have the other 267,000 tons of product ready to be shipped to California. At which time, she along with five staff members, would go to America to support the delivery of the new "green" ink system, wherever it took them.

The remaining scientists would move on to

other military projects controlled by the Generals upstairs. Again, she thought that the Generals would just sever ties at once, but she wasn't entirely sure. They might keep the remaining scientists, and pick their brains forever. After all, they were *hers*, and they were the best and brightest in her country. A mind is a terrible thing to waste, literally.

Angelina looked in her drafts folder, revisited the request to go to America, and modified it to include her top five scientists. Later, after the request was approved, she would have a meeting with her entire staff, and break the good *and* unwelcome news.

Now, she just had to get the materials shipped to America in several container ships, and begin packing for the trip. Soon, she realized that besides the old photos of her family and her computer, she needed nothing else.

Much to her surprise, the Generals' approval for both requests popped into her email box. Both were fully approved and signed! The rest was up to her. Angelina Gear was going to America to work with her team and Yo!

By the middle of the next day, Angelina had copied all the technical data about the i625 and cc625 to her computer. She had also made a backup copy for the remaining team, and another one for the Generals to examine after her departure.

While this had backed up, she had revisited the testing and evaluation of the components. Here are her ultimate results:

1) **Up to what range was a square millimeter lethal?**

   1 meter

2) **How long did someone need to be in that range to receive a fatal dose?**

   Less than 0.1 second - you had about four hours until death

3) **How long would the active radiation last?**

   Until the material stopped moving or being bent

4) **How much time did it take to stop radiation once the two components stopped moving or separated?**

   It was nearly instantaneous

5) **Could the components be dry mixed?**

   **Yes. Very stable
   (Lethal in six months)**

6) **Could the components be wet mixed?**

   **Yes. Very unstable
   (Lethal in two weeks, less if treated)**

7) **Could fire/heat stop this reaction?**

Not usually - most remains were at least one square millimeter

Yes! If vaporized! **See gases!

8) **If burned would it let off toxic gases?**

Yes. If atomized, airborne radiation was lethal for ten miles unless encased in lead

9) **Do freezing temperatures affect it?**

Yes. Cold seems to pause radiation (below freezing)

10) **Was there an antidote?**

Death! Or freezing temperatures will pause the effects

11) **Would a typical radiation suit protect against a large dose?**

Single item exposure = Yes (1-10 items)

Multiple items exposure = No (11+ items)

12) **How long would the radiation last in years on metal surfaces and in the environment?**

metal surfaces = 150+ years

In Env: non-moving item forever = non-reactive

In Env: moving or bending forever = reactive

In Env: airborne = 150+ years

Angelina Gear breathed a sigh of relief and victory. This scary stuff would definitely do a number on Americans!

Half an hour before the end of the day, she

called her staff into the conference room. There was champagne on the table for everyone. She thanked all of them for their demanding work, and announced to everyone they were moving on to Phase II. Her five would go with her to California, the others would be reassigned to a brand new lab facility closer to Hong Kong, where they would restart their lives.

At each setting at the table, there was an envelope containing $500K in the old style US bills, without security threads. The scientists who were going to America noticed they were given $1M. Everyone celebrated for hours, congratulating themselves for their remarkable work!

The next morning, Angelina and her team went to the airport, as the Generals had arranged. The other scientists were taken by train to the new lab facility to get settled in. After their train ride and orientation to the new lab, they would fly into Hong Kong for a month-long vacation. Shocked, but delighted, none of them realized that the $500K was counterfeit. The Secret Service was going to go crazy!

Chapter 11

Yo answered his phone. "Hello, this is Yo. How can I solve your problems today?"

Toby was surprised, but instantly liked the voice on the phone. Maybe it wouldn't be such a long shot after all. "Hi, my name is Toby, and I would like to discuss the ink solutions that you offer."

Yo immediately liked Toby; he got right to the point. "Sure, let's talk."

Toby first inquired about the "green" inks that were available, and asked how long Yo had been in business. Each answer seemed better than the previous one. Instead of a lot of chuckles that he got from the major ink guys, Yo answered honestly and very seriously, qualifying follow up questions. Toby asked how durable Yo's "green" inks were.

Yo informed him that these inks had been tested by the most demanding manufacturers. Whatever didn't work out of the bottle could become useful by adding a proprietary clear coat, which Yo had developed out of necessity. He asked Toby if he had ever seen Tyvek®.

Toby almost dropped his phone. He couldn't believe his ears, and he would need samples. When Toby recovered, he asked, "How much is this clear coat?"

Yo announced, "Free, with the purchase of my inks!"

At this point, Yo could have named his price, and Toby would have signed off on it immediately. But, there was much to be tested and proven before they made this guy a billionaire, Toby thought to himself. He asked Yo to send samples to his office in Washington, DC.

Yo, surprising him yet again, offered to come meet with Toby and his staff to answer any questions they had about his products' longevity, pricing, and environmental data. Yo said that he could be there in two days. Toby couldn't believe his ears again.

This being Thursday, they set up the

meeting for 10am Monday. Toby asked Yo to be available through Wednesday night.

Yo just grinned from ear to ear, and said, "Absolutely!"

They thanked each other, and ended the call. Yo immediately saved the name and number on his smartphone, and assigned a personal ringtone, "Money" by Pink Floyd 1974, to the number so he would be alerted when Toby called back.

Chapter 12

Trent Lester was having another meeting with Toby Lipton. It had been three weeks since their first chat about the recent cost savings project. Trent was hoping for some crucial information to report in his monthly meeting. The news he received from Toby was not the stellar information he was hoping to get.

Toby explained that all the major ink manufacturers were being defeated by the "green" inks, and they were turning out to be very cost prohibitive.

When Trent asked for details, he found out in short order that the ink budget would shoot upwards of $3B more than they were currently using. He also asked if Toby had offered incentives to the major ink guys to work with them on an innovative technology, and give them patent rights in exchange for a lower cost product.

Toby confirmed he had, and again the ink guys turned him down flat. Their suggestion was to ask for a bigger budget from Congress, and they had mentioned something about "you cannot dictate new 'green' technology because you want it." Then, Toby dropped the other shoe on Trent. All the major ink guys were having a durability issue with the "green" inks, which required a clear coating to be applied. This coating was going to cost an additional $6B to purchase.

Trent shook his head, and almost shouted, "Thieves!" Trent knew Toby had something else, because he was not one to bring up a problem like this without having a place to go. So, he bit his tongue, and waited for Toby to save the project.

Toby then told Trent about a Hail Mary play that he was investigating. It was a long shot, but if it worked out, the BEP would have their own supplier, and keep the patents classified, too.

Trent immediately knew Toby had pulled another rabbit out of his hat, and smiled. This is why he kept Toby Lipton employed. Toby thought outside the box. In fact, that gray line, way the hell out there, just over the horizon, was one edge of the giant box!

Toby unveiled his story about an old college friend that he was talking with, and how one thing had led to another, and soon they were talking about technology. He had mentioned his ink problem in general terms, when his friend suggested he look internationally.

At this, Trent visibly cringed, and interrupted Toby. "That's really a bad idea."

Toby raised his finger, and said, "I'm not finished, let me explain."

Trent looked dubious and dejected, but gave Toby a wave to proceed, thinking Toby would be up and flying before his staff would get their first severance check in the new year.

Toby said, "I have set up a meeting with a California based company that sells ink refills for inkjet and laser printers. The owner's name is Eduardo Yo. This guy shows real promise. He will be here next Monday at 10am. I have requested our

staff, and Jack Quick from the Secret
Service office, to run some preliminary
stats and background checks on Eduardo
and his multimillion dollar business. I
know it's way outside the box, but he says
he can handle the job, and we won't be
disappointed."

Trent looked like Toby had lost his mind.
He asked, "What about the ink pricing, and
the coating?"

Toby just smiled, and said, "All we need to
do is buy his ink, and he'll give us the
coating free!"

Trent's jaw hit the floor. "Please put that
meeting on my calendar, and have a great
weekend, Toby."

Chapter 13

Angelina rang the bell at the ink facility and warehouse.

Yo turned on his smartphone, and saw an Asian lady standing in front of the reinforced war door. "Yes, can I help you?" he asked. He had never met, or seen a picture of Angelina Gear, but knew she could arrive any day now. Just to be safe, he waited for the confirmation phrase.

She responded, "Have you inked the deal yet?"

That was the exact phrase he was looking for, and buzzed her inside. The lobby was sparsely equipped with two chairs, a dingy leather sofa, and a coffee table filled with computer technology magazines. At the end of the short hall was a bathroom.

Yo accessed the intercom system from his smartphone, and said aloud, "I'll be up in a minute. I'm in the back of the warehouse." Then, he clicked off.

There was also a very out of place teller window with 2" thick plexiglass for a receptionist to sit behind. Angelina looked inside, and saw a computer, a monitor - turned off, an office chair, and a steaming mug of coffee that looked like it had just been poured.

Yo hopped into the gas-powered golf cart, and raced to the lobby door, another war door, to greet Angelina. The door slid silently open on its 2-ton hinges. Angelina looked at the door, and smiled approvingly. The office and warehouse had been built to incredible standards. She had written the new specs, but not the old ones. It had cost a mint of money, but then again, they may have to live and defend themselves behind these walls.

Angelina introduced herself to Yo, explaining that the other scientists would be arriving in a week or so. Then, she asked if the facility was ready.

Yo decided this was the time to give her the tour. Passing the war door into the office space on the left side, Yo said, "We have 12 individual suites with full kitchen and bathroom facilities." On the right side of the long hallway were state of the art offices next to the fake receptionist office. Each office had a desk with a networked laptop, a docking station, two 27" LED screens, a keyboard and mouse, a chair, speakers, video cameras, a color laser printer, and a speaker phone with a wireless headset. Next to the speaker phone, there was a little box that had big green and red lights on it. The green one was marked TRUE, and the red one marked FALSE. The name on the box read: VoiceStressAnalyzer. The headsets and Wifi were networked all throughout the vast offices and warehouse spaces with 100 Gb bandwidth.

Outside the offices, there was a large common area, with a full kitchen, bathrooms, two large format color copiers, and what looked like a huge color computerized press. There were three state of the art video conference rooms. One looked like a boardroom that held maybe 100 people. The other two looked like they could hold 50 and 20 people, respectively. The rooms had been named: Franklin, Grant, and Jackson. The White House would have liked to have this much secured space and technology within it.

Angelina seemed happy, but not necessarily impressed, until Yo opened the communal area door leading to the secured warehouse.

Now her mouth fell open. There were four state of the art large capacity elevators (20 ft. X 80 ft.), one in each corner of the huge warehouse. Each one of these units could lift a fully loaded semi-truck and trailer up to one of the five levels of the warehouse. Each level could hold and carry 100 fully loaded trucks.

Angelina knew the specs on the walls were able to withstand a nuclear blast from a World War II bomb. The Government had built this bomb shelter facility in the late 1940's, but had mothballed it in the early 1970's, and had been trying to get someone to buy it for decades. When Yo saw it, he knew he'd have to spend more money than they had planned, but for a bomb shelter, it wasn't bad, both in condition, and price. They spent $710M initially on it. Then, added another $400M to modernize it. The toughest part was reinforcing the walls and ceilings to withstand the i625 specs, should the United States figure out how to reverse engineer it, and turn it on them.

On the outside of this shelter, there were functional railroad tracks that could, and would, deliver loaded truck containers to the facility. The Government had recently thrown in a container hoist system to move the trailers off the train and into the overhead rail system inside the shelter. Yo had asked the realtor why they had done this to sweeten the pot. The realtor had replied that they didn't want the deal to fall through, since it had been the biggest complaint during the negotiations.

Angelina Gear just smiled at Yo, and again using her understatement ability said, "It will do."

Chapter 14

Jack Quick arrived at work early Friday morning, sat at his desk, and immediately opened his email. He first noticed a request from Toby Lipton, his contact at the Bureau of Engraving and Printing (BEP). It was asking for a background check on an Eduardo Yo in California.

Jack just muttered, "It never fails. I should be wrapped up in this counterfeit ring in Oregon, and now they need me to do a check on some schmuck, and have it ready for 10am on Monday. Gee whiz, give me a break!" Jack thought about writing back to Toby, and telling him he had real work to follow up on, but he knew BEP service trumped his minor case. He knew Toby had every right to ask. Nevertheless, he'd prefer to chase criminals than to run reports on people.

Jack was a worker bee who needed to get out of his stuffy office, and the thought of the BEP meeting on Monday was even stuffier. The BEP were always so strict and uptight, it was hard to get most of them to smile in a meeting, much less laugh.

Jack found this Eduardo Yo's Social Security number, and put it into his computer search routines which requested any and all data on Yo, his business, and associates. He also requested all business assets to be reported. Jack checked the box on the computer for international data as well. He knew this request might take up to half an hour to generate, so he decided to peek at the counterfeit updates.

"Good grief!" Jack exclaimed. He was astounded at how much video footage they had already collected. Scans of the counterfeit bills were linked to bank ATM and lobby cam videos where all the bills were turned in. Out of 80 bills discovered in the last two weeks, they had tracked down 46 occurrences, all with linked video. In almost every video clip, the bills had been deposited by underage males who appeared as if they had just left football practice, or something just as physically demanding. Almost all of them had a big bottle of water in one hand, and a deposit slip in the other. Some were in a bank lobby, others at the ATM, and several were in vehicles with a parent or guardian. (Too bad the plates weren't captured on the videos.) The banks had all the contact information for every account listed.

Chapter 15

Breaking News! flashed across the TV screen that Angelina Gear was watching at the shelter. She was sitting in the common area, relaxing for a few minutes. She had turned on the financial channel to see what was new in her country, now that she wasn't there. The channel had *Breaking News!* scrolling across as a teaser line, but no information yet, so she changed the channel to the cable news network for real details.

The newscaster was describing another data breach that made the credit scoring breaches look minor and insignificant. Apparently, some international hackers had stumbled onto the credit card encryption keys for all the major credit companies' networks. These keys changed on a minute by minute encryption key system, which meant every minute, the old key was replaced with a brand new one. This code was embedded into all the credit card swipe machines. Basically, if anyone, anywhere swiped their credit card at any store in the world, as soon as that store, or vendor uploaded the transaction data in the machine it would be sent out encrypted. Some big chains held onto the data, and dumped it all at 2 or 3am, when local bandwidth had less traffic on it. Others uploaded the information in real time, which only got to the hackers faster.

Not only did this affect retailers, but also ATM systems, smartphone credit card readers, and any other credit systems such as Wall Street stock exchanges, not to mention any other countries that were on the same network. Most international networks had standardized on the systems based in America or Europe, thinking they were much more secure. At this point, most third world countries did not have the funds necessary for the fees with such networks, so they were relatively unaffected.

Once the hackers had the encryption key sets, they could watch and record the encrypted data streams. Then, at their leisure, they could read the data stream like reading the soccer scores on a sports page.

The newscasters were telling people this would take several weeks to remedy, maybe longer. They suggested going to your local bank, and arranging a manual withdrawal of your funds. However, this threatened to be a run on the banks, and that hadn't happened in decades.

The President of the United States was discussing options with his staff, but none of them offered any get out of jail free cards on this issue. It was a nightmare in the making.

Angelina Gear just sat back and smiled that Cheshire grin. Those hackers had been cheap at $30M! She never expected results would be catastrophic worldwide. Now, they would be beating down Yo's door for the new ink system, for sure.

This was just the start of the true nightmare!

Chapter 16

Johnny Five, the local agent in Oregon, would have surprised Jack. He got the email early Friday morning that Jack sent, and agreed with his assessment of the captured video feeds. Johnny realized that the kids did not have any kind of uniform, but he knew the local teller in one of the banks that four of the boys used.

He headed down the street to that bank, and arrived just before it opened at 7:30am Friday. He called the staff into the conference room, and asked if anyone knew anything about the boys in the videos. Two tellers told Johnny everything they knew, which was surprisingly enough for a strong start.

The tellers easily confirmed each other's story, because it was the bank's policy to spend time chatting with all their clients. Johnny was told that the boys were part of a landscaping co-op for students in the local cities. They also told him that the same co-op had several locations around the surrounding areas. In fact, one teller dashed out to a bulletin board, and returned with a business card. It promised summer money for energetic kids who knew how to mow lawns - an opportunity of a lifetime. It also said to text "WORKER" and "your zip code" to 55555, and information would be sent with details.

A landscaping business? What in the world would a landscaping business have to do with counterfeiting?

Immediately, Johnny texted "WORKER" and the bank's zip code to 55555. Within minutes, his phone was inundated with a slick sales pitch and more questions to ask the workers if they were interested.

CUT MORE GREEN - MAKE MORE GREEN!
Landscaping Jobs $50 per lawn.
Pick your own assignments!
Work as much, or as little as you want.

Type WORKER and your zip code to 55555.
Type DOIT to 55555 to accept these terms.
Type STOP to 55555 to quit working for us.

Type NEWJOB to 55555 to get a job in your area.
Type PASS to 55555 to reject an assignment.
Type ACCEPT to 55555 to complete the job in 2 days.
Type FINISHED TO 55555 when you have been paid.

It was a sweet little business concept, which ran itself as soon as there were 20+ workers in the pool per zip code. What a great idea to get kids by pitching it to team locker rooms. It would take off like wildfire, since a typical kid with a lawn mower might make $15 per mow in this area. $50 would be more for professionals.

Johnny Five immediately signed up, getting an idea! He might not have to subpoena 46 kids, and get their parents' consent. He sent NEWJOB to 55555 after using the bank's zip code to sign up. Within ten seconds, the computer database texted Johnny a name and address about five blocks North. It was now about 9:30am, Friday.

Johnny typed ACCEPT to 55555. Immediately, a return message appeared stating, "Go Mow it! Don't forget to text FINISHED when you get paid."

Johnny immediately drove to the address

he was sent. He rang the bell, and was greeted by a housewife. Introducing himself, he showed her his Secret Service badge. He saw the usual alarm. Still, she asked him to come in, and have a seat. She offered him a drink, but he politely declined. She sat down, looking nervous, and asked what this was about. To her surprise, Johnny asked her about her landscaping service.

She replied that they had tried several professional landscapers in the Home Owners Association (HOA), and all of them were miserably bad. Most had let the grass grow weeks too long, and many only did the job halfway. Also, because they were recommended by the HOA, they charged $100 per mow which seemed extremely expensive for a mediocre service. She then got up, went into the kitchen, took a business card off the refrigerator, and upon her return, gave it to Johnny.

Johnny saw this card was similar to the one he found at the bank, but it was targeting people who wanted the best

landscaper at $50 per mow!

Let us help you go green - Save more GREEN!
Landscaping Jobs $50 per lawn.
We'll cut anything anywhere in 2 days.

Type YARD and your address with zip code to 55555.
Type MOWME to 55555 to accept these terms.
Type STOP to 55555 to terminate service.
Type PAID to 55555 when you pay our worker.
Type SUCCESS or FAIL to 55555 on your satisfaction.
Type PROMO to 55555 to receive $500 cash by mail.

This cash can be used for whatever you want,
but we suggest paying our workers with it.

Johnny was amazed! Who sent cash in the mail these days besides counterfeiters? If it got lost, they could just replace it. It was brilliant... no one knew it was counterfeit, and the people that would be passing it to a bank were completely innocent victims. No way to trace, he'd bet, no return address on the promo cash. Even if Johnny signed up for lawn care, he'd just get a kid who didn't know the scheme. Again, brilliant!

Now, how could he track this operation? Then, it occurred to him, while yes, it could be a local crime, there was no way to prove that it wasn't being perpetrated anywhere!

Sneaky crooks.

Chapter 17

It was early Saturday morning, and Jack Quick was reading Johnny Five's very detailed report which was sent the night before. Jack liked Johnny's report style since it reminded him of himself. The more he read, the more he decided he liked Johnny. At the end of the email, Johnny requested a 9am Saturday video conference with Jack to discuss options for where to go from here.

On the California coast, Yo and Angelina were accepting the cafeteria delivery for the shelter at 4am on Saturday. Angelina wondered how the two of them were going to be able to unload two semi-trucks worth of dry, refrigerated, and frozen goods in a few hours as Yo told her. Promptly at 4:15 am, two trucks honked outside. Yo directed the freezer truck to E1, and the dry truck to E2. He gave each driver a code for the door, and told them to honk when ready to be lifted to the second level. Angelina now smiled, knowing she wouldn't need to carry anything upstairs.

The drivers were amazed at the ease and efficiency of their operation. Both elevators opened on the second level to reveal a rolling conveyor that was positioned at the exact height of each truck's bed. The drivers only had to push the pallets out of each truck. Then, like a train yard, the pallets were taken to the correct holding area as directed by a computer that read the tags and temperature of the products. Several worldwide shipping companies would kill for this technology. Within 15 minutes of the trucks' arrival, the contents were unloaded, and signed for. Now, Yo and Angelina's cafeteria was fully stocked with anything 50 people would need for up to three years. Anything from toilet paper, hand soap, cereal, fruit, frozen meats and seafood, popsicles, alcohol, sodas, staples, paper, and printer ink - you name it, they had it!

9am EST Saturday, Johnny and Jack had just begun their video call. Jack said it was nice to finally meet Johnny in person, and complimented him on a very detailed report. Jack asked Johnny if he had seen the news about the Encryption Hackers. Johnny had. Jack then asked Johnny if he would head up a local and regional Secret Service task force to look further into the "Mower Scam" as he called it. Johnny was rocked to the core! He figured Jack would fly out and take over as every other agent in DC had before. Jack explained that he was going to be busier than a long-tailed cat in a rocking chair factory. This was a field promotion in crisis, these cases could either rocket him to the top, or bury him where he stood. Johnny jumped at the chance for his own case, and was equal to the task. He thanked Agent Quick, and promised he wouldn't disappoint him. Jack believed him. They talked about Johnny's next steps, and Jack congratulated Johnny once more before hanging up.

Toby Lipton was reading Jack's report on Yo, and did a double take when he saw the internship years before. He hoped it was nothing, and even more so, he hoped Jack's organization would investigate, and then let it go.

Then, Toby saved the report to his computer. It was about 11pm Saturday night, and Toby was getting tired, but just then got pinged.

AOD wrote, "Hey! Are you awake?"

Toby would wake up for her. "Yes, kind of."

"I was wondering what you were doing."

"Just catching up on some work. Thanks for that contact. Yo says he can help us."

"Great! - I knew it would work out in the end."

They chatted for a few more minutes, then Toby started yawning uncontrollably, and said, "Good night."

Angelina paged Yo as soon as she ended her chat.

Yo was there in less than a minute. "What's up? Why the emergency page?"

Angelina had wanted to test the paging

system, and it had worked great! - Washington state probably heard the racket - there was no way anyone wouldn't hear it in the facility. Angelina said, "We have a snag. Secret Service agent, Jack Quick, uncovered your internship in our country."

Yo said, "So what? It was years ago, and it's on my school transcript. Why hide it if they could find it easily? I have a cover story for it, and plan to bring it up first thing Monday.

"You, Angelina, will have to ignore everything I say at that meeting to ensure we get this job. If your hatred comes across in the meeting, we will be outed."

Angelina understood that Yo was going to blow off her country in front of her, and had he not told her ahead of time, she would have killed him with her bare hands. Then she asked, "Do you really want to risk me being there with you?"

Yo replied, "Of course. Your fake ID is better than mine, and I'll need a technical scientist to cover the geeky questions they are sure to ask. We will leave 8am Sunday from LAX to IAD, rent a car, go to the hotel, get up Monday, and win the contract that will destroy the United States of America in 12 months. Are you ready?!"

He put up his hand for a high five, and she almost broke his arm slapping it and screaming, "YES!!!!"

Chapter 18

It was 9:55am Monday. Yo and Angelina Gear signed in as visitors in the lobby of the Bureau of Engraving and Printing. Toby was immediately paged to meet his guests.

While waiting, a well-dressed man waved good morning to the receptionist. She instantly brightened and said, "Good morning, Jack."

As Toby entered the lobby, they stood to greet him. Toby introduced himself to Eduardo Yo, and was introduced to Angelina Gear. He couldn't help noticing she was a stunning Asian lady in a red dress. Yo introduced her as his chief scientist, who would be happy to discuss all the technical applications of his inks to the BEP techno geeks. Toby nodded, appreciating the fact, knowing his colleagues were well known to eat average salesmen alive at these meetings with technical jargon.

Toby led them to a nicely furnished

conference room and offered coffee; both requested water instead. Toby excused himself to get the others assembled. He then, asked an administrative assistant to have some waters sent in, and to page Trent Lester to let him know they were ready. Toby called his ink task force to the conference room, and rejoined his guests.

Upon returning, he found Jack Quick introducing himself to both guests.

"Call me Yo, and this is Angelina, my chief scientist. She can help with any technical data questions that may arise during our visit."

Jack just smiled, shook hands, and welcomed them. The Asian lady in the red dress was obviously well educated, beautiful, and he could tell this was not her first rodeo. As the rest of the team entered, the remaining introductions were done cordially.

Toby started off the meeting with BEP's requirements, and Yo and Angelina just sat there smiling, and nodding in agreement, as he ticked off points on a slide show.

After about 25 minutes had passed, Trent Lester quietly entered. Toby paused his presentation to introduce Trent to Yo and Angelina. Trent couldn't believe this was Yo's chief scientist! She should be on the cover of Vogue or Cosmo, not playing in a lab with ink samples. Toby suggested they take a 10 minute break before Yo gave his presentation.

During the break, Yo told Toby and Jack that he had met Angelina in an internship in her parents' country. She was the director of the internship program at Caltech at the time. Since then, they had kept in contact as she was getting her PhD. Yo described his internship as a chance to see a third world country at its worst. He had wanted to see if he could offer them any options to bring it out of the third world status. He realized that it was not a possibility in that "bass ackwards" society, and gave up. Still, he got to see, do, and taste things that America would not have shown him in books.

Angelina was glad he had prepared her earlier, since that backwards comment would have caused her to chop at his jugular, killing him on the spot. Instead, she was laughing and chuckling at what Yo had described. Clearly, Toby and Jack were buying into this rehearsed line, and Angelina just smiled deep down inside.

When the meeting kicked off again, Yo pulled up his slides and began answering Toby's questions as he progressed through his presentation.

Jack was instantly wary something was amiss, but he couldn't figure out what. He noticed the slides from Yo's deck were in the *exact order* as the questions from Toby's deck - what were the odds! Yo had stressed that he had prepared his notes over time, and that these points were identical in each and every large-scale installation they had done... although, none of their installations were anywhere near this one in magnitude! All the bullet points that Toby brought up were answered in exactly that order, and Toby's scientific staff was almost drooling, looking at the samples Yo and Angelina passed out.

Toby asked about the durability of the clear coat, and Angelina took over. She explained that without the clear coat, the paper or fabric (in this case) got too wet with the "green" inks, and when dry, became brittle and ripped easily. However, with the one millionth of a millimeter-thick clear coat, it became part of the note, strengthening it to that of a strand of superhero's hair.

Once the other side of the note received the clear coat, it too, would bond to the other side, and now nothing less than a torch could hurt it. This meant that the current notes that must be recycled within 18-22 months, now would have a longevity of 120-180 months. This would allow them to save money for years to come, since they wouldn't be replacing hardly any in the first 84 months.

Toby looked at Trent from across the table. Trent's smile said it all! Toby broke the gaze and asked, "Enough already, what's the shocking news?"

Yo and Angelina looked at each other, and

then Yo asked, "What shocking news?"

Toby frowned and asked, "How much will all this cost per year?"

Yo looked at Angelina, who winked at him. (That was their *go get it* sign between them.) Yo answered, "With a year's supply of our ink, proprietary clear coat, and our technical service over the phone and in person as needed, $650M per year, with no multiple year contract required!"

There was dead silence in the room for almost a complete minute. Did Yo kill them? Angelina urged Yo to wait patiently. Earlier, they had discussed that once the price was revealed, they would wait quietly until the BEP staff responded.
(Shut Up! Say Absolutely Nothing! Wait for them.)

Trent stood up, reached over to Yo, and said, "If it checks out OK - we accept your offer." A cheer that Jack thought he'd never, ever hear from this building erupted, and people were ecstatic!

Yo looked at Angelina and smiled. It was

almost noon, and Yo's sales pitch had been accepted. Damn, he was good!

Trent took everyone to his favorite restaurant for lunch to celebrate. Yo and Angelina were exhausted, but happy. Everyone lost track of time, and after lunch, the rest of the day flew by. Everyone had tons of things to do.

Toby pulled Jack aside, and asked what his gut feeling was on the intel dump on Yo's business. Jack smiled, and said that the only issue he was concerned about was that questionable internship.

Toby exclaimed, "I knew you'd pick up on that!"

"Well," Jack said, "I'm willing to overlook it for now. I still have to check up on the rest of Yo's staff, but for now, start printing!"

Back at the hotel, Yo and Angelina were discussing the events of the day. Yo thanked Angelina for getting a copy of Toby's slides on Saturday.

Angelina replied, "No problem, but next time, you better mix up the bullet points. I saw Jack's face contort when your presentation was exactly the same. For a minute, I thought we might have lost the edge."

Yo asked, "Was that what his look was? I saw it too, but just kept plugging."

"Good thing you didn't ask anyone for questions," she winked!

Chapter 19

Tuesday morning came way too early for Yo and Angelina, but as soon as they arrived, the BEP people were ready to mix the samples and print money. They were rushed into a lab to mix the black and green inks, so the BEP could run a manual set at the DC facility. They printed one hundred 32 bill sheets with the sample inks. The first 50 sheets, they left with no clear coat. On the last 50 sheets, they applied the clear coat as directed to both sides. Adding the clear coat would be an extra step in the BEP's process, but was easily accomplished with very little fuss. Once the sheets were dried and cut into separate bills, they took the samples into the conference room to show Yo, Angelina, Toby, Trent, and Jack.

Jack was the first to detect that the smell and the consistency were off from the new process, even though the fabric was the same as normal currency. Angelina stated that the smell and the feel would come back as the clear coat dried completely (12 hours after coating). This, Jack noted, would have to be added into the QA testing.

Trent and Toby thought this was a fantastic catch, since none of the scientists had discovered this in the initial testing. It was decided that they would dry the money, and revisit the clear coated money tomorrow. Now, they could play and test the non-clear coated money. Much to Yo and Angelina's delight, the untreated money looked flawless, but when they tried to tear a bill, it tore very easily. Everyone in the conference room agreed the bills would definitely need the clear coat to survive in America.

Wednesday arrived way too soon for everyone! The BEP wanted more time to discuss Yo's proprietary clear coat, but Yo said that they would have more time to discuss that on his next visit.

Yo and Angelina could not believe the access they had in the BEP. The BEP scientists had arranged a white glove introduction of their facility, including some of the non-classified security features, as well as a look at their custom presses. After the 3-hour tour, they rejoined the others in the lab.

Everyone was in the BEP lab playing with the new coated bills. They had all been given separate bills from the lab, and were trying to destroy the bills in any way possible, using their bare hands. Jack was astounded. The smell and feel of the bills were that of a fresh crisp dollar. He was thrilled, because the Secret Service wouldn't have to rewrite any processes due to changes in smell or texture.

Shortly before 5pm, everyone gathered in the conference room, and summed up the very successful visit. Trent asked if anyone in the room was able to tear or destroy any new bill. No one could! (Except by mechanical tools: knife, scissors, or shredder.) The new bills were of the superhero caliber. Trent congratulated everyone in the room, announced that he believed this would stop the impending Reduction in Force (RIF), and thanked Yo and Angelina personally for their fantabulous product. Yo and Angelina just thanked the team for letting them be part of history.

After Yo and Angelina had returned to their hotel, Yo got a phone call on his smartphone. He recognized the number, and turned on the mobile camera viewer on his phone. He saw five people outside the war door, 4,000 miles away. "May I help you?" he asked.

"Have you inked the deal yet?"

Yo replied, "YES! We have much work to do! Please come in, and get settled." He buzzed the door open, waited about 30 seconds, checked the lobby camera, and opened the door. He announced over the intercom, "Badges are in the communal area on the table of the office space. Find an office and bedroom. The cafeteria is on the second level, fully stocked. Angelina and myself will be back there late tomorrow night."

When he saw Angelina at dinner, Yo told her that he'd let in the staff at the shelter.

Chapter 20

It was now Wednesday night, and the President of the United States was about to address the nation on the Encryption Hackers that had devastated the worldwide banking system. When the TV cameras turned to him, and the red dots came on to show they were live, he began.

"Our nation has been targeted by several types of terrorists in the past. Some of them physical and brutal, and others of them like last week's cyber and data breach attacks. While some in the past have only touched a few of you in America, the ongoing attack is ruthless and will be shut down in the near future.

"Homeland Security and the Secret Service are working together with many other agencies to stop the people responsible for interrupting our lives. Rest assured, we are doing everything possible to keep your hard-earned money safe and secure. As always, I urge all Americans and other nations to work with the banking system, and not panic. I understand we all use money or credit to buy items to sustain life, rent, food, medicine, gas, energy, and even entertainment.

"Our country will get through this crisis. I am signing a new bill that will give creditors and citizens a one-month grace period for all debt. By then, the credit card networks should be back online (hopefully within a week), and currency will be flowing once again. Until then, reserve your cash to buy necessities only: food, gas, and medicines mainly. Once again, remain calm. We have been through much worse in our past, and we will overcome this, too! Thank You. May God bless America. Good night."

As soon as the President got off the stage, he asked the Vice President if anyone was close to nailing these bastards to the wall. The VP replied that the transmissions had been narrowed down to somewhere in Korea, but they weren't sure if it was North or South, yet.

"Tell them to get on it!"

"Nice play to give all Americans a one month grace period to pay their bills! How did you ever get Congress to sign off on that?"

"I haven't, it's a bluff, but it's the only thing that makes any 'cents'! Even Congress should be on board with this looming threat."

Back in Oregon, Johnny Five, was assembling his task force requesting people from the Federal Reserve Bank, local law enforcement officers, and local bank managers to help isolate where the bogus currency was showing up. He also requested several of the bills to examine in his onsite lab.

His first impression was that these were top rate knock-offs of the real hundred-dollar bill. Someone had gone to great lengths to make this funny money, right down to the micro-printing. Old-style bills did not have any security features such as security threads or holographic images when you held them up in the light. This series was way too old for those features.

The raised ink surface and the smell were correct, but the actual paper was just 60-pound bond, not the 75% / 25% cotton with embedded fibers. Had a perfume manufacturer been able to reproduce the money's scent as a fragrance? Looking closer at the bills, he realized the money had random red and blue flecks of color, barely visible, printed on them.

Aside from the BEP fabric mix, these bills were very clever indeed. The fact that they used a thicker bond than average paper fooled the untrained senses!

Looking online, Johnny discovered there were several scent manufacturers out there that specialized in a new money scent. He found oils, sprays for houses and cars, and even candles you could burn to smell like new money.

He took several of his strongest scented bills, and sent them to a lab near DC to ask them where the scents had originated. He knew this particular lab could detect what kind of dog peed on a fireplug after three winters had gone by, and tell you the owner's scent, too. He hoped they would be able to track down the specific manufacturer based on the surrounding scents on the bills. He marked urgent on the form he printed from the website, and included the Secret Service account number. Then, Johnny saved a copy of his results to his computer, and emailed his findings to his task force. He also included a copy to Jack Quick in DC.

Jack was amazed someone was going to such great lengths. He congratulated Johnny again in a return email, and told him to keep digging, and to keep him posted.

Minutes later, Johnny smiled as he read Jack's compliment.

Unknown to Jack, Johnny, and Trent, when Toby had emailed Jack for the intel dump on Eduardo Yo before the meeting, a trojan had been sent to Jack's computer. It stored data on searches, emails, and files, and gave Angelina Gear access to Jack's and Trent's computers. Now, Johnny's computer had just received the trojan from

Jack's email, and it was phoning home for the first time.

Angelina saw the announcement email, and said to Yo, "They have found the counterfeit money from the mower service promo cash. They have no clue where it's coming from, but they sent the sample bills to be analyzed by... *Holy Cow!* That *bad news lab* in Virginia!"

Yo's eyes looked at Angelina, and he said, "It's just a lab. Besides, I assembled the money in our throw away lab in Washington state. Even if they find that it came from there, they can't tie it to you or me, just the druggie running the mower scheme. Relax, he doesn't even know who we are! They'll be chasing their tails for months. By then, it will be too late for anyone!"

He smiled at Angelina, and she returned the smile saying, "So true!"

Chapter 21

Upon Yo and Angelina's return, they entered the shelter, and stood there with their mouths wide open. The five scientists had settled in, and then some! They had unloaded the first shipment of 80 containers off the rail cars by themselves, 40 of i625 and 40 of cc625.

Yo was the first to recover, and asked, "How many workers were needed, and how much time did it take to unload?"

One scientist answered, "80 containers, two operators, and one hour all on level two. It was a piece of cake. The new hoist system that the US government provided made things very simple indeed. It unloaded the rail cars automatically, and using the robotic arms, loaded the containers into the shelter's overhead rail system. It was all point and click on a computer screen. Actually, the two operators, slowed us down. The next shipment will be in two days. I believe I can write an automated script between the hoist system and the overhead rail system controllers to load the third level without operators, and be considerably faster."

Angelina then smiled and said, "We're in business!" She looked at Yo, and asked him to show the scientists the secret tunnel, and how to access it from both sides.

Yo nodded and said, "Follow me." Yo stood by a wall with large pillars of steel pipe that were driven into the ground, then reinforced with concrete. These pillars were in every warehouse known to mankind to protect trucks and forklifts from hitting walls and doors. However, Yo swiped his badge on the side of a specific pillar. Silently, four pillars disappeared completely into the ground and the floor retracted, leaving a gaping tunnel sloping downward.

Angelina and the scientists marveled at the silent operation. Yo led them down into the lighted tunnel, swiped his badge at a card key reader, and a copy of the pillar and floor system opened into his ink factory. Yo explained that everything would be shipped out of his ink factory, in case there was satellite or surveillance coverage. From now on, everyone was to enter and exit through the ink factory. All cars were already parked there. He asked if everyone understood. They nodded in agreement.

Yo then explained that the front lobby was a prison in disguise. It had reinforced concrete walls, and two war doors providing a makeshift prison, in case anyone uninvited showed up.

Chapter 22

9am Friday, at the shelter, Yo received a shipment of inline mixers from his ink supplier. He wondered why Yo, his best customer, needed it, since he sold him premixed colors, but it was none of his business. He was into supplying, not questioning, his clients. All the same, these inline mixers were rated at well over 300 gallons per minute. That's one heck of a lot of ink - more than what a computer printer would ever need. Then again, Yo had some feelers out on some very large quantities of ink. Maybe Yo would benefit from buying in bulk.

Just then, the supplier's mobile rang - speak of the devil. "Hey Yo! I was just thinking about you. Did you receive those mixers yet?"

Yo said, "I just inspected them, and they look perfect!"

"So why call me? I know my mixers are the best."

Yo laughed and said, "I need to place a small order. I hope you can handle it."

The supplier's bravado did not stop, "Come on, who ya talkin' too... Name it."

Yo said, "I'll need my *green* environmentally friendly inks in the following colors and amounts:

GRN33284	300 tons
BLK33284	300 tons
CLRcoatYO	600 tons"

The supplier dropped his phone, and sat down in the nearest chair. "Are you kidding me?" he asked, after finding his phone under his desk.

Yo said, "I thought you could handle big orders. I could go find a co-supplier, if the order is too big."

The supplier recovered and said, "No, we can handle it." He looked up the numbers on his computer and said, "Hold everything, Yo. These are classified inks, only sold in very small quantities."

Now, it was Yo's turn to laugh! "If you

have any difficulties, please contact Toby Lipton at the BEP," and rattled off his mobile number.

Yo's supplier said, "Well, damn! There are going to be a lot of people that will be upset about not winning this contract. Keep eyes in the back of your head, my friend. Some of these players play for keeps! Oh, and Congrats!"

Yo asked for a delivery date, and to be billed.

The supplier continued, "If Toby Lipton has the power to sign, the inks will arrive in five days by railcar. Then you will receive one more shipment in ten days by ship and railcar. We'll split the order down the middle: 150, 150, and 300 tons, assuming your check clears."

Yo said, "Actually let's do that now. Give me your account number." Yo was enjoying this way too much!

His supplier dropped his phone again, but soon returned to the line. The ink supplier gave Yo the bank name and account number, and said, "The total comes to $82M."

Yo keyed in the amount, verified he had both accounts' information correct, and then tapped confirm. A message appeared on Yo's screen announcing that since funds were available, and the ink supplier's account was using the same bank, the transaction was instantaneous. Yo said, "Cool! Done!"

The ink supplier quickly checked his account and said, "Hold it! You sent $83M. That's $1M too much."

Yo laughed again, and said, "Keep it as your commission!"

They talked for a few more minutes, and then said goodbye.

"What a day," the supplier was thinking, and now he thought, "That's why Yo needed those inline mixers. But it was still premixed ink... It must be a top-secret requirement for the BEP security protocols."

Angelina walked by, and waved to Yo.

Yo called her into the office, and said, "We'll have half GRN33284, BLK33284, and CLRcoatYO in five days, and the other half will arrive five days after the first shipment. Oh, and it's paid for!"

Angelina cocked her head like she misheard him. "What?!"

"I asked him for his bank name and account number. He didn't even blink. So, after we print the money, your hackers can get us a rebate of everything they've got."

"Absolutely!" Angelina agreed. "Great thought!"

Chapter 23

It had now been one full week, since the Encryption Hackers had pulled off their stupendous hack of the worldwide banking system. When the hackers first thought about this job, they decided that they would buy two houses. The first house was located in a third world country that was hated by their host nation. They would set up a secure house and server to remote into it via another secure house and server located in Washington state. Both were booby-trapped with hundreds of pounds of high explosives that could be detonated remotely by phone or computer. Although it was not based in the same place as the Mower Scam, it was in the same city. But the hackers didn't know anything about the mowing operation.

This plan of two houses meant the United States government would be hunting in a country where there were no diplomatic ties. There would be no local agencies to help locate the hackers in the third world country. With any luck, it would lure the troops that killed Angelina's family 30+ years ago into that country covertly. Not having the local government's assistance would mean it would be that much more complex to breach. When the secure house was breached, hundreds of pounds of high explosives would put those troops on the moon.

Angelina was in a quandary! She wanted the hackers to keep all the agencies busy, but she wanted her revenge on the agencies worse. She would contemplate this more thoroughly. She didn't want revenge at the price of her i625 project. She wanted both.

Angelina picked up her mobile. It was time to check in with the Encryption Hackers near DC, in Virginia. She dialed the number from memory, and it was answered on the first ring.

Steve Stevenson answered the call, and asked how they were doing.

Angelina loved their progress to date, and asked, "What's next?!"

Steve replied, "My team is setting up a secure website in a country with no extradition, and will be sending out account information to all your players soon. The site will have billions of accounts in clear text posted for the world to download after the banking system supposedly resets all the codes - Yeah Right! And the Easter Bunny exists too! The list won't be released to the public until the house in the third world blows up. That is what will trigger the website data release."

Angelina was impressed. She asked, "Did you make sure our data will not be published?"

Steve said, "Don't worry, I would not leave you in the lurch like that."

Steve Stevenson was a techno geek from the day he could use a computer. He was well beyond typical hackers because he worked at Homeland Security. Steve was currently on the second week of his long overdue vacation. Each and every time he'd leave for a vacation, his boss, an

Admiral in the Navy, would call him back to duty because "some crisis" arose the moment he left. They had breached his vacation schedule nine times in the past four years. This was beyond ridiculous!

This year he asked the President, a family friend, for a pardon by email. The President knew Steve was burning out, based on what his son and daughter had told him. The President of the United States thought this request was over the top, but so was no vacation for four years. He had his staff write the pardon. Most thought he had lost his mind, but they completed the request anyway. Later he signed it, and as requested, emailed it back to Steve.

So, when the Admiral called him up last week, Steve emailed the pardon to him. Since then, Steve had not been bothered by the United States government. Instead, he was moonlighting for $30M under Angelina's direction.

Angelina was back in her office, thinking about her scams, hackers, projects, and her family whom she missed the most. While she was lost in thought, she looked at her computer screen. Her list of taps was growing, and she still hadn't opened some of them yet... It wasn't time.

They were sorted by email address:

fivej@secretservice.or.gov.net
lestert@bep.gov.net
liptont@bep.gov.net
potus@whitehouse.wdc.gov.net
quickj@secretservice.wdc.gov.net
stevensons@homelandsecurity.wdc.gov.net
yoe@inks4life.net

Chapter 24

It was a rainy Friday night in Oregon, and Johnny Five was having dinner at one of his favorite restaurants. He was chomping on his pineapple burger with BBQ sauce, sweet potato fries, and Dr. Pepper®, thinking about how he could find the well-hidden source of the counterfeit money invading his territory. He had already set up an account, sent the PROMO message to 55555, and had received the bogus $500 in cash. As he expected, there seemed to be no way to track those crooks.

He noticed that the mailer had been sent supposedly from Washington state. After calling the Postmaster General of that area, Johnny told him the story. The postmaster had said that unless the package was special in some way, it would be unlikely to trace the package via video surveillance. He also reminded Johnny that there were hundreds of drop boxes around the city with no surveillance on them. If the counterfeiters were smart, they would disguise their drop, and make the packages as generic as possible.

Johnny just then realized that the envelope was not metered, but stamped. He originally had asked his local police station to try to lift fingerprints off of the envelope, but nothing had come back useful. All at once, Johnny asked for the check, paid, and ran outside in the rain with a long shot in mind.

When he got home, he carefully removed the stamp, and got out his fingerprint kit. He then lifted a partial print from under the stamp. Hopefully, it was from the person who had mailed it, and he hoped they were in the system, any system.

Johnny scanned the print into his computer by taking a picture of it with his smartphone. He then logged into the Secret Service database with cross links to other agencies all over the world. Within minutes, he had 60 names of potential matches. Really, 60?! But 60 was much better than the 1.2B people in the United States that he had an hour ago. In fact, he reminded himself that these 60 might not be who he was looking for at all. Still, undaunted, he was making progress.

Johnny got a cold Dr. Pepper® from the fridge, and started searching through the names. He found 37 were still incarcerated, and ruled them out. It was highly unlikely a prison mail scan wouldn't have found counterfeit bills. He chuckled at the thought of that actually being possible. Of the 23 that were left, six of them had died within the last nine months, thus they weren't going to be caught by Johnny. Down to 17 possible names, now he had to start reading through case files.

He read the first one, groaning and hoping he could find a better way. This one was a DUI with a fatal accident - a 2014 Mustang lost control, crossed a divided interstate with a steel barrier, launched over it at an estimated 130 MPH, and landed in the middle of a hay wagon trailer being pulled by a pickup truck with 25 kids and a chaperone on board.

Why did they think they could pull an open trailer on the interstate in the first place?!

Mike Parry

Some people... Apparently, all the kids survived untouched, but the 42-year-old chaperone was crushed to death by the Mustang. Johnny screamed in frustration! The 19-year-old kid driving had been sentenced to three years. He'd have been out in about five months, if they would have kept him, but no, they released him 27 days ago...! Johnny ruled him out, but made a note to take a ride and check on his rehabilitation. Legally, Johnny couldn't do anything, but he'd still check him out.

The next nine to be dismissed, were in and out of county lockup over the past 17 months. He ruled these out because once they got out, they went right back in over probation issues.

This left Johnny seven possibilities. He reminded himself that this might not pan out, but he didn't have a hot date tonight, so he'd be bored. Johnny went to the fridge, got a refill of Dr. Pepper®, stretched, and returned to the sofa, noticing it was just past midnight. Turning his attention back to the seven that were left, he felt this was doable.

120

Right away, he noticed that the next one was a security clearance fingerprint. It belonged to last year's winner of Teacher of the Year from a school in Georgia. He deliberately dismissed this record and moved on.

His search showed that the next three were home invaders, not related to each other's crimes, all separate. They were committed 4-5 years ago. All three were released due to overcrowding conditions, and serving the remaining 3-11 years under house arrest anklets. One of the three had left the range radius of his anklet to go get groceries, because seven grocery stores in that area had been hit with arson. Johnny couldn't make this stuff up if he tried! He decided to overlook this one for now.

The three remaining likely matches were druggies, mostly crack or meth lab entrepreneur wannabes that had been caught, served time in county jail, and then were released to rehabilitation centers (6-12 months) to complete the court orders.

Two of them went to the same high school,

not far over the Oregon border, in Washington state. Johnny decided to look up their current addresses, but found fake addresses in the system file. He checked IRS records, thinking rehab was a great tax write off, but found nothing. He signed into classmatesRus.net and looked up both of their photos for all four years. In both cases, it was all six years of high school. The drug business must have been great behind the football stadium.

The last one was unique, Johnny thought. Steve Stevenson had been arrested on drug possession and incarcerated in a local town in Virginia, near DC. He was released early by a Federal Judge. Steve had worked with the DC Police Department for three years, and he has held a very high-level clearance job for Homeland Security for the past five years. Johnny recognized what this was. He was looking at a CIA cover story for drugs, and they had used the fingerprints of the Washington state kid as part of the cover. He read further down though the file, and found notes saying that David Jones of

Washington state had agreed to lend his prints to his cousin Steve Stevenson in exchange for a lighter sentence for drug charges. The weight of Steve Stevenson's testimony alone swayed the Washington District Court Judge.

It was very unlikely that the Homeland Security guy's cousin would be involved with a counterfeit ring. So, Johnny scratched both names off, and decided to go with the other high schooler as his prime suspect for now.

Chapter 25

Jack Quick was in his home office researching the intel on Yo's Inks4Life.net business. Specifically, Angelina Gear was a mystery to him. Her credentials all checked out flawlessly; too well for him. She was born in Oregon, and moved to California to live with her guardians after her parents went back to their homeland for a six month long work-related assignment. Soon after they had arrived in their homeland, they had become casualties of a peacetime operation surrounding a classified American Seal incursion. Apparently, a whole village was sanitized, or something akin to that. Jack could not be sure between the redactions and the classified intel. Angelina Gear never saw her relatives from that country again. It was a truly sad story. Jack was amazed at her laughing at that "bass ackwards country" that Yo spoke about, although he did realize that she had tried to soften his words after they came out. Yo didn't seem to fight her on it either.

After she graduated high school with honors, she attended Caltech and received her Bachelors of Science Degree in Physics (Magna Cum Laude) with a 4.000. She continued her education to earn a Master's in Computer Science, and her PhD in Engineering - again with honors and a 3.985 average.

This lady was a rocket scientist for all reasonable expectations!

Why was she wasting her life on computer inks and dyes, when she could be making millions for NASA or the United States Department of Defense as a US citizen?

Jack's gut was gnawing at something, but he didn't have enough information to say "No" to Trent and Toby's request on Yo and Angelina's intel dumps.

Jack emailed Trent and Toby, and notified them that Angelina's background check had come back solid as a "T Bill". He did mention that with her education, she could be making millions as a NASA consultant, but instead she was playing with ink... why?!

Angelina's email chimed, and she was notified that Jack had just cleared herself and Yo on the project.

Radical Payment Project was underway!

Chapter 26

Back at the Bomb Shelter in California, Angelina's staff had just unloaded the second shipment of 80 containers of i625 and cc625. As promised, her lead techie scientist was able to automate the containers off the rail cars into the shelter on level three. It took all of 40 minutes, and it was indeed choreographed well, unloading two containers (or one railcar) per minute. Not even the dock workers were that fast in her parents' country.

After the loading doors were shut, and the shelter was secured, Angelina called a meeting to discuss their plans for moving forward. Yo and the scientists were all comfy in the common area, some with coffee, most with water.

Angelina started by congratulating them on getting this far, and then emphasized for them to stay focused and vigilant. If they had questions, or thought of a new angle while working - share it! Angelina asked Yo to discuss the operation of the ten inline mixers, and the overall process and operation.

Yo started by saying they would have:

2 mixers dedicated for the i625 + BLK33284
2 mixers dedicated for the i625 + GRN33284
4 mixers dedicated for the cc625 + CLRcoatYO
2 spare mixers that could be used if one should fail

If more than two mixers failed during the project, another mixer could only be used after it was thoroughly cleaned and dried, since mixing the components would kill *all of them*, if not done correctly!

They all hoped Yo's ink supplier really did supply the best quality mixers money could buy, so that the project would run smoothly.

Yo compared the inline mixers to a zippered coat. The two sides of a zipper are joined by a trolley, creating the closed zipper. As the (i625 and the inks) or (cc625 and Yo's clear coat) would proceed through the inline mixer, a combined product would be made. The final products would be vacuum sealed in a very thick plastic bag inside a metal pallet and secured. The metal pallet, a requirement of the BEP for security purposes, would ensure the inks and the clear coating had not been altered in transport. Yo reminded his scientists that once mixed, the combined products, could not be separated. Although there was plenty of i625, inks, and clearcoat (enough for four complete projects), they didn't want to run out!

This brought up another conversation - what if the project went smoothly? What would be done with the excess? Angelina asked for suggestions, and some of the scientists' ideas surprised her.

Durable inks were very useful in manufactured items that sat on a shelf for a long time such as: retail items, grocery boxes, board games, boxes in toy stores, and printing for books in a school, bookstore, or library.

Printed Interstate road signs on metal posts blowing in the wind would cause movement and cracking of the paint. Radiation would be left on the metal, irradiating vehicles as they passed under, or near them. 600-1,000 signposts later, death of the vehicle occupants would occur.

Again, all of these items would be extremely difficult to pinpoint, and the actual cause of death may never be found. Angelina thanked her staff, and told them to keep thinking. These were all excellent ideas!

Chapter 27

Trent and Toby were in a meeting together. Trent was congratulating Toby once again for saving his staff and his department. As a token of his appreciation, he was giving Toby a bonus today of $25,000, and a two-week vacation after the new money was in circulation as an incentive.

Toby was honored he could help save so many jobs, and suggested his money be divided up amongst the workers who would be doing the heavy lifting part of the project.

Trent was way ahead of him, as always. Trent explained that with all the money they were going to save, all the employees in his department would see an 8% raise by Christmas Eve. Toby was stunned!

Trent continued, "Even you will see it. On behalf of myself and our staff, we thank you." Moving on, Trent asked where they stood on the ink deliveries.

Toby informed Trent that Yo's ink supplier had requested the classified ink ***33284 in very large quantities. Toby also noted, maybe too large, but better to have too much, than not enough, especially in a project of this magnitude. Yo and his staff should receive half of the ink three days from now, and the rest in eight days. Also, the engraver had the specs on the new ink trenches which would have to be modified for the thicker "green" inks viscosity, which should be ready in two weeks.

"By the way," Toby asked, "how did the monthly meeting go this time?"

Trent just grinned and said, "I didn't approve the bonus and raises. Who do you suppose did?"

Toby was stunned again. All he could get out was, "Woooow!" Recovering, Toby asked if Trent had seen Jack's release on Inks4Life.net.

Trent nodded, and said, "Yes, it is a mystery why anyone as beautiful and talented as Angelina would be happy playing with ink, but I for one am not going to question her motives until our new bills are in circulation."

Toby then asked him if there was any progress on the Encryption Hackers' system breach.

Trent slapped his hand on the table, and said sarcastically, "They are still looking into it! No progress yet, we sure could use the new bills now."

Toby said, "Have mercy on me, Boss. We just got the ink approved! You know it's going to be 2-3 months from now. Maybe Santa will grant your wish on Christmas Eve."

With that, they concluded the meeting, and Toby went back to call Yo for an update. By the second ring, he had Yo on the phone.

Yo said that the inks should be in his facility in three days, and they would immediately start their standard quality checks on the "green" inks to make sure they met his personal standards.

Toby suggested they skip that step, and

send the ink directly to DC. This way he wouldn't have to pay for storage fees.

While Yo thanked Toby for the kind offer, he insisted his staff would test and inspect the ink for flaws before it got to his customer's site. It was all part of his services.

Toby reluctantly agreed and said, "If you change your mind, we can arrange it at any time in the future." They talked for a few more minutes, and ended the call.

Toby sat back, thinking about plans for his bonus. What did he want to do with it? He'd give that some thought.

Chapter 28

By 10am Monday morning, Johnny Five was in Washington state at the high school where his two druggies had attended several years ago. He first checked into the Principal's office. She had been with the school for the past 17 years. During that time, her school had seen its share of troubles, with the growing youth backlash that every school had seen in the past 15 years. Gangs, metal detectors, and drugs were on the rise, regardless how many people and sheriff deputies were thrown at the problems. Actually, she called them resource officers, but they had been deputies before coming to her school.

When Johnny asked about David Jones and his buddy, the Principal called the guidance counselor into her office, and brought up the old school files on her computer.

Upon entering the room, the counselor was introduced to Johnny. He recalled David Jones and Sam Henderson doing everything together, especially smoking joints 24/7/365. "It's a miracle they ever left, always high as kites on a windy day."

Johnny asked if anyone knew what happened to either of them.

The Principal said, "I had the counselor as their point of contact, since they respected him."

The counselor said, "I just told them the truth, and tried to get them involved with other things besides drugs. Sam had shown interest in Science and Chemistry for the obvious connections to his lab. David seemed to like computers and technology more than drugs.

"I remember talking to David's cousin in DC when David got arrested. He too had come to the school to try to help David get straight, and it worked for about a year, but there was a snag of some sort. David said his cousin was more of a druggie than him. It made the papers, maybe five years back. The gist was, there was a drug sting in a nearby town, and both David and his cousin were arrested on weed charges.

"David got out almost immediately, but the cousin, Steve, I think, was extradited to Virginia to serve four years, as I recall. That pretty much did in David's hero figure. After that, David didn't care.

"Sam, however, somehow turned his life around after high school, and went to college with a full scholarship. I never saw that one coming! A druggie with a full ride to a Virginia college! Sam's SAT scores were off the charts, near perfect, and one of the drug manufacturers sponsored him through college. He's working on his Master's now. Last I heard, he has a wife and a daughter, and is doing quite well."

Johnny asked if Sam Henderson might know where to find David.

The counselor looked up Sam's contact information on his phone, and gave it to Johnny. "Tell Sam that you got his info from Freaky Fred. That's what they called me in high school, because I was always trying to get them interested in freakin' school."

Johnny smiled, thanked them for their

time, and said, "I think you did remarkable things for Sam. It's great to hear there are still professionals that care for the kids!"

Fred said, "If you ever want to get involved, call me and I'll give you a list of schools in Oregon that would love to have a Secret Service agent of your caliber as a mentor."

As soon as Johnny got in his car, he dialed the number for Sam. To his amazement, he heard, "Hi, it's Sam. What can I help you with today?"

Johnny said, "I got your number from Freaky Fred."

Sam said, "Gee whiz, talk about a name out of the past - how is Freaky?!"

Johnny chuckled, and said, "It still sounds like he's looking after kids."

Sam was helpful. He said he had lost contact with David right after that bogus sting.

Johnny asked him for details, but Sam just said to check out a newspaper archive.

Sam said that he had tried about a year ago to contact David and strike up a friendship again, but David was too far gone, and Sam didn't want back into the life. He'd cleaned up, and his wife and daughter meant the world to him now.

Johnny asked if there was a way to contact David.

Sam said, "You didn't hear it from me, but if you help him get out of the life and get him straight, I'll tell you how."

Johnny answered, "I'm not going to lie to you. Your friend is in some serious trouble with the law, and he may have to serve time. Freaky Fred said that both of you were worth saving. I'll do what I can - no promises though."

"Good enough," Sam replied. "I'll take it! Thanks!" He continued, "Use your mobile phone and text this to it: IWANTTOWORKWITHYOU to 55555. The server will text you his current address."

Johnny dropped his phone. Picking up the phone, he thanked Sam. "I will do what I can for David. May I call you back later, or can David, if he wishes?"

Sam didn't think David would want to call, but Sam said, "Sure, anything for a friend! Always."

Chapter 29

Johnny dialed Jack's mobile number, and Jack answered on the second ring. Jack couldn't believe how fast Johnny had whittled down the list of 60, and got "lucky" from an old high school connection. He was amazed to hear about the text to 55555 to get a real address from a crook. Most crooks are not too bright, but this one seemed to outsmart himself.

Jack asked Johnny if he needed anything.

Johnny said, "I have a Federal Judge signing the warrant now. The closest SWAT should execute the warrant in about four hours."

Jack said, "Sounds like you've got it under control. When you file your paperwork, send me a copy, please."

As soon as he ended his call, he headed to a King of Burgers restaurant where they had free Wifi and Dr. Pepper® with his combo meal. There, he typed his report, and sent a copy of the warrant as an attachment. He emailed this to Jack and his field office in Oregon. Then he sat back, enjoying his burger and relaxing before the bust.

Angelina's email chimed while she was in Yo's office. She glanced down, and saw a warrant for Washington state. "What the Hell?! How did they find it so fast?"

Yo looked up and asked, "What's up?"

"Our Mower Scam is gonna be busted by SWAT in about three hours." Angelina asked, "Do we have a burner phone close by?"

Yo calmly walked over to a cabinet in his office, and said, "I don't know. What do you think?" He unlocked the cabinet, and opened it to reveal four power strips with eight plugs each, one per shelf. Each shelf had eight powered off cell phones. Picking up two, he said, "Let's go."

Angelina asked, "Where?"

Yo refused to turn on either of the burners until he was at least 30 miles away from the shelter, just in case they searched to see which tower sent the text. It wouldn't do to have the Secret Service snooping around the shelter looking for a burner phone. They drove some 45 minutes into downtown LA. Yo powered on the phone, and texted, "GETOUTNOW call 999-555-1234 when out and secure!" to 55555.

They turned off the first phone. Yo removed the battery and SIM card, turned on the other phone, and waited for a call. While they waited, Yo opened the trunk, took out the tire iron, and destroyed both the first phone and the SIM card. Then, he went to the closest sewer and dropped the phone in it. He kept the SIM card for disposal later.

As he walked back to the car, he heard the phone ring. Angelina handed him the phone, and he answered the call. The voice on the phone, David, said, "I'm moving to warehouse two."

Yo said, "Correct." Then he asked, "Is everything still in the truck, or did we lose some product that you left behind?"

David confirmed he worked out of the

truck exclusively, which was the plan. It made getaways like this smooth.

Yo said, "Ok, we gotta find out how they found you so fast."

David replied, "You do that. It would be nice if I had a secure location for more than three months at a time."

Yo said, "Just be glad you don't know me, and you're not staring down the business end of an M16 and SWAT."

David said, "Thanks," and hung up.

Angelina asked, "Do we know where warehouse #1, #2, and #3 are?"

Yo nodded and smiled, then said, "Not yet Angelina! You and your 9mm will wait until warehouse #3. #1 and #2 were always part of the plan to keep the Secret Service busy."

Angelina said, "You always make me wait!"

Yo once again removed the SIM card from the second burner phone, and destroyed both the card and phone, near a different sewer, nine blocks from the first site. He kept the SIM card for his special place.

On the drive back, Yo and Angelina discussed how "lucky" this Johnny Five was getting. Yo said, "Give me the word, and we can put some wet i625 in his car, or house."

She said, "Now don't be like that. We want the Project to succeed, not draw more attention to it. No, for now, Johnny will just be our nemesis. We'll just have to be more clever than he is."

Chapter 30

Johnny and the SWAT team were outside the warehouse #1 location one hour before the warrant was set to be executed. What they didn't know was that David Jones had vacated the location two hours before the warrant was to be served. Johnny, plus the 8-man team and four local PD units, were getting ready to breach the warehouse. Local Police were to provide a perimeter around the warehouse, and keep civilians safe. SWAT would breach the doors, and surprise the counterfeiters.

It was going to be a surprise alright! Johnny smiled. "3,2,1 - GO!"

Everyone stormed in! The building had two stories plus a basement, so it took almost five minutes of tense searching before people called, "Clear!"

Johnny was disgusted and angry! The SWAT team thanked him for the practice gig, and chuckled at the thought that they might have been able to have some fun today. It beat desk work, but Johnny was so sure he'd hit pay dirt.

Seconds later, one of the SWAT guys called Johnny over and said, "Look at this!"

Johnny walked over, and there was bag of soup and a sandwich from a grocery store that was not far from the warehouse. It had a receipt taped to the bag, dated today, less than three hours ago. Johnny snatched up the receipt, and raced to his car. He had a local PD unit follow him with lights and siren.

Upon entering the store, they went directly to the manager's office, and requested the security footage for the last four hours. The grocery store's camera system was state of the art. Finally, a break! Johnny had the security manager pull up the time from the receipt on the video. Sure enough, there was David Jones, about five years older than the yearbook photos, buying lunch for what looked like two or three people.

Johnny asked the security manager to email him the footage, and then went to the deli to talk to the lady who had served David.

Jane had remembered David because he was super happy. Apparently, an old friend was coming to work for him, and he needed a special lunch of soup, sandwiches, and potato salad. Jane had suggested some cookies, but David wanted cake. He asked Jane to write: So good to see you again Sam.

Johnny couldn't believe that code was just between Sam and David. Crap! He had probably lost his edge on locating David by going through Sam's personal code.

Johnny called the local PD, and asked them to run a scan on the cell towers for 55555 messages. The sergeant said, "Good luck."

Nothing was discovered. His lucky streak was gone. Back to the drawing board.

Then, Johnny had another idea. He called, and got Steve Stevenson's voicemail which said that he was on a long overdue vacation. Leave a message and he'd return it, if he ever came back from his vacation. No hint of when that might be.

Chapter 31

Johnny thought about yesterday's defeat. He was sure that he would have surprised David, between the text message with this address and a four-hour window. Maybe Sam had a change of heart, and warned him.

On that note, Johnny called Sam.

Sam answered, "Hey, Johnny! Tell me you're getting him help. When are visiting hours? I know he'll be upset, but I want to support him!" It was obvious that his friend was definitely not the one responsible for warning him off.

Johnny said, "Not yet." He told Sam of his dismal failure to catch David at the address. "We missed him by maybe an hour, since his celebration lunch was still warm."

Sam knew his friend must be ready to talk to him, especially after Johnny described the cake. "So, you called me back just now to see if I had a change of heart, and warned him off?"

Johnny felt even worse, "Guilty as charged."

Sam told Johnny, "Dude, you are my only hope that David will get out of this drug business alive. I have no illusions that any other agency would do anything for David, but lock him up and throw away the key. Agent Five, I made a promise to myself to help David get out of the evil life, and help him back to being normal. You are my only hope in 5+ years, and I will hold you to it at all costs! Don't give up on David or me! Now shake it off, and use that brilliant brain of yours."

Johnny now knew Sam was right. He said, "Dude, thanks for the pep talk, I needed it."

Sam chuckled and said, "No worries, Johnny! I just used the same one that Freaky Fred used on us several times! It's pretty good! Huh?"

It was Johnny's turn to laugh. "You missed your calling!"

Sam asked, "Who did you tell about the

arrest?"

Johnny answered, "Jack, his field super, local PD, SWAT, and of course, the clerk, and the Judge."

Sam asked, "Did you talk to them, or email them?"

Johnny asked, "What's the difference?"

Sam said, "In my business there are email bots that steal email by keywords. They will send out one email, and leave everything else alone. It's very hard to detect them with current antivirus and malware scanners."

Johnny thought about that. He had sent an email out just before the arrest. "Thanks! I'll get an IT techie to check for me. In the meantime, I won't let you and David down again."

Sam said, "I'm here anytime. Call if my therapy can help motivate you again."

They said goodbye, and Johnny thought about Sam. He knew now that David had a true-blue friend in him. Things would be hard for David, but with Freaky Fred and Sam in his corner, he had a great chance to straighten out his twisted life.

Johnny thought, "I wonder if David thinks Sam gave him up?" He still had a code for the text, and resent it. To his amazement, a new address popped up in less than 30 seconds. This time, Johnny was not taking chances. He'd investigate it alone first.

It was three blocks away from the other site in the same derelict business district. He could be there in 45 minutes. He grabbed a Dr. Pepper® as he headed out the front door. Thirty-eight minutes later, he was driving past the location. He parked, and walked around the block. There was no one in sight, no cars but his.

He walked up to the front door, and pulled on it. To his surprise, it opened. He walked in. Carefully looking around, he unsnapped his holster, but did not draw his gun. He was all alone, in the front office. Just as he was about to open the door leading into the warehouse space, he heard the front door open behind him.

He swiveled, and saw David Jones coming in the front door with a pizza and a 12 pack of Jolt Cola®. Johnny said, "Hello."

David just stood there with a questioning look on his face. Then he said, "Hi, can I help you?"

Johnny couldn't believe his luck was improving. Slowly, he walked over to David, and introduced himself, offering his hand. David set the pizza and colas down, and shook his hand. Holding his hand, Johnny spun him around, and cuffed him. "David Jones, you are under arrest." Johnny frisked him, and found no weapons or drugs, but he did find a well-stocked wallet with about $4,000 cash of funny money.

David Jones was completely understanding and compliant. (Almost mellow came to Johnny's mind.)

Johnny asked, "Who else is coming?"

"No one. I work completely alone, and I'm tired of it."

Johnny read him his rights, and asked if they could talk. To his surprise, David agreed, but suggested they eat while they talk. He explained that he had just picked up a pizza with everything except anchovies.

Johnny locked the front glass doors with the twist lock, and then uncuffed one of David's hands, and cuffed him to the chair. Johnny played it extremely cool, for he had a gold mine in front of him, and since he brought the pizza and drinks, why waste them?

He started by saying, "We have a lot of evidence against you, and if you cooperate, it will be much easier."

David agreed to waive his rights, and talked freely. Johnny listened as David spun his tale for the next ten minutes, nonstop except for the occasional bite of pizza. David also mentioned that for the last two months, he was trying to stay off drugs.

Johnny said, "You have three friends in this world that want you to survive this and get your life back."

David was shocked! "Who?"

"Freaky Fred, Sam, and myself."

David recalled Freaky Fred and said, "Man, I forgot all about him. I was hoping to see Sam yesterday when I got paged." Then, he realized that Johnny must have talked with Sam, and Sam gave up his best friend.

Johnny confirmed this saying, "Sam would be happy to give a glowing recommendation to the Judge, if it would help."

David got misty, and said that Sam was the best friend he'd ever had. It had been a mistake to make him choose between their friendship or Sam's wife. He asked how badly he was screwed.

Johnny replied, "Pretty bad, but if you'll help us, we can help you!" Johnny described jail time of 5-20 years for passing counterfeit money intentionally. If David were to help catch the real counterfeiters, he might be able to get that reduced to just rehab time.

David wanted to hug Johnny to thank him for the rehab deal - anything to get him off drugs. Taking a long drink of the Jolt Cola®, he said, "Caffeine is the only thing helping with the withdrawals."

They talked for almost an hour. Johnny thought this Mower Scam was brilliant. The IWANTTOWORKWITHYOU code to 55555 was an automated response. Johnny asked if he knew where the server was.

David said, "No, I don't even know who hired me. They just told me where to pick up the truck, and where the keys were. The phone tells me where to send the cash. The printer prints the label, and I stamp and send it."

Johnny uncuffed David, who in turn embraced him in a hug of appreciation, and then led him on a tour of his truck. Johnny was amazed. Inside the truck was a laptop with a Mifi device to connect to the internet remotely, a label printer, several boxes of envelopes, nearly 100 rolls of forever stamps, and a pallet of funny money.

David had orders to send five $100 bills to each address that was printed, and in turn, mail them out from various locations in Washington state. Also, if David found a worthy cause, at his discretion, he could pass more money as long as he didn't get caught. David told Johnny that every chance he got, he'd drop a paper bag with $500 at a bus stop or a park bench.

Johnny was impressed, not for the first time, that this operation was brilliant! Now, if he and David could just lure the bosses out. Johnny wondered how many trucks they had in operation.

David only knew of his in this area, but guessed there may be some in other states.

Johnny shuddered at the thought of nine more trucks like this, and the damage they could do...! These past two hours had proven to be extremely beneficial for both Johnny and David. This was one time he was glad he acted upon his instinct.

Johnny called the local PD, and had them pick up David. He told them to go easy on him, as he was a cooperating witness, and he would need to be hospitalized for drug addiction. Sergeant Hangry told Johnny he would personally take care of this witness.

Johnny had met Tom Hangry the day before, and the two had talked at length about the case. Johnny, finding the truck keys under the mat where David told him they were, followed the Sergeant to the station, and locked and logged the truck into the evidence lot.

Before leaving the station, Johnny checked in on David and watched him get photographed and printed. He told him that he would be in touch, and not to lose faith. David smiled weakly, and thanked him for helping him get out of this trap.

On the way out, Johnny talked to Sergeant Hangry and said, "You may want to put a suicide watch on him. I don't know what drugs he uses, or the effects of coming off of them, but he is too valuable to lose that

way."

Chapter 32

Johnny decided to call Jack Quick personally. Getting Jack's voicemail, he said, "Call me when you get a minute," and hung up.

While he was waiting, he called Sam. Like always, Sam said, "Hey Dude!"

Johnny said, "I picked up David, and I think he'll be a great candidate for amnesty and drug rehabilitation. He was very helpful, not to mention, very cool under pressure."

Sam said, "Yeah, David's always been a cool cucumber, even when he was caught. He could talk himself out of walking the plank on a pirate ship. I was always the nervous one. Hey! Thanks for doing this for us."

Johnny tried to push it off, but it really did mean that much to both David and Sam. Johnny said, "I just want to put an end to this crisis, and if I can help get people back on track, it's better than making

American's foot the bill for a prison stay."

Sam agreed, thinking how much he paid in taxes. "Too bad not all people are willing to help others fix this world."

Johnny gave him the PD phone number and visiting hours, and said for him to call if he needed anything.

A short minute passed, and Johnny's phone rang. It was Jack. Johnny told Jack of the disaster two days before, and that he had no idea where the leak was, but there was a huge one somewhere. Then, he told Jack about casing the second location by himself. He told how he had met David Jones, and the ensuing conversation, and the discovery of the mobile truck.

Jack, again, couldn't believe how good Johnny's luck was on this case. "Congrats, Kid! Not bad for your first field promotion."

Johnny asked Jack for a favor. Jack liked the idea and told Johnny to run with it.

The next call Johnny made was to his IT

department. He asked if someone, or something, could be spying on him and his computer. The techie was drooling after telling him how many dreadful things could be on his system without his knowledge after three minutes. But this was the Secret Service's laptop. Surely, they had software running to prevent that from happening.

The techie said, "Unfortunately, not as much as we would hope. About 120,000 new threats hit the world each day, and those are only the ones that get reported."

Johnny described the events that happened, and that his friend, Sam, suggested he check his computer for a keyword bot.

The techie was impressed. Keyword bots were the latest in theft software on a computer, and he said that they were new, even to him. He ran the latest scanner he had, and then looked for software after the scanner came back clean. He looked at the incoming and outgoing data in real time, and saw something, but lost it. It was stealthware that the Homeland Security was toying with, but had not yet deployed. The techie whistled, and said, "WOW! I've read about this in the Secret Service updates we have recently received, but I didn't think I'd ever see it in my lifetime!" He explained it would send out data (which was keyword emails, files, and photos) on the suspect's computer, encrypt them, and send the package out in a microburst of less than a second to an undisclosed location.

Johnny had a brilliant thought! "Wait, don't remove it!"

The techie said, "Who, me? I couldn't even if I wanted to. The program is booby-trapped to wipe the data and fry the motherboard in the event that it is removed."

Johnny clarified, "So, it would physically damage the computer?"

"Worse, it would *Brick it!*" the techie said. He told Johnny he'd better talk to Homeland Security about this directly.

Johnny let that sink in... "Homeland Security... is investigating me, or all of Secret Service laptops." Either way, this was rather a new development in the light of recent events.

Before hanging up, Johnny asked one more question. "Do you know anything about the Encryption Hackers?"

The techie replied, "Not much, but I'd bet they could write or hack this easily."

Johnny said, "Thanks, you've been an immense help."

Immediately after ending his call, he called Jack. He asked him to check his computer for the signature the techie gave him, to see if he had it on his machine.

Jack reported, "No." They talked for a bit, and Jack again congratulated the field agent on outstanding work. They planned a video conference call with Homeland Security to quietly discuss this new wrinkle. Johnny told Jack over the phone not to email anything, just in case. Jack agreed.

The following day at 2pm EST and 11 am PST, Jack initiated a video conference call with an Admiral of Homeland Security and Johnny. Johnny calmly explained the issue he had with his machine.

The Admiral was flabbergasted! This software was not supposed to exist yet, and never on another law enforcement agency's computer. "Scallywags! I'll have them court martialed for this. Computer techies always think they can skate by and do whatever they want to test something. They don't always understand 'National Security Protocols'. I would have my best man come on your system and remove it, but he's on a vacation and cannot be disturbed at present."

Jack and Johnny both started to protest, but the Admiral wouldn't budge! Johnny said that when he was on vacation, they could call him anytime.

The Admiral agreed. "It's a long sad story, but numerous times in the past four years, we called and cancelled his vacation for things just like this. It got so bad, he requested a pardon from the President of the United States, and gave it to me a week ago when the Encryption Hackers hit."

Johnny and Jack both laughed, and said, "Four years without a break... you're lucky he didn't go postal on you!"

The Admiral chuckled and said, "He's the best, and we should treat him better - this time we are."

Jack was about to end the call, when Johnny asked the Admiral if he could help with finding another assistant.

The Admiral said, "For you two, name it!"

Johnny said that he was looking for a Steve Stevenson.

The Admiral almost choked! "He's the one on vacation!!!!!"

Chapter 33

Back in California at the bomb shelter, Angelina Gear, Yo, and their five scientists were busy. Yesterday, the shipments of inks and CLRcoatYO were delivered, and placed on the 5th level of the shelter. They had begun mixing the inks with the i625, and the CLRcoatYO with the cc625. These new mixtures were stored in vacuum sealed plastic bags inside metal pallets that were welded shut by Yo. They were then moved into Yo's warehouse for storage, by way of the secret tunnel.

Angelina and her team had this procedure down to a choreographed science, and within 24 hours had mixed all of the first shipment of inks, clear coats, and *death!* Angelina congratulated her staff on accomplishing these tasks three days ahead of schedule, without one mistake or error.

In the back of Yo's Inks4Life.net building they had three loading bays where they had three non-descript semi-trucks waiting. Painted on the sides of the bay doors, were BLACK, GREEN, and Clear Coat labels. Each kind of pallet was to be shipped in a different semi-truck to prevent accidental mixing. If the trucks were in a traffic accident, or some other cataclysmic event, they didn't want accidental mixing to occur. This also meant the trucks would all be taking separate routes to the BEP, where possible.

This secure arrangement was also satisfactory with the Secret Service and the BEP scientists. No one wanted a semi-truck that had all three components in the same vehicle, in case one got stolen.

Yo had been working on these plans with Jack, Toby, and Trent over video conference calls in his office. The gadget on his desk had proved to be invaluable during these calls because anytime there was stress in the voices on the call, Yo's red light had come on and warned him someone was worried, or not happy. This allowed Yo to be completely dialed into the video conference participants' moods. This made him look extremely professional, and he was able to reassure everyone at the BEP and the Secret Service that everything was going as planned. Now, if he could only make this gadget portable, and use it on poker night at the Elk lodge!

Angelina came into his office and said, "I haven't seen any messages from 55555 in the past three days since the move to location two."

Yo thought this was odd, since most people never hesitated to request free cash from their promo. He said, "I'll check it out. Have you seen any emails from that Johnny Five agent? Maybe he got lucky again."

Angelina said, "Everything has been unusually quiet between Johnny and Jack. But then again, you've been keeping Jack occupied." She said that she needed to check in with Steve Stevenson today. She'd ask him later.

About 4pm, Angelina called Steve, who answered and said without preamble that the new server was up and functioning, and he would be sending out access rights to them in 25 minutes or so.

"Excellent!" She wanted to play with some accounts to keep a Secret Service agent busy who was messing up her plans.

Steve asked if it was Jack, or Johnny.

She replied, "Johnny. He's made some pretty good guesses, and that's why I called." Angelina told Steve about the Mower Scam, and how they were using it to stir up counterfeit issues in Oregon.

Steve was amazed! This lady was beyond smart, and ruthless too!

Angelina said that she had set up a druggie who seemed computer savvy enough for her scheme. She continued to tell Steve that she got an alert from Johnny's email that the Secret Service had found his first location. She had warned him to bug out to the 2nd location of the three sites they had set up.

Steve whistled, "Yeah, you need to give this Johnny guy a new puzzle."

Angelina agreed and said, "Your data will allow me to do just that. In the meantime, can you look at Johnny's machine and see if anything looks out of place? He hasn't sent any emails in three days, and I'm pretty sure, it's just my paranoia."

Steve said, "Sure, I can do it with you on the phone. I don't need to even get on Johnny's machine to do this. Everything was captured in that microburst transmission, and system log files were sent, too." Steve was silent for a few moments, then said, "Uh-Oh!"

Angelina felt a knot tighten in her stomach.

"I have good news and bad news. Bad news is that he called Tech Support and told them he suspects an email search tool on his system. Also, the Tech Support guy found it, but couldn't remove it. My secret recipe would brick his machine. The good news is, I can modify his code to gather more intel video to continue to spy on him."

Angelina asked, "Well if he's infected, and he knows it, won't he just not use it?"

Steve replied, "That may happen, but I'm willing to bet he wants to trick us into revealing something by pretending he doesn't know, but we do know! So be on your guard, Angelina!"

She thanked Steve and told him to stay on it. He'd keep her posted.

Ten minutes later, Angelina and Yo got an email with the access to the data site and a text file attachment with all the key players' accounts listed for easy retrieval.

Right then, Steve started wondering how his cousin David was doing. Wasn't he still in Washington state? He went back to Johnny's logs, and on a hunch, did a keyword search on "Jones". There were 49 hits! Steve looked closer, and immediately sent an email back to Angelina.

She called him 12 minutes later, asking, "What's up now?"

Steve said, "I think we have what you may call a cluster in the making."

Angelina's knot turned into a clove hitch!

Steve explained that he had a cousin, David, living in Washington state that grew up on the wrong side of the tracks.

Angelina said, "Holy Cow! Is his last name Jones?"

"Yes," Steve confirmed. "How in the world did you select my cousin for your scheme?"

Angelina said, "I have no clue. Do you have any ties to him?"

Steve told Angelina, "Yes. My Homeland Security profile uses his fingerprints as mine, should anyone check me out."

Angelina remembered this, but her access wouldn't reveal the notes. That's where they found the druggie. She asked, "What does this mean?"

Steve thought about it. "Nothing. No one knows who did the Encryption Hack yet, and so I have a cousin, no biggie." Steve added, "I was digging around Johnny Five's caseload online, and noticed that he arrested my cousin last night. What does David know about Yo and you?"

Angelina assured Steve, "David does not know who hired him, just a voice on a burner phone, and those phones are destroyed now."

"Ok, I'll keep my guard up. You do the same, and we should be fine. Make sure you give Johnny a tough time for me, and David too!"

Angelina said, "Count on it!"

They disconnected, and she went to break the news to Yo.

Chapter 34

Jack was on a video conference call with the BEP staff and Yo. Jack had called the meeting because Yo was ready to ship the first nine trucks. There would be 120 tons of BLK33284, GRN33284, and CLRcoatYO. Jack told everyone on the call that Secret Service agents would be escorting the three trucks across the country, disguised as wide load transporters. One SUV would be in the front, and one in the back of each set of trucks. The agents would be trained semi-truck drivers who were licensed to carry in all states. Each vehicle would have two occupants, so they could drive straight through. Each semi-truck was armored, and had bulletproof tires, doors, and glass. The BEP had this arrangement with all its vendors for the engraving plates, and the paper as well. There were secure GPS, Top-Secret sensors, and gadgets on board to detect smoke, heat, water, mist, and radiation levels. This was all monitored by Homeland Security while in route.

Jack took his transporting mission the same as guarding the current President, since he had to guard billions of dollars at the same time! The shipments would begin at 7am at Yo's Inks4Life.net building the next morning.

Yo found Angelina. She said, "It won't be long now!"

She called Steve while he was eating lunch, poolside. It was still his vacation *after all*. No one was around for miles. They all worked for government agencies across the river in DC. He had checked before renting this place for a month. He didn't think he could use a month's vacation all at one time, but he was going to see how far that pardon would get him.

Angelina said, "I had a thought about Johnny. Aren't there signatures that antivirus companies use to detect who else has it? If Johnny sent that signature file to Jack, and maybe the BEP staff, will we lose all our intel dumps?"

Steve laughed, "Yes, usually that is how it works, but my secret recipe generates a new random signature file for each computer it's set up on. Meaning, there are no similarities passed from one system to the next. This gives Homeland Security the classic deniability to protect themselves against lawsuits from the civilian population. That was a requirement from my bosses, and the Presidential mandate."

Angelina breathed a sigh of relief and said, "Great! One less thing to think about. By the way, thanks for giving us the highlighted text of our enemies in that file you emailed to us. Any day now, Johnny is going to say, What the Hell?!"

Chapter 35

Johnny was paying for his breakfast on the way to his office for a meeting with his boss, when the waitress came up and told him his debit card was declined. Johnny wondered, but asked her to wait a minute. He didn't have cash, so he tried his other credit card. In a minute, she was back, saying it was also declined. He started getting worried. He picked up his smartphone, checked his banking application, and said, "What the Hell?!"

His banking app said he was $4,853.72 in the hole. He checked the recent transactions, and noticed someone had systematically drained his debit account. Then, when the Secret Service direct deposit hit, they had drained that too, leaving him owing the bank for his check that cleared yesterday. He looked up, and saw the waitress getting impatient. He gave her his Secret Service expense credit card. Again, in thirty seconds she was back with his card. "What the Hell?!" His expense card had no reasonable limit.

$250,000.

This was not good! But, then he thought about it, and it hit him. He had struck a nerve with the counterfeiters. He was making somebody very nervous. Nervous enough to come after *him*. He grinned and apologized to the waitress. He said that he'd pay her back. He flashed his badge, and told her he'd be back with cash.

She laughed and called Earl. Earl could have played professional ball with the Raiders, and he'd be two centers!

Johnny asked to see the manager, who he found out was Earl. He explained his slight problem, and gave Earl a signed business card.

After about 15 minutes had gone by, Earl said, "Anything for the Secret Service."

Johnny was now 20 minutes late to his meeting. He told his boss that he got under someone's skin, and asked if he could get a $500 advance until he got it straightened out.

His boss said, "Get $2,000. You're going

on a trip." His boss explained that he got an email from Jack Quick in DC, requesting Johnny's help with a convoy tomorrow in California, after which he would be temporarily reassigned to the DC office under Jack Quick. He continued, "Pending your approval and Jack's, you will be moved to outside DC, probably Virginia, to a staff house with a pool and perks, helping Jack with whatever he is working on. Fantastic job, Kid! This is how the Secret Service is supposed to treat people - enjoy it!"

Johnny was stunned. "Ok, where's the convoy?"

"Jack said to call him, and he'll send the address of Inks4Life.net."

Johnny got his $2,000 advance, called Jack for the address, and headed to the airport where his plane awaited to take him to Inks4Life.net in California.

When Johnny arrived at the ink facility, he rang the buzzer and Yo answered it.

He buzzed Johnny into the Inks4Life.net

lobby and said, "I'll be up in a few minutes, have a seat." Yo turned and looked at Angelina. "You're not going to believe this...!"

Yo and Angelina both took the tunnel. They shut it behind them and locked it, so no scientist could use it when Johnny was taking his tour. Yo introduced himself and Angelina Gear, his lead scientist, for Inks4Life.net. Johnny was struck by the beautiful lady in a white lab coat, and immediately wondered why she did it.

Yo led him on a small tour of his shop, and asked if he'd had any trouble finding them. Johnny laughed, telling them about his morning at the diner, and then his surprise assignment to escort the inks across the country to his new posting.

Yo said, "Messed up finances are a real pain to clean up. I hope you have better luck than I do. That Encryption Hacker thing two weeks ago has threatened my livelihood. Thank goodness, the President gave everyone that extra month to straighten it out."

Angelina and Yo opened the back door, and introduced Johnny to his new colleagues. Soon after the meet and greet, the convoy set off with Johnny in the back of the BLK33284 convoy with the other two Secret Service agents, Tom and Harry. Both of them had been doing these runs for the BEP for eight years, with only a flat tire for a story, and they were serious about keeping that record.

When Yo and Angelina returned to the shelter, Angelina said, "I know you are supposed to keep your friends close, and your enemies closer, but this is CRAZY!"

Yo had told Angelina that Jack was going to invite a very special agent to ride along, but he thought that was just talk. Yo said, "Well, at least we'll know what he's up to now that he's working with us. He doesn't know anything about this project, and we don't have counterfeit anything around here, so everything is cool, right?!"

Angelina could make this work. It was just the challenge she was craving at this moment in time.

At the first gas break, Johnny ran into the store, and got a cold case of Dr. Pepper®, water, and munchies for Tom, Harry, and himself. Then, they settled in for many miles to come.

Chapter 36

For Johnny, the cross-country trip flew by. They stopped every two hours for stretch breaks, and six hours to change drivers. They made excellent time. Each time they pulled into a weigh station, they always got a friendly wave past, and wondered if all truckers had it this good.

After the second day, they were beginning to see fatigue creep into their routines. Some of the trucker pairs were getting back into their "I hate passenger car drivers" mentality, although it never was a problem, just a running joke on the radio frequencies. By the third day, everyone was glad to see a sign that read Washington, DC 74 miles. A cheer could be heard on the radio six counties away. The other trucking teams cheered too when they got close. Johnny informed Jack when they were about 30 minutes out. Jack and the BEP staff would be ready for their arrival.

Within three hours, the BEP was buzzing

with activity that made a beehive pale in comparison. Forklifts and trucks were everywhere, as far as the eye could see.

It was October 15, and the BEP staff were all a twitter with the anticipation of a new bill seeing fruition. After six hours, the BEP had set up the connecting hoses to the ink presses for the three main components BLK33284, GRN33284, and the CLRcoatYO. The other hoses connected the spot changing ink colors for the other security features not changing on the bills. They ran several tests with plain paper, but the real test would be soon enough. After all the testing and bleed problems had been tweaked and corrected, Trent gave the OK to start a run going full production. They ran nonstop for six hours, and printed just over $500 million in cash. Every last bill was flawless, no defects or errors could be found on any of the notes. Trent and Toby were shocked at Yo and Angelina's product.

After this run was complete, the press staff changed out the three new components with forklifts, and put the empty containers in the area marked return to Inks4Life.net to refill. No one noticed that the valve on the hose connecting the CLRcoatYO was in the off position, and the forklift driver couldn't tell that his pallet was still full of the CLRcoatYO. The next day, the new money was sent out to the Federal Reserve Banks as was their standard operating procedure. This money then replaced the recycled bills that were taken out of circulation.

The inspection process at the BEP had not been changed, due to an oversight of an overworked BEP employee. This meant that the checks for the durability of the bill were not in the procedure to test the Superhero caliber of strength. This and the shutoff valve that was overlooked on the CLRcoatYO meant that the cc625 never met the bill at all, and this set of $5B ($500M x 10 printing days) would never be radioactive... ever!

Chapter 37

Johnny had just finished getting his ID card made by the Chief of Security for the Secret Service. (Now that Johnny had been assigned to Jack, he needed new credentials for the new DC office and the BEP.) The next item on his agenda was to go with Jack to the BEP where he would be introduced to the receptionist and the key players on the project. This was the first time that Johnny had seen the BEP, and he was in awe of the size of the facility. Johnny had to keep reminding himself that this was his new office, too. Jack had told him to expect 40% / 40% / 40% in each location. DC BEP / Fort Worth BEP / DC Secret Service. Johnny just smiled, knowing Jack was going to depend on him like Trent did Toby.

Johnny was fine with the idea. Maybe he'd find a girlfriend later, but for the first year, he'd have to pay his dues. He never in a million years thought he'd be assigned to DC! One could always hope, but that was like hoping you'd get the chance to protect

POTUS.

This morning's activities and instructions seemed to fly by, and before he knew it, Jack was taking him to lunch. Toby would be joining them since they weren't printing money today.

During lunch, Jack and Toby listened to the details of the Mower Scam counterfeit ring. When Johnny finished his story, Toby winked at Jack and said, "You've got a great protege here." Looking at Johnny, Toby said, "If you do half that well in DC, I'm willing to bet you'll have your own staff outside of three years."

Jack joked, "I've got $20 US *real currency*, he'll do it in two years!" Johnny's mouth dropped open when Toby took the bet.

Later that day, Jack and Johnny returned to the Secret Service office. Johnny's day had been both productive and educational, but he was beginning to realize how long it felt.

Jack suggested he take the rest of the day off to go look for a place to hang his hat.

"There's a delightful place just across the river in Virginia. Traffic could be bad, but there are multiple ways to come into the city." Jack knew this place, since he lived there, too.

Johnny, thankful for the opportunity to find housing, said, "See ya tomorrow, Boss," and split. He drove out to the address, making amazingly good time, and was surprised to see new construction in the subdivision. Finding the leasing department, he inquired about furnished units.

The agent said there was no waiting list, which he found impossible to believe! Amenities included a pool, tennis and basketball courts, a health club, and the prices were about the same as Oregon. He figured more in Oregon, actually. Next, the leasing agent asked if he was looking for an apartment building, or a villa.

Johnny didn't care, he just needed a place to be. In the end, he decided on the apartment, since it was closer to people and the pool. Not that he'd have time to enjoy it, but he could still dream. Forty minutes later, he had his new apartment keys, and was on his balcony checking out the traffic at the pool from the fifth floor.

Next, Johnny used his map from the leasing office and his GPS to get his bearings on the local shopping area. First order of business was to find an excellent Mexican restaurant. Then, he could pick up a few groceries and several cases of Dr. Pepper®. It was nice to finally be home, even if his stuff hadn't arrived from the movers yet.

The next morning, Johnny thanked Jack for a great tip on housing, and told him he was in unit 5555.

Jack laughed and said, "You're kidding, right?"

"Nope!" Johnny couldn't believe it either!

Jack just grinned. Johnny and Jack had decided to work on the Steve Stevenson issue today. They called the Admiral to find out if anyone could assist them with Johnny's laptop while Steve was out of the office. The Admiral told them to stop by, and he'd have his second-best expert look at it.

By 10am, Jack and Johnny were in a lab facility with Winston. Winston worked with Steve and his team often enough to know almost as much as Steve, but just like the Secret Service techie, he said, "I don't see a way to remove it without bricking it!"

Johnny said, "Don't worry, I have backups and a new Secret Service machine. Give me a receipt for this, and you guys keep this one here. Find a way to disarm this! Something tells me we'll need the solution sooner, rather than later."

Winston gave Johnny a receipt, and showed them into the command area where the Admiral's office was. Needless to say, the Admiral was quite disappointed with the results. He mentioned keel-hauling Stevenson, but that would have to wait until he returned from Bora Bora, or wherever techies go to escape life.

In the car, Jack and Johnny continued to discuss current events. Johnny asked if there was any news on the Encryption Hackers.

Jack said, "Unofficially, we have narrowed the location down to North Korea, but it doesn't look good for a seal team incursion. Delta is looking at it, too. The President wants it blown off the map, but there are issues with that approach."

"Someone put a lot of thought into this electronic assault, too much, if you ask me," Johnny said.

Chapter 38

Three weeks had passed since the scientists left the hidden lab facility to move outside of Hong Kong. Over the past two weeks, they had set up their new offices, and now they were getting ready to have the time of their lives on a well-deserved vacation.

Within six days, funny money was discovered at the Hong Kong banks from places such as: ships' casinos, real estate agencies, race tracks, movie theaters, and dance clubs, to name a few. Most of these places didn't check the currency to see if it was counterfeit. Casinos want your money, so dealers take money at the tables when you enter, stuff it into the table slot, and give you chips to play with.

Only one of the remaining 12 scientists got caught for passing counterfeit US bills. He tried to pay for a house out right with his $500,000 in funny money. Things for that scientist did not work out well. He remains in a Hong Kong prison, waiting for his time in front of a Judge, most likely before he is sentenced to life in prison.

One scientist discovered that his longtime friend had been arrested, and went to the jail to talk to him. Nearly impossible to do, somehow, he got one of the policemen to let him speak to his friend who warned him that Angelina had set them up, and if they weren't careful, they would all end up like him behind bars. He explained that the $500K was expertly counterfeited money. He told his buddy to be careful and to warn the others quietly not to alert the Generals of their country. He knew he was safer here in prison, than on the outside where the Generals would just kill him and his friends for bringing disgrace on their motherland. The two talked for several minutes, but did not discuss the charges and plans to get him out of jail. Those Generals were scared men, as Angelina had put it, and these two scientists knew it meant death if they found out.

Back in California at the shelter, Yo and Angelina were having a status meeting with her five scientists. All the ink and clear coat had been mixed, and was ready for shipment as soon as the BEP could decide where they wanted it delivered.

The BEP had two locations that printed money, DC and Fort Worth, TX. Currently, Trent and Toby were contemplating if they should split up the shipments between the two sites, or keep everything in DC for the moment. They decided to give it four months, and then start in Fort Worth. Toby agreed this sounded like an excellent thought for now.

Everyone had been very happy with the first ten day run of the new bills. (They were unaware they had printed approximately $5B worth of weak currency without the clear coat being applied.) The nine semi-trucks were about to go back to get more ink and clear coat from Inks4Life.net. They would send the empty pallets back to get cleaned and refilled for the second ten day run in November.

Toby had contacted Jack, and told him it was time to schedule a return trip back to California. They would return the empties, load up the trucks, and get the shipment back before the second week of November.

Jack had been expecting this request for the past week. Actually, he was surprised they had waited so long. He told Toby that he would need an updated bill of lading for the trucks' return and approximate weight for the weigh stations.

Toby calculated this number based on the number of empty pallets they were returning per truck. Then, he emailed the data to Jack, who in turn emailed it to the weigh station system.

The next day, the nine trucks were loaded, and the Secret Service crews (minus Johnny Five) left for California by 7am.

The Secret Service agents had an ongoing bet for $1 per man on whether the state's weigh stations were opened or closed when they passed them. Nine trucks, three different routes, thirty men; that meant it could be quite profitable, and that made the trip pass by quicker. The first four weigh stations were closed. Tom and Harry were in the lead, but they were also in the CLRcoatYO truck convoy this time, by chance.

The fifth weigh station was open. Normally, they just got that friendly wave, and went about their trip. Not this time. The attendant flagged all three semi-trucks over to the impound lot. Tom was driving, so Harry called Jack instantly. Jack and Johnny, in DC, were on the call together. Harry explained that all three trucks had been placed in the impound lot, and several officers were coming outside to inspect the trucks.

Immediately, Jack called the weigh station master to let him know who they were. He asked what the problem seemed to be.

He was told that all three trucks were massively overweight, and the bills of lading were wrong. Jack explained they were transporting empties, and should be close to the weight of the truck plus 3 tons.

The weigh station master said, "No sir, they're all roughly 77,000 pounds!" So much for Tom and Harry's flat tire record - this was going to put a dent in it.

Jack called Toby and asked him if they were missing any new containers of the CLRcoatYO.

Toby replied that nothing was missing or out of place, except all the empty containers weren't present as expected.

Jack and Toby talked for several minutes, and Jack finally told Toby what the issue was.

"That's impossible, Jack!" Toby replied.

Jack knew something was horribly wrong. The next question Jack and Toby had was, "What was in all those containers?!"

Chapter 39

Angelina Gear's email chimed, and she looked down at her phone. "What the Hell?!"

Yo looked up from his coffee and danish in the cafeteria and said, "What's going on now?"

She had just received a forwarded email from Jack's tap. "Apparently, one convoy was impounded due to the trucks being overweight of the bill of lading. Each truck weighed in at about 77,000 pounds, but should have been returning to us as empties!"

Yo said, "That's impossible. The empties might weigh 3,000 pounds, if even!"

"It gets worse. Jack called Toby and no product is missing. Something's not right, that's for sure. Any chance they filled the empties with water, and shipped them with water in them?"

"Who knows!?" Yo, looking at Angelina, said, "Pack your bags, I sense a technical troubleshooting session in our future." Yo walked into his office and said, "Sounds like an appropriate time for a courtesy call to the BEP. My guess is, you'll get to see Johnny up close and personal sooner than we planned."

Angelina didn't like Yo's idea, but they'd have to call and find out soon. She nodded, and Yo dialed the number. Yo's call went straight to voicemail, and Yo just played it cool. "Hey Toby! Yo, here. Just checking on the progress of the project. I noticed on the calendar that your tenth day of printing was a couple of days ago. I just wanted to make sure everything is still golden. Give me a call when you have a few minutes. Thanks! See ya."

Much to Angelina and Yo's surprise, Toby never called. He was too busy to check his office voicemail. It took him a full 24 hours to call Yo back.

Yo answered his mobile and said, "This is Yo. How may I solve your ink problems today?"

Toby almost laughed. "Sorry," Toby said,

"yesterday was stinking crazy."

Yo played his part well. "Something wrong?"

Toby assumed someone would have emailed Yo, but then he realized that it would have been him, if he'd had time to do it.

Toby began, but was soon interrupted by Yo saying, "Let me get Angelina in on this call." Ten seconds later, Angelina was conferenced in.

Toby began to spin the tale of the overweight trucks being impounded. It seemed that it was only the CLRcoatYO that had the incorrect amounts. The other trucks flew through the stations without incident.

When Toby took a deep breath, Angelina asked, "When your staff changed out the CLRcoatYO pallets, did they try to rinse them out with water?"

Toby paged the press operator, and he was in the office within two minutes. Toby put the question to him.

His response was, "No, Sir! We just switched out the pallets with a new one. We took the empty, and placed it on the stack labeled empties: return to Inks4Life.net. No one on my team would try to clean them. If it's not on the checklist, as we've found out in the past, we don't improvise!" Toby thanked him, and let him get back to work.

It was a real mystery. Yo asked, "Where are those trucks now?"

Toby replied, "They got impounded, and are still at the weigh station waiting for a new bill of lading."

"Are you going to return them to us, or are you recalling them to the BEP?"

Toby thought about that. "Hold on a minute - let me conference Jack in on this." In a moment Yo heard Jack and Johnny's voices on the call. Toby posed the question to Jack, who hesitated before answering.

"Return them to the BEP." Jack then asked, "Yo, can you two join us out at the

BEP tomorrow?"

Yo and Angelina agreed to catch a flight out ASAP.

Jack said he would revise the bill(s) of lading, and have the impounded trucks turn around. They should be returning to the BEP by tomorrow.

Everyone agreed not to touch anything until all the parties were represented at the opening of the pallets. Johnny asked if Hazmat should be there as a precaution. Jack and Toby thought that was an outstanding suggestion since nobody could be sure of what was in the pallets.

On the way to the BEP, Angelina and Yo were both trying to figure out what the BEP could have done, and what they put in the containers. "We'll just have to be ready for anything! Story of my life," Yo said with a smirk!

The next morning, all the players were there by 11am. Hazmat was standing by; Toby and his staff were waiting. Yo and Angelina drove up, and right after them,

Jack and Johnny arrived.

Everyone took one collective deep breath, and opened the first truck. Toby and Angelina stepped inside to examine the pallets. As expected, all the seals were broken, but recapped as per the checklist required for empties. Angelina took a sample of the CLRcoatYO with a syringe, and looked at it in the sunlight. She then asked for a beaker, and emptied the syringe into the beaker, smelling the sample. It wasn't water, it was the CLRcoatYO in its original state!

Wanting to save face for Toby, they climbed down, and went into the conference room where she asked Toby to bring "all" procedures with him.

Yo followed her and whispered, "Do you know what it is?"

She nodded and whispered back, "They never used it in the first batch."

Yo muttered, "There's no coat on the first $5B they printed?!"

"Seems that way. Now, Hush! We've got

to let Toby find this out, so he can save face."

Yo knew she was right. If they just said you forgot a step, it could cost them the contract, and her revenge!

Toby walked into the conference room with all the new documentation. His staff impatiently waited outside to find out the verdict.

Angelina, quietly pulling Toby aside, said, "It's the original clear coat formula."

Toby looked at her like she was crazy.

She asked him to show her the new documentation, and he highlighted all the new sections with an orange highlighter. Next, she asked if these were the exact documents on the floor at each station of the presses.

Toby said, "No, these are my copies."

Angelina, unable to help herself, exclaimed, "Field trip!" They all walked the route of the presses, and the documentation at each station was checked against Toby's masters. They noticed that the process document to the press that did the clear coating was different... it was the *old* document. Next, they checked the hoses going into the press. Toby noticed the shutoff valve was in the "OFF" position. The press had never used the clear coat!

Where was the QA testing procedure? They went into that particular lab, and looked up the checklist. It too was the *old* document! So, the clear coat was never applied, and QA never tested for the Superhero attributes of the new money.

Toby found a new bill still in the vault. It looked as flawless as all the rest of them, but when he tried to tear it in half, it tore right away. No effort was needed. Toby was disgusted, livid, and raving towards his staff. Once he regained his composure, he thanked Angelina and Yo for their assistance in discovering the flaw in the process.

Angelina said, "There needs to be one more check so that this doesn't happen again. Weigh the pallets going back. Nobody detected they were full, because they used mechanical lifting devices to load them. Forklifts, hoists, cranes, all of these won't tell you if you're lifting 100 or 2,000 lbs."

Toby apologized for the miscommunication, and thanked everyone present for their patience. The good news was: the money was no worse than the current money, and could still be circulated. The next batch would be of the Superhero caliber, and Angelina didn't add *Deadly!*

Chapter 40

The following day, Toby asked Yo and Angelina to stay on for the next week, so that they would be ready to go as soon as the BLK33284 and GRN33284 arrived in five days. Angelina did not like the idea of sitting around babysitting the BEP employees that long, so Yo told her he could stay and look after their interests. He suggested she go sightseeing in DC, since in six months she wouldn't be able to.

Angelina liked that idea, and decided she could do some intel collecting herself. Toby, hearing that Angelina was going sightseeing, suggested she go with someone, but she said that she wanted to explore by herself.

Angelina hailed a cab, saying, "Take me to the number one tourist spot in DC."

The cabbie asked her, "Is this your first time in America?"

She replied, "No, but in DC, yes."

Then he suggested he could drop her off, and return to carry her to each new site for a small extra fee.

She liked this guy, and she was sure Archie would suit her purposes.

He dropped her off at the White House after giving her his mobile number. "Call me 15 minutes before you're ready, and I'll meet you back here."

Angelina wandered around, visiting some other sites nearby. About three hours later, she called Archie. "Can you recommend a good place for lunch?"

A short distance away, he dropped her off at a park that had seven lunch carts. She walked over to the one with the shortest line, and ordered the special and a water. It was something called a falafel. She thought it was delicious, so she went back and ordered the same for Archie. Then, she called him, and soon she heard a horn honking behind her. Angelina saw him wave, and got in the cab.

Archie inquired about lunch.

She was amazed that something not from a real kitchen could be that good. She then surprised Archie by handing him the food she had bought him.

Thanking her for the thought, he politely declined stating, "I only eat falafels."

Angelina smiled and said, "I guessed right then."

Archie couldn't believe it! None of his clients had ever bought him lunch. He thanked her, saying, "I'll eat after I drop you off. Where to?"

She thought for a moment and said, "I'd like to see an Aerospace Museum."

Archie knew exactly where to take her. Soon, he pulled under a nice shady tree, and let her out. Archie was the best guide she'd ever seen. He pointed out all the sites and monuments they passed, and said, "If you're here tomorrow, I can be your guide again."

She walked into the museum, and marveled at the jet planes and space ships that she saw. About two hours later, she called Archie. When he arrived, she told him that she could spend a month in there and still not see everything. Now it was time for her to return to the BEP.

Archie dropped her off. She reached into her purse, pulled out $500 in cash, and handed it to Archie. He argued, "$100 is more than enough, but $500 is way too much!" Archie lost his argument. He thanked her for lunch, and said he hoped he could help in the future.

Angelina said, "Stay by your phone tomorrow." She entered the BEP, where she showed her pass to the guard, and found Yo, bored to tears. "I told you so...!" She smirked.

Yo asked if she had fun.

She told him about the White House, lunch in a park, and the aerospace museum. She had also made a new friend in a great cabbie. She told him of Archie and his talent that they could put to beneficial use later.

Yo raised his eyebrows and said, "You

gave him your mobile number?"

"Yes, but it's a burner!" she replied.

"Ok, was the $500 the special?"

"Nope, it was the real USD. Like I said, we can use him later."

Yo wasn't sure, but it wasn't a big deal yet.

Angelina asked, "How'd Toby treat you?"

Yo told her that he barely saw him, but he did check all the stations and procedures, and they are now correct.

"So, no more CLRcoatYO mishaps?"

"They are a thing of the past!" Yo stated. "Toby said I should go sightseeing with you tomorrow. He was feeling guilty for keeping me here all week over something so minor."

"Great! Tomorrow you can meet Archie, and give me your take on him."

When they returned to their hotel, they went out on the balcony. Yo asked her, "What in the world do you want to use a cabbie for?"

Angelina said, "We can use him to send out cash to people here in DC, like David did in Washington state, but it won't be counterfeit. Lots of people want to come to DC for trips. He already has a printer and smartphone in his car. We supply the envelopes, stamps, and cash - He's completely mobile all the time."

"Brilliant!" Although, Yo liked the prospect, he asked, "Why won't he just take the money and run?"

Angelina said, "He's honest! He wants to earn his keep. We throw $5K a week to him, and he's ours! He can work as a cabbie, and work for us if he likes."

The next morning, Angelina called Archie and told him that she and a colleague would need a tour guide, and would be in front of the Grand Hyatt.

Archie laughed and said, "On my way!"

While they waited, Angelina asked Yo how hard was it to change the text number on the server in Washington state.

Yo said, "Child's play - if the base number is not taken already. What number are we thinking of?"

"SEEDC or 73332"

Yo loved it!

Angelina said, "Now, when the money becomes active, the CDC will get involved too!"

As if right on cue, Archie drove up. Angelina introduced Yo as they entered the cab. She asked him to drop them at Congress, so they could see their hard-earned dollars at work.

Archie chuckled, "You get what you pay for sometimes!"

Yo laughed, saying, "Maybe yes, maybe no, but we're going to find out if it's worth keeping them on the payroll."

Archie said, "You know the drill, 15 minutes. Have fun!"

Yo found some passes to the gallery, and they watched and listened for ten minutes.

That was enough for both of them for a lifetime - *Gee Whiz, so boring!* Toby and his crew weren't this bad. Next, they visited the Rotunda, and saw the Declaration of Independence. Then, they called Archie and said they wanted to go to the Library of Congress... Angelina was excited to see what it was like.

Yo couldn't believe how vast the Library was, and stated, "It may take several lifetimes to visit each volume, and if you wanted to read each one, it would be closer to an eternity."

Two hours later, they called Archie, and told him they would like to take him to lunch. Archie tried to argue, but lost again. The three of them decided upon a nice, but small, kabob place. The food was exquisite!

Archie definitely knew this town, and how to get around. He never sat in traffic for more than three minutes, and seemed to know people and places very well. Street vendors and small shop owners waved as he drove past.

Angelina looked at Yo and smiled. "What do you think? SEEDC will work?"

Yo nodded, and then asked Archie how busy he was as a cabbie.

Archie stopped at a red light and looked back at Yo. He replied, "Sometimes business is good, other times there are no tourists. I wish I could do another job while waiting for fares."

Angelina just winked at Yo and mouthed, "I told you so!"

Yo asked Archie to find a place to park. Archie was worried something was wrong. Yo said, "I want to offer you a job, but I don't want you to have an accident while driving."

Archie parked under a big shade tree. The trio got out, and walked to a park picnic table.

When they were settled, Yo began the pitch. "Angelina and I are working with the DC tourism bureau on the side. We are getting discounts from them to get people from outside DC to visit and promote it as the place to enjoy for vacation. We need someone who we can trust to mail out envelopes to the prospective vacationers. This is something you can do while you're waiting for your next fare, or you can just work for us. Your choice, either way, you will be based here in DC, working out of your cab."

Archie raised a finger and said, "I do not own my cab."

"If you take our job, we will get you a state of the art new cab, and do all the paperwork for your independent medallion."

Archie was having trouble processing why anyone would make such an offer. "I am not even an American citizen. Why would you help me like this?"

"Because we need an honest hard-working person we can trust who knows this city backwards and forwards."

Angelina placed her hand on his arm and said, "We could really use your can-do attitude, Archie."

Yo explained that the job would pay $5,000/week and Archie could keep the car if he left after three months.

"So, I work for you for three months at $5,000/week, and keep the cab and medallion if I decide to quit?"

Yo said, "Unless you wish to work longer for us."

Archie knew this was too good to be true; he was wary. "What must I do - Kill people?!"

Yo and Angelina laughed. "Of course, not! Just put envelopes in the mailbox."

"Is this drugs?"

"No. Cash, $500 per envelope."

"When?"

"Whenever the printer prints out a label."

"Like my receipt printer in my car?"

Yo said, "Yes, exactly like that."

"This $500 per envelope comes out of my $5,000 a week?"

"No, that is yours to do with as you wish."

Archie said, "What is the catch?"

"None. We will pay an additional bonus of $1,000 for each month you work for us." Yo clarified, "By your third month, you will be making $7,000/week."

Archie looked deeply into Angelina's and Yo's eyes as his started to water. "This is fantastic! Why me?!"

Angelina said, "Simple - you were very kind to me. I want to be able to help you."

Archie said, "I would be honored to work for you."

"Great!" Yo said, shaking his hand. "Let's go find ice cream to celebrate!"

Archie found he had new friends with these two. He still didn't believe it until Angelina pulled out $5,000 cash, and said, "We'll be in touch tomorrow to get started. It might take as long as a week before you get the car. We'll go shopping tomorrow."

Archie dropped them off at their hotel, and

asked what time he should pick them up.

Yo said, "8:30am is good. See you then."
As Yo and Angelina walked toward their
rooms, Yo said, "I think you made his
day."

"I think I made his life, and hopefully we
can convince him to leave at the appointed
hour."

Yo said, "You really like him, don't you?"

Angelina replied, "I may be cruel, and want
revenge on America, but I can save who I
think is worthy, right?!"

Yo smiled. "It's your show!"

Chapter 41

Jack, Johnny, Toby, and Trent were on a video conference call together to follow up on the progress of the shipment. Jack told everyone that the drivers had made excellent time to Inks4Life.net, and were on their way back to DC. They would arrive Saturday night, and unload. They'd be ready to print Monday at 8:30am, full tilt.

Toby informed the others that Yo and Angelina would be onsite for Monday's run. Jack and Johnny looked at each other, and Johnny nodded to Jack that he understood. Jack would see to the shipment, but Johnny would track Angelina's movements over the next several days.

It was Thursday morning, and Archie's cab was out waiting for Angelina and Yo by 8:31am. Johnny was watching with curiosity. It was just Angelina today. Yo had said that he wanted to check out some sites for himself, so they spilt up.

Angelina asked Archie how he slept, and he admitted to having a restless night. When she questioned him about it, he acknowledged that he was very nervous about working for so much money for such a minor job.

She asked, "Will you feel better if you are getting $100/week instead?"

Archie said, "No, it is just hard to explain."

Her next question startled him. She asked, "What kind of cab would you like? Minivan, Sedan, Limo, club van, SUV?"

Archie was too surprised for words. He answered, "You choose, you're paying!"

"Ok, you had your chance! Let's go the Chevy dealer."

Johnny followed the cab, but couldn't figure out why an ink scientist would be walking around with a cabbie at a car dealership. Maybe she needed wheels for while she was here, and didn't like rentals. No, that wasn't it.

Johnny wished he had brought another

agent whom she wouldn't recognize, so they could find out what she was up to. He sent Jack a text requesting assistance.

Jack's return message read, "All agents are tied up, do your best."

Johnny snapped a picture of Angelina and the salesman with the cabbie by her side. It almost looked like she was asking Archie for his opinion of which vehicle to lease. She wouldn't buy one now, would she? The salesman showed her all kinds of models, and it didn't seem to matter what color they were. How many women did he know that didn't care about color? This was odd. Johnny wished he'd taken that lip-reading class back in college. Note to self: next time, bring a parabolic mic. He texted Jack a list of the equipment for tomorrow. Also, a bottle of water, or Dr. Pepper®, would really hit the spot. Some secret agent he was.

Now the salesman was getting a little perturbed with Angelina. The cabbie was waving his arms, and saying, "We don't need it today."

Johnny must have misheard him. The cabbie has a car. At that, Johnny snapped a few photos of the cab, the company name, and the number on the medallion. Then, Johnny turned his attention back to the salesman who looked like he might lose the sale any minute. He held up one finger, like wait a minute, I've got an idea. He led them to the back of the dealership where they entered a garage, flipped on the lights, and shut the door.

The salesman said, "All of these vehicles are ready today, Ms. Gear."

Angelina said, "Thank goodness, you're finally listening." She looked at Archie whose eyes were bugging out of his head. He tried to say one more time, he didn't need it today. She just put a finger over his lips, saying, "You had your chance to decide, now it's my turn!"

Slightly embarrassed, he quieted.

Turning to the salesman, she said, "Keys!"

He replied, "They are in it. As I mentioned, all of these are completely identical

Suburbans, and very pricey. But, they are available today."

There were 48 in the garage; all jet black with the blackest tint available and every gadget known to mankind inside.

Angelina smiled and said, "Sold!"

The salesman's jaw hit the floor. Then, picking it up, he said, "You haven't heard the price!"

Angelina looked into his eyes and said, "It doesn't matter!"

The salesman began to stammer, and looked at the cabbie, and said, "You reason with her!"

Archie had seen enough, and he knew not to try. He just smiled, and put one finger over his lips.

Finally, the salesman asked, "How would you like to purchase this vehicle?"

She pulled out a black American Express card, and said, "This should take care of it."

The salesman went to see his manager to run the transaction, and was more than shocked when it went through without even a request to verify. His manager was pumping the salesman's arm up and down. Johnny couldn't understand why. Then, the salesman disappeared once again into the closed garage where Angelina signed the credit card slip. Archie glanced over her shoulder, and immediately opened the rear door of the Suburban, and sat down. $2,480,000.00 for his new taxi!

The salesman had said that it was the Presidential model, but he thought that was just the package name.

Angelina knew this would be a fortress for their mobile printing station, and that even if it had to carry $5M in cash, it would be safe! She asked the dealer, "Who in the area does the best paint wrapping with the quickest turnaround time? Please deliver this vehicle there today, and alert them I will be calling with details later."

The salesman promised he'd do it, and asked her to come back soon as he opened the cab door for her.

Johnny said to himself, "I guess she was just window shopping." He started his car, and followed them to a restaurant.

When they came out an hour later, Archie looked like he was the happiest man alive, but at the same time looked like he was going to have a heart attack. Was the food that bad?!

Next, Johnny followed them to a museum where Angelina went inside. After about 20 minutes, Archie went to get a drink from a street vendor, and talked for a while. Suddenly, the street vendor came out of his cart, and called to a mounted police officer. The cop looked bewildered, and then nodded his head. He rode up to Johnny's car, and tapped on the back glass window, since the front one was down, pulling his revolver as he did so.

Johnny slowly raised his hands, and said, "I'm Secret Service."

The cop requested ID. Johnny complied. The cop announced, "The street vendor thought you were dealing drugs!"

Then, Johnny noticed that the cabbie was gone. *Oh my gosh, that cabbie knows too much.* Johnny told the officer that he was tailing a cabbie, but now, he thought he had been played. He sat there for a few minutes while the officer talked to the street vendor.

Johnny was just about to start the car when the passenger door opened, surprising him. "Listen Officer, I thought this was done." He then realized it was the missing cabbie. Archie was staring at him.

"Why do you follow me?"

Johnny couldn't believe his operation was blown by this cabbie...?!

He tried to play it off, but Archie said, "NO! Do not lie to me! Why you follow?"

Johnny was debating, lie or truth.

Archie said, "Outside hotel, car dealership, restaurant, and now museum."

Johnny showed Archie his Secret Service

badge, not knowing that Archie was a self-taught speed reader. He only flashed it for a second, but it was long enough for Archie.

"What does Johnny Five want with me?"

Johnny couldn't believe this guy knew who he was. He finally said, "Not *you* - your passenger."

Archie nodded his head and said, "So you spy on all foreign people? Why are you interested in Angelina? Did she do something wrong?"

Johnny just said, "I'm trying to find out more about her."

Archie said, "This is a very hard way to get a date!"

Johnny laughed, "I wish!"

"Please stop following us, Agent Five. There is nothing illegal about shopping in America."

"Alright. You win."

Archie got out and walked to his car, three

cars behind Johnny's. Jack wasn't going to believe this! Would Johnny tell him? Yes!

As Johnny drove away, Archie's phone rang. Angelina asked, "Was that enough time to finish your errand, Archie?"

"Yes, I will be there in a minute."

When Angelina got into the car, she asked if anything was amiss.

Archie said, "Maybe, do you know anyone at the Secret Service?"

Angelina's blood went cold and said, "Yes, I know Jack Quick and Johnny Five."

Archie raised an eyebrow and said, "Johnny Five was tailing us all day."

She couldn't believe it. She hadn't seen him, but Archie had!? Wow, she could pick them!

"I asked him to stop following us, and he said he was trying to get to know you better. I told him it was a strange way to get a date!"

Angelina chuckled and said, "That probably irked him."

"Quite," Archie agreed. "Why is the Secret Service checking up on you?"

Angelina didn't even blink. "We are working with them and the BEP to try to develop the next generation of money. Our side business is the vacation promo."

Archie looked at her and then said, "You are telling the truth."

"Yes, I am, but how do you know that?"

Archie answered, "I am a retired agent myself, Israeli Intelligence for 15 years."

Wow, she *could* pick them! "Do you have a problem with my job offer now?"

Archie said he still had many questions, but he was game, if she was.

She weighed her project and his working arrangement carefully in her mind. "I picked you for your intelligence and honesty. I believe you can do the job as required and succeed. Now, I want you even more on our job."

"Very well, I am at your command."

Angelina said, "Great. Now if you see others tailing us - just tell me."

"Where to? The hotel?"

"Not yet. Let's go visit that paint wrap guy."

Archie remembered the address from the split second he saw the salesman give it to Angelina. He read it from his mind as Angelina looked down at the address on the card. Again, Angelina was yet amazed!

When they arrived at the paint shop, she went directly to the manager's office. He said, "Yes! That sure is some vehicle!"

She asked for samples of cab logos they had done in the past.

He told her they had handled most of the cabs in the city.

She then asked if any of them used TXT exclusively.

The manager told her that they use Phone, Text, and email on all their cars.

Angelina told him that she wanted the paint to be their brightest greenish-yellow mix, with black bold text on the hood, trunk, roof, and doors which could be read from 1/4 mile away, and by air.

TEXT PROMO to SEEDC
SAVE $500   (73332)
On your next trip to DC!!

The manager asked Angelina, "Windows too, with that see-through dot wrap?"

"Yes, please!"

Archie asked, "Are you sure about this neon green, instead of black?"

The manager sensed the sale was about to be blown, and said, "We'll work on this tonight, and it will be ready in the morning."

Angelina looked at Archie, and said, "Visibility is our friend. People will be afraid to hit you in this city."

Archie chuckled, "Oh, they'll see me!"

The manager suggested that since the wheels on the Suburban were so large, maybe they should dye the rubber green, too!

Angelina looked shocked. "Won't it look bad in three weeks?"

"Bring it back anytime if it fails within three years."

"Do it!" she replied. Angelina paid the bill, and Archie returned her to the hotel.

A few minutes later, Yo walked in, and Angelina told him to stay on his toes. She informed him of Jack and Johnny's surveillance.

Yo just said, "I told you they'd watch us like hawks. How did you spot them?"

Her next surprise made him almost faint!

Yo exclaimed, "Archie was Israeli Intelligence?! Can we trust him?"

Angelina replied, "I'd say he proved himself worthy today!"

Chapter 42

7am Friday morning, Johnny knocked on Jack's door. Jack waved him in asking, "Johnny, you feeling OK?"

Johnny took a seat, and said he really screwed the pooch yesterday.

Jack, sensing a long story, tried to convince him that it couldn't be that bad.

Johnny told him it was even worse. He told Jack about the car shopping, and how he couldn't get close enough to find out anything. Next, he told him about waiting at lunch, and about the museum where the street vendor thought he was dealing drugs.

Jack replied, "You just had a difficult day. Shake it off."

Johnny then continued describing his all-knowing visitor.

Jack's mood changed to a very dark one. "Did you get his name, the cabbie?"

"No, but he got mine, and I'm sure he shared it with Angelina by now."

Jack immediately asked for his medallion number, ran a background check, and cursed! Johnny did a double take. Jack said, "He goes by Archie. No one knows what his last name is, but we think he used to work for Israeli Intelligence."

Johnny was speechless. "Why would he be interested in Angelina?"

"I haven't got the foggiest clue," Jack replied. "I ran into Archie on a counterfeiting ring in Israel several years ago. He is brilliant, to say the least, but I always had the sneaky suspicion that he was the one involved in passing the funny money in Israel. Unfortunately, I could never prove it. A couple of months after I saw him there, he said he caught the counterfeiters and disposed of them, but he never returned the notes. His story was that they were destroyed in the fire."

Johnny whistled. "Why would Angelina and Yo be involved with a counterfeiter?"

Jack said, "The question is, what is *he* doing with *them*? My bet is, they don't know who they are dealing with!"

"Ok Johnny, your assignment hasn't changed. Follow them covertly, or befriend them, I don't care, just keep tabs on them. Here is the equipment you requested."

Johnny asked, "What's Archie's address?"

Jack looked at Johnny with amazement... "Agent Five, if we don't have his last name, what leads you to believe we'd have his home address?!"

"Wow, he *is* a professional! I can check with the cab company, but it's probably a dead address."

Johnny left Jack's office with the equipment, went to his car, and dialed the cab dispatcher. After Johnny got the office location, he made a bee line there. He walked into a small, but busy office with 15 people working in a space designed for five. Flashing his badge, he asked for the manager's office. They just pointed to the only closed door. It sounded like an angry, grizzly bear was inside. Johnny knocked and waited.

The manager opened the door without looking, and shouted, "Which one of you flaming idiots doesn't understand that I said, *Don't Disturb Me*?!"

Johnny held up his badge at eye level.

The grizzly bear said, "Oh crap! What does the President want this time?"

"Simply a name and address."

The manager invited Johnny to come in and sit down, slamming the door closed behind him. "How can I help you, Agent? It's been a rough day, my best cabbie just quit."

Johnny's hair on the back of his neck stood on end.

The dispatcher asked, "Whose address are you looking for?"

"Archie's."

The grizzly bear grunted, "If that don't beat

all!"

Johnny said, "Excuse me?"

"Archie was the one that just quit. He walked in, handed his keys to me, and left."

"Did he leave a forwarding address?"

"Nope. Told me to use his check at a bar, he didn't want, or need it."

Johnny inquired, "Did he up and win the lottery?"

The manager sneered, "His dream job, only, far better he said! You just missed him by 30 minutes."

Johnny then asked if he had any address for him on file.

"Yes, but I'll betcha it's a bogus address."

"Why's that?"

"Because it's 1602 Pennsylvania Ave."

Johnny said, "Thanks," and left.

Chapter 43

On Thursday afternoon, while Johnny was being introduced to Archie, Yo had registered the medallion for Archie's neon-mobile. He couldn't believe that a DC medallion cost close to $460,000. Yo hoped Angelina knew what she was doing, but he'd never openly question her about anything. She was a deadly shot under 40 yards with that 9mm! She'd done fine so far, hopefully she'd keep it going.

As Johnny mulled over the events of Friday morning in his mind, he drove to Angelina and Yo's hotel, and asked the doorman if he had seen them. The doorman chuckled, saying it was hard to miss them. They had stepped out of a brand new cab that was bright green. He had overheard them saying something about a lunch buffet by the fountain. Johnny gave the doorman a ten spot, and thanked him. Then he went down two flights of stairs, and looked in the restaurant.

The host suggested a relaxing table next to the fountain, and Johnny noticed Angelina and Yo two tables away. Chancing it, he walked up to them and said, "Surprise, Surprise!"

Angelina and Yo looked up, saying, "We just sat down. Would you like to join us, Agent Five?"

"I sure would." Johnny grabbed the offered chair, ordered a Dr. Pepper®, and asked, "So, are you enjoying your stay in DC?"

Angelina, deciding it was time to put her cards on the table, told him she had done some shopping and sightseeing in the area while Yo was checking back home. "I heard that you were very interested in me. Yo and I are just working colleagues, so if you would like to take me out, may I suggest tomorrow night at 7pm?"

Johnny almost snorted Dr. Pepper® through his nose. His mind raced as he thought, "So, Archie did inform on me. Why, what was his game? Better still, what is Angelina's game?" Snapping out of his daze, Johnny replied, "That sounds like a delightful suggestion. We're both new in town, maybe we can discover places together. Yo, would you like to come along? The more the merrier."

Yo declined, saying he had other customers in the area that he needed to visit. Then Yo suggested, "Maybe Sunday afternoon, we could go see the Nationals play if you can get tickets."

Angelina requested that they get four tickets, because she wanted to bring a friend.

Johnny said, "Done! Now let's hit that buffet. I'm starved!"

Angelina and Yo agreed it was time for food.

By 6:50pm Saturday evening, Johnny was dressed in his best suit and tie that he wore during festive events for the Secret Service. It held everything, including his gun, very neatly and discretely. Precisely at 7pm, he saw the elevator door open, and his jaw hit the floor. Fortunately, he recovered before she noticed him. "Wow! That's some dress."

Then she said, "It will do." She looked down, and waved it off. Then said, "Oh, that's right, you're new here, too." She told him she had worn it to the sales meeting at the BEP.

"No wonder you got the contract."

She just winked at the young agent, wondering if he was wearing a vest tonight. No, he wasn't. She had hugged him. She gave him a quick kiss on the cheek, which he returned. The things he had to do for his country!

For the next four hours, they went to dinner and two different clubs. The first club was too current, hip-hop. The second one was a throwback to the 1980's. They both seemed to enjoy it better. By 11:30pm, Johnny suggested they return to her hotel, where he kissed her on the cheek. She asked him to come up, but declining he said, "Good night," and walked her to the elevator.

Angelina went to Yo's room.

Yo asked how it went.

"It was nice. We had dinner, and danced at an 80's club. If he didn't work for the government, we could use him, too."

Yo said, "Hell, NO! Archie- fine, but Johnny is playing you."

Angelina looked straight into Yo's eyes, and said, "I know he is. He came armed tonight! Did you brief Archie about Johnny and the ball game?"

Yo answered, "Yes, and Archie's completely on board with it. Besides, he really doesn't know what he'll be doing anyway, right? We told him some, but not all the details. The game starts at 7pm, so let's meet in the lobby at 6pm."

Johnny drove home to his apartment, locked his car, and started walking up the path to the building. As he opened the door, a guy in workout clothes said, "Someone had a night better than me," and held the door open for him.

Johnny just chuckled and said, "Not as good as I would have liked. I'm still going to my apartment alone."

The workout guy smiled knowingly and said, "You'll get that red dress yet!"

Johnny laughed and headed for the elevator. As he turned the key in the lock, he wondered, "How'd he know about a red dress!?" He ran to the balcony, but realized the guy was gone. He watched the surrounding houses and cars for ten minutes, but gave up. As he was watching, he replayed the scene in his head. It definitely was not Archie: wrong body type, and age was wrong, too. He knew he was missing something, but what? He shut his eyes, and replayed the details in his mind. He knew that face from somewhere, but who was it?

Chapter 44

While Johnny and Angelina were having fun at the 80's club Saturday night, Jack was overseeing the unloading of the BLK33284 and GRN33284 inks at the BEP. This time went much quicker and smoother than the first time.

Sunday morning arrived too fast. Johnny used the morning to catch up on sleep, and then decided to look for the mystery workout guy. Soon, it became clear he would have to give up until Monday, when he could speak to the security manager.

About 2pm, he called Sam Henderson, and asked if he'd seen David, and how things were progressing. Sam welcomed Johnny's call, and told him that he had visited David twice. Both times he appeared to be in high spirits. The first visit was at the county jail, and the second was upon his admission to the rehab center. The center facilitator had taken Sam's name as David's sponsor since he had no living kin. Linda, the administrator, explained it was best for the first 12 weeks to let the patient enter the program quietly. Be there for support during a letter writing campaign, but it always worked better to let them adjust on their own.

Johnny asked if either of them needed any kind of support. Sam assured him the government program had covered all that, and they were fine. He asked how Johnny liked DC.

Johnny just grunted, and said, "It sure ain't Oregon!"

Both laughed, and ended the call.

Steve Stevenson's phone rang. "Hey Angelina. What's up?"

Angelina warned Steve to keep on his toes because things were rapidly changing in DC.

Steve said, "I saw your boyfriend last night. I even poked him a bit on it, and then vanished."

She just said, "Don't get caught. Having fun is one thing, but if you blow the project, I'll kill you."

Steve laughed it off, not realizing how serious she had become.

Angelina then told Steve that she had called to let him know they had recruited a driver for the DC campaign: Text PROMO to SEEDC and save $500.

Steve replied, "You didn't let me check him out! Who is he?"

She told him she thought Israeli Intelligence.

He whistled! "Are you sure we can trust him?"

"Yes! Confidently," she said. "Just check him out."

Steve asked for his full name, and got Archie. "His *whole* name?"

Angelina replied, "That's all we've got!"

"Wow!" Steve didn't like this; he'd have to call into a Homeland Security server and cover his tracks. "Ok, give me 24 hours. I'll email you." Then, Steve told her that the President and his people were still trying to locate suspects for the strike on North Korea in regard to the Encryption Hackers' first location.

She just said, "As soon as they breach it, send them to space! Just make sure you see troops outside first. If local robbers hit it, don't waste the explosion on them."

Steve understood, and assured her that he was on top of it.

Sunday evening, everyone assembled at the hotel at about 6pm. Johnny's eyes bugged out of his head as Archie approached. He was wondering if he should draw his gun, and escort Archie to Jack's office. The look on Archie's face made Johnny wait. He was walking straight toward them. Angelina and Yo introduced Archie and Johnny.

Yo said, "Archie was hired by Angelina, and he will be working for us."

It took every muscle in Johnny's face not to give away his feelings.

Angelina looked at Archie and said, "I think you two met the other day outside the museum, briefly."

Johnny just nodded, and shook Archie's hand.

Archie flagged down a minivan cab, and they all piled in. When they got to the skybox, Archie said, "It's much better in the cheap seats."

Johnny suggested they chat here first, and later go check out the regular seats. Johnny was interrogating the group strongly in the skybox, and didn't think anyone noticed.

Yo abruptly turned to him and said, "Enough talk, Agent Five. Let's watch the game."

Johnny instantly relaxed his posture, and to his surprise, he started enjoying the company of the others.

After about 90 minutes, everyone agreed it was time to go out to the seats. Archie took them to a section just on the first base line, at almost ground level. To Johnny's surprise, he pulled out four tickets and handed them to the usher.

They were in the first row; they could taste the chewing tobacco! Archie pointed out their seats. He told them there were cold drinks under their seats, if they were interested. They all had shocked expressions on their faces. Archie gave them a knowing wink, and shouted, "Enjoy!"

Angelina had a tall glass of chilled red wine. Yo had a large iced cappuccino. Johnny had an ice-cold Dr. Pepper®, and Archie had an ice cold Israeli beer. With drinks in hand, they toasted each other. Johnny just looked at Archie in bewilderment. He wondered, "How had the cabbie done so much homework on everyone, and had everyone so thoroughly penetrated?" He was in way over his head!

As the game ended with a win for the Nationals, the home team seemed to party on the streets. The group made their way back to the hotel, and split up from there. Johnny waited outside for Archie to come out, but he never did. While he was waiting on Archie, he noticed a really bright green cab driving past him. Gosh, what an ugly (or was it vivid) paint job! He continued to wait 15 minutes, and then figured Archie slipped by him somehow.

Johnny drove back to Virginia, and stopping in Jack's driveway, called him.

Jack asked, "Johnny, how were the Nationals live?"

Johnny said, "Fine. Can we talk?"

Jack, sensing unwelcome news said, "Sure, come on over. I'm at the house."

Johnny told him he was hoping he was. He parked and walked up to Jack's door, and rang the bell.

Jack opened the door with a cold Dr. Pepper® in his hand for him.

"Not you, too!"

Jack smiled with a sly grin on his face, acting surprised. Johnny took the Dr. Pepper®, and threw his tired bones on a chair in the living room. Jack had a cold beer. Johnny proceeded to tell Jack about the mystery fourth ticket holder. Jack was truly surprised!

Then, Johnny said they had adjourned to the "cheap seats" as Archie led them to the first base line, and told them to enjoy the ice-cold drinks. "We had been at the game for over 90 minutes! How did he get the cold drinks under the seats? Archie knew everything before I asked my questions!"

Jack laughed, "It really got under your skin? Huh, Kid?"

Johnny asked, "How did he know me that well?"

Jack replied, "Every agency has bio files on everyone, Kid. Shake it off. We have to find more out about Angelina and Yo! We know Archie is a big player. How he fits in, will be anyone's guess."

Johnny told him about losing the spook at the hotel, and then about seeing this monster neon green and black Suburban.

Jack said, "Tomorrow, after we're done printing for the day, let's go check out that dealership."

Johnny agreed, said good night, and went home to sleep it off. Yes, it was a strong Dr. Pepper® night!

Chapter 45

Monday morning was beautiful in DC. Everyone arrived at the BEP by 8am. Trent, Toby, Jack, Johnny, Angelina, and Yo were preparing to start the real printing operation in one hour. The presses started rolling, and they checked to be sure that the clear coat was being applied to both sides this time. Each bill had that distinct smell that Jack predicted. In 12 hours, they were going to have strong currency. Everyone else smiled knowingly. Yo said a silent prayer for those who would be the first victims. Angelina seemed to glow.

After a 6-hour run, the BEP had $500M in new currency, which they were letting dry. Everyone decided to come back tomorrow, and adjourned for the day. Angelina and Yo left for the hotel and a nice dinner. Trent and Toby finished paperwork at the BEP.

Johnny and Jack quietly left on their own for the Chevy dealership. When they arrived, Johnny found the salesman who

Angelina and Archie had dealt with. Meanwhile, Jack went to find the owner of the dealership.

Johnny couldn't believe that this worthless sleaze of a salesman actually had an office inside the dealership. Most sales people were lucky to have an assigned chair on the sales floor. He knocked on the open door. The guy held up one finger, and told the person on the phone that he had a customer, and had to go. Hanging up the phone, Sweeney got up, and introduced himself. Johnny, in turn, introduced himself as if he were a customer interested in a vehicle for his girlfriend. He described her in full detail.

The salesman then surprised him, saying his clients deserved the utmost respect and privacy, and he refused to discuss any transactions without their consent. "If you want more information, I suggest you ask your girlfriend."

Johnny was livid, but it didn't show. He thanked Sweeney for his time, and moved on to a friendly salesperson he had noticed earlier that day.

Johnny walked out to the lot, and up to a guy wearing a nametag that read *Joe*. Introducing himself, Johnny said that Sweeney was too busy to help him look for a vehicle for his girlfriend.

Joe said, "Come with me. We'll find the perfect Suburban for your girl."

While they were perusing the cars, Johnny asked how Sweeney got set up in that new office.

Joe replied, "It was a pure stroke of luck. He sold a Presidential model to some lady that walked in off the street, and the rest was history."

Johnny thought it was way too easy of an explanation. Suddenly, his phone rang, and Jack was telling him to come back to the car. Johnny said he'd have to go, but he'd be back, and took Joe's card. He looked at it, and as expected, it had Sweeney's name scratched out and Joe Simpson's name written in. Joe and Johnny shook hands, and Johnny walked away.

When he got into the car with Jack, he could tell Jack didn't have much luck either... He was fuming! Jack had flashed his badge upon meeting the owner, and found out discretion was high up on their list of client services. The owner all but threw Jack out of his office, telling him not to come back without a warrant.

Johnny said, "Sweeney basically had the same attitude." Johnny then told Jack that Joe had told him how Sweeney got that promotion after selling a special edition car to some walk-in.

Jack asked, "What was special about it?"

"It was a Presidential edition."

They were obviously missing something, but Jack shook it off and said he'd have an intern check on it back at the office.

Johnny had a better idea, and took out his smartphone. He took Joe's card, and put in the website for the dealership. Then, he looked up Suburbans. He told Jack, "There are basic, sport, luxury, and deluxe models. The small print says, *Please request a quote for the Presidential model.*"

Johnny, clicking on the link, was taken to a picture of a black, plain jane, Suburban, and was directed to fill out a form. Information on the form consisted of the usual suspects: name, address, contact phone, and email. Then, something caught Johnny's eye that was different. A credit check, and a PO number request field that was mandatory. He showed it to Jack.

"That's weird! How does the average bank executive order one?"

Johnny decided to use his cover name and address from the Secret Service. He entered BuyforLincoln in the purchase order field. After tapping submit, Johnny's cover email pinged, saying they would get back to him after the credit check and PO were validated. He said, "Well, that will probably fail. My cover name is in Oregon, and my limit is $50K."

Jack drove Johnny back to his apartment, and told him he'd pick him up at 7am in the morning to drive him into the BEP, where they had left Johnny's car.

Chapter 46

On Monday night at 9pm, all the networks were showing a special report from the President of the United States.

Everyone was wondering about the Encryption Hackers, and whether they had been found yet. The President started his briefing with the sad news first. They had yet to determine who the guilty parties were, but there was a location in Asia where they had been targeting their reconnaissance.

Next, the President allowed the banking investigators to give their briefing. They basically had reprogrammed the banking network infrastructure to be ten times more secure, so that this could never happen again. A month had passed, and everyone should have had their credit cards chipped, and delivered to them by now. All of the smartphone apps, banks (direct deposit), and vendor swipe machines had been updated for the new cards. They gave out an 800 number for those who had questions.

The President then said he was going to grant another two-week grace period to make sure everyone had enough time to clear the delays. He said, "Again, we have prevailed by sticking together, and working as one nation. Friends, thank you for your support! May God bless America, and all nations."

Steve Stevenson was replaying his copy of the digital report on his computer. While he did this, he sent an encrypted email to his team, stating there was another $30M up for grabs, if they cracked this new beast of a system.

Three people responded, "Absolutely!"

Steve set a meeting at his vacation house for Tuesday morning at 11am.

Tuesday morning at 8:30am, Trent, Toby, Jack, Johnny, Angelina, and Yo were all in the BEP's conference room looking at yesterday's dried notes. Jack instantly recognized the texture and scent were back, as they should be. Toby was trying to tear one bill with pliers. It didn't tear, or for that matter, stretch.

Yo was watching Toby with consternation. He caught Angelina's eye and whispered, "Did we test for friction?"

She looked over to Toby with a look of horror, and then immediately hid it under a neutral expression. Angelina excused herself to go to the ladies' room, and texted her lead scientist the question of the plier friction. He said he'd get back to her.

Less than three minutes later, he replied. "The samples we had in California did not have the softer paper, so we cannot be sure. So long as the pliers were dry, no water, oil, etc. on them, they should be safe."

Angelina thanked him, and told him to start testing on friction samples, so they could collect more data on this new development. She went over to where Toby was, and picked up the pliers to examine them.

Toby said, "I wanted to see how strong the product was. I couldn't tear or stretch, Hell, change the bill in any way. The clear coat protected the image below it, and that was remarkable!"

Trent suggested to Toby that they should put it in a tensile strength machine, and just see where it fails.

Angelina said, "That's not necessary. We performed that test earlier at a different client's facility, and it was upwards of 500 pound fishing line."

Toby and Trent said they didn't think their labs were set up to accommodate tests in that range, so they'd take her word for it.

Yo immediately followed up with, "But I wouldn't use it to fish with, since the CLRcoatYO is water soluble after two weeks."

Trent slapped Toby on the shoulder, and congratulated him once more. Trent knew Toby was a keeper for life.

Johnny's phone chirped, and he left the conference room to take the call. He answered in his cover voice and name.

The man on the phone announced that he was Sweeney, and he wanted more information on the credit application.

Johnny tried a Hail Mary attempt. He told Sweeney that he had given his monthly credit limit, not yearly.

Sweeney's attitude changed drastically. "Oh well, in that case, we can do a 70 month term at $30K, with a balloon payment at the end of the term for $551,777! If this is acceptable, you can come down today to pick it up."

Johnny said, "Let me discuss it with my boss, and I'll call you back." Johnny needed to sit down. He found an empty chair, and dropped in it. When Johnny had composed himself, he went back into the conference room, and gave Jack a signal.

Jack told the others that it was about lunch time, and he and Johnny had a meeting in their office. Johnny waited until they were securely in Jack's car before telling Jack his news.

Johnny began, "I just tried something dumb, and it worked! Sweeney called my cover name, and was going to tell me to stick it, when I told him $50K was my monthly, not yearly, limit. The Presidential model is 70 months at $30K, with a $552K balloon payment! We can pick it up tonight if the terms are acceptable."

Jack had just taken a sip of water in his car, and spewed it all over the steering wheel. "Shit! That's a lot!"

"I calculated it to be close to $2.6M, for a Suburban?! Question: Why would Angelina and Yo need a ballistic vehicle?"

Jack said ominously, "More to the point, why would Archie?! If they have it, where are they keeping it? Those things are too big for this town! No wonder they threw us out of the dealership."

Steve Stevenson opened the door to his vacation house. Standing there with the Admiral were Peter and Peggy. Steve welcomed them into the Encryption Hackers' Lair. He shook the Admiral's hand and said, "Sir, how are things going?"

The Admiral replied, "Son, that
Presidential pardon was a work of art! It
saved my bacon many times in the last
month, but we'll need you back soon."

Peter and Peggy agreed that the pardon
had worked great, and their father was still
clueless as to what he had caused by
granting it.

Steve made sure all his guests were
happy, and brought out the munchies and
drinks. "Ok, so how do we crack this next
iteration of security around the banking
systems? Do we lay low, and play it
cool?"

The Admiral was the only one who said to
lay low.

They were all sitting around a poker table
in front of the fireplace, and Steve had a
keyboard and mouse. Pressing a recessed
button on the table, the fireplace wall
disappeared, and six 60" LCD's appeared
on the wall. Peter, Peggy, and the Admiral
Oohed and Ahhed, and said, "You sure can

design computer layouts!"

Steve brought up the satellite images of the North Korea hideout and noticed seven unmarked vehicles within one block of the house. He had used the Homeland Security data to get facial recognition on the drivers of all seven cars. None of them were US Military forces.

Peggy thought they should drop hints to the Seals or Delta to get them to breach. Peter wasn't sure how they would do that convincingly. Steve and the Admiral agreed with Peter. No matter how long it may take, they'd have to stumble on the house themselves.

Peggy said, "Do we really need to kill our own highly specialized troops?"

"It does seem like a waste," the Admiral agreed. "If we don't, your father won't put any more money into the training budget."

Peggy hated politics, and how people had to die to get more people to help.

Peter looked at Steve, and asked how the printing was coming.

Steve said, "The first $500 million dried today. In six months to a year, Homeland Security and other agencies will have a blank check to spend on training and tactical advancement."

Everyone nodded in agreement that this was still the best course of action for now, not knowing how badly it was going to get out of control. They knew some of the plan, but not to Angelina's extent. She had told them that they'd be able to use an antidote to stop the carnage. The truth was: *Leaving the country was the only way to survive!*

Chapter 47

Wednesday morning by 8am, Angelina and Yo were at the BEP asking Toby if they could arrange to buy some of the new currency. Toby said that he could arrange it for them, and asked how much they would need.

"$100K," Angelina said without emotion.

Toby told her that it would take a couple of hours to do the paperwork, and suggested that they come back later in the afternoon with the cash for the exchange. Starting off for their sightseeing tour, Angelina and Yo thanked Toby for taking care of this personally, and wished the BEP success on Day 2 of the printing schedule.

Not wanting attention outside the BEP, Angelina and Yo decided to walk a little bit before calling Archie. Once they were four blocks away, they called him for a pickup. At Yo's request, they drove directly to a computer store where they purchased a high-end laptop, a Mifi device with unlimited service, a mobile printer, and a laptop stand for the center hump, like those in police cars.

Next, Yo had Archie pull into a friend's driveway in Virginia. Steve came outside when he heard them drive up, and opened the garage. They pulled inside, shutting the door behind them. Yo gave the laptop, Mifi, and printer to Steve. It took him just minutes to work his magic to set up and configure the backdoor, 73332 (SEEDC) text codes, and label printer. Archie was impressed by how quickly Steve completed the process.

Stamps were already mounted on the security envelopes that had SEEDC flyers in them, which Yo had already loaded into the back panels of the Suburban. He showed Archie how to access them, and how simple it was to load in the five $100 bills, and seal the envelopes with the wet roller. To prevent paper cuts, Yo suggested he use disposable gloves, and do each day's labels in a batch, rather than each one by themselves. Archie made a note to pick up gloves, but Yo was ahead of him again, showing him the other side panel had boxes of gloves, spare ink for the printer, and spare labels.

Archie was amazed that the mobile business concept was going to work this well! Just then, Steve walked into the garage with his goodies. He bolted the laptop into the secure stand that had been welded in a place that suited Archie. After mounting the label printer under the dash, Steve showed Archie how to change labels and inks. Everything was simple and easy to maintain. Steve then showed him what would happen when Archie used his phone to text Promo to 73332 (SEEDC). Moments later, Archie got a text message requesting his full address. He typed in a fake one. His printer hummed for a second, and a second later, they were pasting his fake address label on an envelope. Archie was amazed! He'd never considered using technology for a business like this! No one else had either!

The foursome went into the house to review the plans for the SEEDC business. Yo walked over to the fridge, and asked Archie what he wanted to drink. Archie said he was happy with water.

Steve, nearly choking on his beer said, "Dude! This is a vacation house, live a little!"

Archie said he was driving, so water it was. Steve couldn't believe it, but then told Yo that the water was in the first fridge in the garage. Angelina requested a cabernet. Yo started his cappuccino, got ice-cold water for Archie, and brought all the drinks on a tray over to the poker table.

Once everyone was relaxed, Angelina said, "It's time we brief Archie in full!"

Yo, Steve, and Archie all looked shocked. Archie was the first to speak. When he told Angelina that his alliances were still with the Israeli government, Steve nearly dropped his beer. Angelina asked him how he felt about most Americans and their culture.

"Blah! Rubbish! Americans think they own this world, and have no idea what true freedom entails!"

Steve quickly asked Archie, "If there was

an assassination attempt on a high ranking official here, would you be compelled to report it?"

Archie asked, "To your government, or mine?"

Steve replied, "Either!"

The hair on Archie's neck stood on end, and his blood temperature dropped by 20 degrees. Archie answered, "It depends. I would like to know more before I commit to an answer."

Angelina smiled.

Steve exclaimed, "Wow!" Then said, "You found him on the street in a cab?"

She just nodded, knowingly.

Steve then asked, "Ok, does your country use US currency freely over there?"

Archie was puzzled. "No, we have our own currency. You can exchange it for a fee, and in some tourist spots, they have money exchangers on site. But, I hate the way many tourists defile our sacred places, thinking they can trash them with empty bottles and wrappers, like here in America."

Steve asked one last question, "How does your government feel about spending more money on training new agents, or military defense?"

Archie said, "They are narrow minded men who think they don't need to spend money in that regard. Fools!"

Smiling like the Cheshire Cat, Angelina asked Yo if he had any questions for Archie.

Yo had just one. "If someone could guarantee that they could thin out a population, which two would you choose?"

Archie's blood dropped a bit more, and finally he said, "Arabs, North Koreans, and Americans."

"Wow! I can live with that," Yo exclaimed.

"Steve?" Angelina questioned.

Steve pressed the button on his table, and the room darkened, and six huge LCD's appeared from nowhere. Archie's jaw made a cracking thud on the table. His whole life: real, imaginary, covers, family, *everything* was on those screens. His own agency didn't have this much intel on him. He instantly understood that these people were well connected and funded. These questions had implied real threats. What had he stumbled onto???!

Angelina said, "Impressive, *Yes?*"

To her surprise, Archie took a deep breath, and stated, "It will do."

Steve and Yo stood up and welcomed him to the team, shaking his hand firmly, but cordially.

Angelina then told Archie all the details about the counterfeit money in Washington state, about getting the new isotope set up in her parents' nation, shipping it to California, mixing it with the inks and clear coat at the shelter, and selling it to the BEP as the new "green" ink with up to six months of a safety zone.

Letting Steve take over, he described the Encryption Hackers' scheme to make people wary of credit systems to promote the new cash, and to gain funding from the US government when they discover the cash plot. But by that time, there would be several million less people in the US population.

Angelina informed Archie that they would need him to help distribute money packs to random people all over the US. Some of this money would undoubtedly travel overseas, but that couldn't be helped, or controlled.

Archie put on his professional appearance. These people really did have everything handled, and ready to go in six months. He asked, "Radioactive money is what I will be carrying around for three months!? Talk about a *Radical Payment!*"

Angelina said, "Indeed!"

Yo said, "You can continue as long as you wish, but three months of random money drops should be enough for the circulation numbers we have. Again, we will ship your

Suburban anywhere you wish to live after three months. In six to twelve months, the United States is going to be one scary place to live! Then, this country will never stop funding defense, ever again!"

Archie felt this was a lot to take in, *but he liked it!* Inside, he was still on the fence, but now he definitely would not say that to their faces!

Angelina Gear explained how all of this had started some 30+ years ago for her, when her parents and family were summarily executed with their entire town.

Archie interrupted and asked, "In China?"

Angelina knew Archie understood, and was now with them until the end.

Chapter 48

By 5pm Wednesday, the trio were back in the Suburban to go collect the money from Toby. They instructed Archie to drop them off where he had picked them up earlier. When they arrived, Archie pulled over, and all three got out. Yo had Archie open the back of the vehicle. Archie watched as Yo typed in a key code on a panel under the carpet near where the spare tire would be, if there was one. They heard a metallic thud, and a large vault opened.

Yo said, "We have one more surprise for your safety." The vault had one more keypad with a selector switch on it. *Funny*, *Real*, and *i625* were the marked selections. Yo explained that funny had no code. He'd get the codes for Real and i625 from Steve later. Yo put the selector on Real, typed in an 8-digit code from memory, and opened the middle compartment. Underneath was a lead enclosure, just like the other two. Archie's eyes went wide as doorknobs; he was carrying over $4 million in cash! Yo pulled out $100K, and gave it to Angelina, who turned, and started toward the BEP.

Archie said, "No wonder you wanted someone trustworthy."

Yo just smiled, and told him this was just the tip of the iceberg.

Archie said that his government would never transport that much cash in a car.

Yo corrected him, saying it was a tank with nuclear shielding, inside and out!

When Angelina found Toby in his office, he had her sign the transfer, and they made the exchange. Toby unbundled her currency and placed it in a bill counter, saying, "It pays to be sure."

Angelina just pretended to be miffed. "What, you don't trust me?!" Batting her eyelashes for effect, they both laughed. Thanking Toby, she asked how today's run went.

He said, "Flawless again, and this is just day two!"

Angelina informed Toby that she and Yo would be returning to California in the next couple of days unless something else was needed.

Toby laughed, and assured her all was well. "Enjoy your trip home. Oh, by the way, Jack and Johnny were looking for you earlier today."

"OK," she said, smiling to herself. "I bet they were!"

Angelina decided to walk back to the neon office, as she had been calling it.

"Any problems?" Yo asked.

"None, except Jack and Johnny were looking for us."

Archie, Yo, and Angelina all started laughing! Yo slid the selector switch to i625, typed in his personal 8-digit code, and loaded the $100K into the vault. Next, he closed the vault, and selected Funny. They heard the thud without putting in a code. Opening the compartment, he showed Archie over $10M in funny money.

Archie said, "It's all fake?"

Yo and Angelina just smiled. She said, "Yes! If you think you're being tricked or spied on, you can use this to throw others off the trail. Real money can be used if you find a Secret Service spy. Steve will be calling you to set up your own personal codes for the Funny, Real, and i625 vaults. Any questions?"

Archie said, "Yes. Let's talk over dinner."

They agreed, and as always, Archie took them to a fabulous Israeli place that they all enjoyed.

Chapter 49

Steve was watching the 3rd world server house, intently by remote video, after an alarm had sounded signaling intruders. He had observed several people entering the house, but wasn't sure they were American Special Forces. With his finger on the remote trigger, he phoned Angelina, and requested her to join the video feed on her phone.

Angelina said, "Wait. We want to make sure they are US Special Forces." Minutes later, she saw the uniforms she had been waiting for. "Fire in the hole!" Angelina shouted. The picture on her phone vanished.

Steve went back to the live satellite feed of the city, and zoomed in. Eight square blocks had *vaporized*, and there was nothing but wreckage visible! All the support vehicles were nowhere to be seen. Steve said a prayer for those lost souls in the chaos that knew nothing of the mission.

Angelina just shouted, "YES! Eat that, you US pigs!"

Before ending the call, Angelina asked Steve to keep tabs on the newsfeeds to find out how many casualties there were, and to forward the information to the group. Also, she asked if the website was up and operational to anyone in the world.

Steve had already checked that, and replied, "We are live!" After a couple of minutes went by, the Homeland Security feed chimed with the estimated fatalities in the server house. Seven operators of Seal Team Five, and six of Delta were all presumed dead in the massive explosion. As many as 2,000 nationals who worked and lived in the area were also missing, and unaccounted for. Witnesses swore that every structure in that eight square blocks had been lifted vertically 20 meters before crashing down to the ground.

Angelina and Yo were on their way to the airport to return to California, when they received the Homeland Security alerts from Steve. Several of the news organizations were reporting a massive explosion of epic proportions in that 3rd world country! Many of them wondered if the POTUS had ordered a military strike that killed those 2,000 poor souls.

The President of the United States hit the airwaves immediately! He insisted that he had not retaliated on that country for the Encryption Hackers' scheme. He did, however, tell the world that this was their headquarters for the operation. The President failed to acknowledge the presence of Seal Team Five and Delta at the location. He was hoping he could keep that a secret until the next President could address it.

About two hours passed before the media caught wind of the Encryption Hackers' clear text dump on that foreign website. By morning, there was chaos everywhere. Not only had the accounts been revealed, but Social Security numbers, and passwords to the accounts were also in clear text. This meant that most people's data was now unsecured, because unless they had a unique password for every account, anyone could look up this site and try passwords. Bosses could look at employees' personal accounts for AOL, Gmail, Yahoo, Hotmail, Facebook, Twitter, LinkedIn, Dropbox, cloud services; you name it, it was most likely public knowledge by now.

This opened a totally new can of worms for all the major data providers and services that used a username and password. It was going to be a race to see who got there first; a nosey friend, ex-spouse, lawyer, hacker, *or* the real account holder to change the passwords!

Chapter 50

8:30am Friday, November 7th, the BEP staff was getting ready for day three of printing the deadly money. With Thanksgiving coming up, they wanted their staff to have time with their families, if at all possible.

Angelina Gear and Yo had returned to the California shelter a couple of days ago. Yo had been busy with his staff, getting more ink containers loaded into the Inks4Life.net building in preparation for the December and January shipments of ink.

Angelina had begun taking day trips to several sites in California, mainly banks. Sometimes, she requested new currency to exchange her old bills. Other times, she opened a safety deposit box account, placing $1,000 worth of 20's in each box. She placed five freestanding stacks of ten bills each to line the front and sides of the box. Next, she would wad up a couple of notebook pages to fill the back of the box, so that the money would be pressed to the front and sides. Then, she would kindly thank the bank staff, and take her leave. She would do this at over 50 banks in the California area. In each city with a major bank, she would carefully wash and dry one hundred $20 bills. Using the extra bank envelopes that she had picked up, she filled them with ten bills each, and made five sets. Then, she left them in well concealed, but easily accessible locations: under park benches, in alleys where homeless were common, at interstate rest stops, and in mall parking lots. She placed them anywhere there were a lot of greedy people.

If it was sunny and dry, in about two weeks, she'd have news reporters scurrying for coverage. If it was wet and rainy, she'd see coverage several days sooner.

Yo would take the same approach, but he was to cover Nevada, Texas, and Florida. Her five scientists were given $40K, and chose two states among: Washington, Michigan, Wyoming, Kansas, Georgia, Tennessee, New York, Illinois, Maine, and Delaware.

Although Yo and the scientists did not get safety deposit boxes, they did have orders to cover concerts, theme parks, toll booths, stores, and local fairs. Angelina encouraged them to have fun with it, and see who could come up with the best ideas. They would vote on them when they met in a week to compare notes.

Back in DC, Jack and Johnny were hard at work making sure all their protected clients had changed their passwords for work and personal accounts to prevent further damage from the Encryption Hackers' data dump going public. Countless Public Service Announcements (PSA) encouraged people to change and review the passwords for their work and personal accounts. Changing your password became mandatory for most of the major businesses as soon as you logged in. This had the desired effect on law enforcement, FBI, Secret Service, and Homeland Security. All of them seemed too busy chasing the hackers, leaving less time to branch out on other work assignments such as Angelina and Yo's activities. What was once a priority, now fell to the bottom of the stack.

POTUS demanded a review of what had happened at the 3rd world server headquarters because his re-election was in danger of failing. No one believed that he was not behind the destruction of the Hackers' headquarters. Even though he wasn't - he had been framed well. Maybe it was time to give up, and go fishing for the rest of his life, but no, he liked the feeling of power. Soon though, he may change his mind.

Chapter 51

It first happened on a drizzly Friday afternoon. Just before dinner, Sam was playing left field at his neighborhood ball field, when big, bad Lester hit one over his head. That was it! Lester had won the game for his team, and everyone decided to go home for dinner. Sam climbed over the fence, and retrieved the baseball 30 yards from the fence line. Golly! Lester could hit for a sixth grader. Sam would take the ball home, and return it tonight to its owner at his big brother's football game at the high school.

Sam's brother, Willie, was the Quarterback voted most likely to join the NFL. Sam wanted to be just like his older brother, but that changed the moment he spotted the envelope under the park bench. He opened it, and saw $200. The envelope had no ID, or writing on it. Pocketing it, he'd talk to his parents about what to do next.

At dinner, it was chaos. Apparently, Willie

was to report to the field two hours ahead of the 9pm game. In the past, several players had shown up late, causing a forfeit. His coach would not allow that to happen again.

Mom was preparing dinner in the kitchen, and was almost done when she was informed of this hiccup. It was arranged that Mom and Willie would leave Dad in charge of dinner with Sam and his sister, Lisa, who was in fourth grade. Later, they would meet Mom in the stands at the game. Sam forgot all about the items in his pocket. His dad was helping Lisa with a mismatched sock debacle.

After dinner, the trio got into the car and drove the ten minutes to the high school game. Dad paid for the tickets, and gave Sam the change from a fifty-dollar bill. It was common knowledge that Sam could not sit still for more than 15 minutes at best. His dad would give him money so he could be their "runner", getting sodas and hot dogs for the family, usually a couple at a time during the game. This made Mom and Dad happier, and gave Sam something to do.

After about 45 minutes, Lisa wanted a soda. Sam was up and ready. He raced up the steps at breakneck speed, bored, since no one was scoring. He got to the concession stand, and saw Cindy was working tonight. Cindy asked, "So what does Sam want tonight?"

He said, "Two dogs all the way, two cokes, and a plain and a peanut M&M's."

"That will be $19.50." Cindy left to go get the items. She put them in a tray container for Sam to carry back to his seat. Sam noticed he was short by three dollars. Remembering the envelope, he put his dad's money back in his pocket. He opened the envelope discretely, taking out one $20 bill. It seemed to catch more on the other bills in the envelope, almost like it was magnetic, but not really. (If events in life had sound effects, you would have just heard the loud rattle of a diamondback rattler, violently shaking, as the bills in the envelope rubbed together coming out.) Sam had just been dosed with a lethal amount of i625. The clock was ticking.

Adults took 3-4 hours to succumb to the effects of the radiation. Sam was skinny and fast for his age, but maybe 85 lbs. wet. He didn't notice anything wrong until he started feeling queasy while eating his hotdog in the stands.

About that time, Willie scored a touchdown pass of almost 83 yards! Most likely, it would be the winning play. Sam was up again, this time to go down to collect Willie's game ball, so it wouldn't get lost.

On the way back up the stadium stairs to his family, Sam abruptly stopped, and sat down on the stairs, catching his breath. Nobody noticed because their team had just made an interception. Everyone was on their feet. Sam got up shakily, and only had seven more flights to climb. For him, it was child's play, but after taking a step, he fell, dropping the ball. He tumbled head over heels down the stairs, some twelve flights. After the crowd quieted down, someone noticed Sam sprawled on the stairs, and screamed for 911. The paramedics on the field rushed over to Sam, and the game was halted.

Willie's eyes focused on the downed person on the stairs, and noticed a familiar t-shirt. He leaped over the four-foot fence like a gazelle, and was by Sam's side in nine seconds. He flagged down his parents, who knew something was very wrong.

The paramedics worked on Sam for a few minutes, and then placed him on a gurney. They transported him by ambulance to the regional medical center.

Unbeknownst to anyone, Timmy had gotten to the body first, while everyone was cheering. Timmy was the class bully, and despised Sam for being an excellent athlete like his brother. Before all the commotion, Timmy saw the envelope half out of Sam's pocket. Noticing a local bank logo on it, he swiped it, and ran off before anyone saw him.

This was Angelina's first of many lucky breaks!

At the hospital, Sam's family couldn't believe the doctors. All of them said he was gone, and had no explanation for his sudden death. The twelve steps had skinned him up, but had not caused any major damage. His family was devastated, to say the least!

By 8am Saturday, Sam's death was leading the news on all the major networks. Everyone wondered what could have happened to an active twelve-year-old boy with no known illnesses to mankind.

Living five blocks from the stadium, Timmy ran directly home after the game. Using the key around his neck, he let himself into a dark, deserted house. He got a soda out of the fridge, and took it to his room. He wasn't supposed to have food or drink in his room, but his old lady was a flight attendant, and was working tonight on a weekend stay over in Hawaii. She wouldn't be back until Sunday night. She had made Timmy independent over several years, and perhaps that had made him a loner and a bully at school.

Timmy took the money out of the envelope and counted it, like he was a big-time dealer in a card game. Each time one bill rubbed against another, the diamondback rattlers sounded, but Timmy could not hear them - just like Sam. After playing for 20 minutes, he put the money back in the envelope, and hid it by taping it to the back of the ceiling fan blade. The ceiling fan had been broken since they had moved into this house 18 months ago. Timmy opened the soda on his bed and lay back, thinking of how to best spend his new $180.

Suddenly, he dropped the soda in his lap, but for some reason he didn't care. He had drifted off to an eternal sleep. His last thought was that his mom was going to read him the riot act for bringing a soda to bed with him. He was wrong.

She had an unexpected delay which kept her out of town for an extra week, due to a volcanic eruption, but she didn't worry once about her son. She had taught him how to survive on peanut butter and jelly, and he'd be going to school every day.

Chapter 52

Yo decided to go to Texas first, then to Florida, and later Nevada.

First, he stopped at Lubbock, dropping off several washed and dried sets in the park, community youth centers, and industrial districts where there seemed to be a lot of foot traffic. He dropped about 20 special packets, and then moved on to other cities. He decided to visit Austin, Fort Worth, Longview, Houston, and on a whim, Baton Rouge, LA.

One of those special packets found its way into the hands of a devout Christian man named Ted, who was currently out of work. He was collecting aluminum cans to recycle from the trash bins at several parks close by. He was making a good living at it, for what it was worth, and still providing for himself and his wife. As he was looking for cans, he noticed one in the bushes. He picked it up with his claw stick, crushed it, and threw it in the garbage bag. Then, Ted spied the envelope, and picked it up. Opening it, he found there was no ID. He looked around and saw no one. Thanking God for this amazing blessing, he carefully put it in his pocket, and continued on his afternoon route. After filling four bags of crushed cans, he took them to the recycling center, and cashed them in, making about $46.75 for two hours' work, tax free. He went home to show the missus the wonderful bounty that he had discovered, and they both thanked the Lord.

The following day was Sunday. Ted and his wife attended their church for the am service, and were greeted by many friends. The Minister was a down on his luck Evangelist, who had seen much better days before his TV ministry went bankrupt.

During the offertory, Ted decided to thank God by double tithing, and put $40 in the plate. After a couple of minutes, one of the ushers waved to the Evangelist. Recognizing the sign, he stopped the service.

The Minister said, "Brothers and sisters,

we all have needs." He called the ushers forward, reached into a plate, and pulled out the two twenty dollar bills that Ted had donated. First, he waved one in each hand, and then he put them together, rubbing intensely, like sticks to ignite a fire. Right then, the diamondback rattlers sounded loudly, but even with the powerful microphones and speakers, neither he, nor the congregation, heard the warning. The Evangelist said, "This just won't do."

Many times, in the past, he had urged his flock to give until it hurt to help the ministry of God. Today, he gave that same message, and then asked the ushers to pass the plates again. He had a balloon payment coming due on his Beamer, and this wouldn't cover it.

Ted looked at his wife, and she nodded. Ted took the cash out of his pocket, kept $40 for groceries, and put the rest in the plate as it went by. Again, the diamondback rattlers sounded loudly, but no one heard them. This time, Ted and his wife were in the kill zone.

On the way out, they stopped to talk to good friends who were having harder times than Ted. They were just getting by. Their mortgage payment was due, and they didn't know how they'd pay it. Ted knew they lived close by, so he told George to stop by Monday morning. He told him he would show him the can route, so he could save his house.

Ted and his wife chatted with George for a few more minutes, and wished him a good afternoon. The two drove to the grocery store where they bought milk, eggs, bread, and fresh produce. They handed the remaining $40 to the cashier, who returned $5.50 back as change. They smiled, and told the cashier to enjoy the rest of her day. By some miracle, the cashier never got dosed.

Ted's wife was feeling good, and suggested they go drive around the old places for a few minutes. They did. Ted drove a few towns over, where they reminisced about their first date, and the house where they had raised their four kids, now each with a family of their own.

Life was good.

Suddenly, it hit Ted like lightning. He grabbed at his left arm, saying, "Oh my," and blacked out.

His wife grabbed the wheel, and expertly guided the car into a field, and then killed the ignition. Pulling out Ted's cell phone, she dialed 911, and told the person who answered what had happened. It was 20 minutes until the paramedics arrived. By that time, she had expired as well.

Meanwhile, the Evangelist was just leaving his favorite steakhouse, and feeling queasy. He got into his Beamer, and started for his mansion. He loved his powerful convertible. He usually kept it under 75 on the interstate, but not this fine afternoon. He pushed it up to 100+ MPH, zipping right through traffic. He started over a very long overpass, when he too, lost control, careened off the center metal guardrail, and punched through the right side concrete barrier causing a six-car pileup on the street below.

The congregation was in distress the

following Sunday upon hearing about both tragedies. Everyone knew Ted and his wife were singing with the other angels in the choir, but no one was sure where the Evangelist ended up.

Chapter 53

Friday night before Sam was discovered, Angelina was on the computer, and got pinged by Toby. She answered him, and asked how life was.

"Life is Great! That ink supplier really worked out well for us, and is helping to make the world a better place with all the credit card fraud going on. This new money will be a Godsend, and it will help people gain their lives back."

Angelina smiled at her keyboard, glad this was just a text chat, and not a video or audio chat. She replied, "How so?"

She didn't really expect him to go into details, but Toby threw caution to the wind; he wanted to impress his old friend, Angel_of_Death. "We are using it in the new US currency, and it is the strongest paper money to date. There are so many security features in the new bills, that counterfeiting will be a thing of the past. Any average person will now be able to detect if it's real or fake just by holding it up to the light. It's eco-friendly, too."

Angelina just fell off her chair with that last comment! "Wow! You and your staff did all this in the last two months? Impressive, Death_Hiding_in_Plain_Sight! Excellent job! I hope you get a raise."

"As a matter of fact, I will, and a sizable bonus!" Toby typed.

"Bonus, do I get part...?" Angelina asked.

This was Toby's big break! He said, "YES!" Toby proposed a vacation spot in Hawaii where two very old gamers could meet and have fun together. He told her they would have separate accommodations, and no strings attached.

Angelina smiled again and typed, "OK! When?"

Toby yelled, "Yes!" so loudly, he figured she heard it. "When does it work for you?"

Angelina responded, "Maybe March."

Toby said he could wait that long; DC in March was miserable.

Angelina laughed again, and said to herself, *You don't know the half of it - Buddy!* Then she typed, "This sounds like a really promising idea. I need a real vacation. Work is too stressful; it's like death warmed over! Let's start making plans somewhere with a nice pool and beach access. Do you know how to surf? Maybe we can learn together!" she added. They talked for about 30 more minutes, and then she signed off.

Next, Angelina called her team on a video conference that she had prearranged Wednesday. Everyone was there, and all were getting their first state ready. They all assured her they knew how to access the real funds electronically if they ran out, so they could request more new money from the local banks. She reminded them not to be stingy, and have fun. "Be relaxed, no one should see your brow sweating while you're spending money!" She thanked them, and dismissed everyone except for Archie and Steve.

"Archie, how many requests have you fulfilled by mail?" she queried.

"Today's drop will be seventeen, I just got three more in the last hour."

"Great! Any problems?"

"None," replied Archie.

"Steve, how's the website coming for SEEDC, and how many search engines are on board?"

Steve smiled and assured her it was up, and for any search that used "DC", theirs would be the first site on all the engines.

Archie was going to need a whole lot more money, sooner, rather than later. "I'm guessing by the end of the week, I'll be out."

"Excellent!"

"Steve?" Archie asked. "Can you order more for me? I don't want people getting suspicious of an ex-cabbie asking for $200K worth of new money, even if I am driving a green monster!"

Angelina agreed that it was an excellent point. Next, she asked Steve about his return debut.

Steve had called the Admiral, and they had agreed that he would return Monday - two days away. He added, "I don't know how I'm going to work with those idiots anymore, but I'll try."

Angelina just said it was imperative for him to remain on the inside of Homeland Security for at least three more months, just like Archie!

She asked if there was any other news. Steve included a piece from Hong Kong about a gang of high tech counterfeiters who were dropping bills in the city. Five scientist types had been jailed, screaming they were framed by another country. All of them were waiting on sentencing in a month, but the expected sentence was going to be life in prison. Archie wondered why Steve had mentioned that, and then remembered the $10M in his SEEDC vehicle. Were the two related? Interesting.

Angelina ended the call, and went to bed.

Chapter 54

7am Monday morning seemed way too early to be up getting ready for "work" after being on vacation for a month. Steve needed another vacation to recover from his vacation. He was definitely not ready for the shit storm that was going to happen today, but happily told himself it would all be over in 12 hours, and his next vacation of eight hours would be here soon enough.

When he rolled into the parking lot, he saw a lot of friends going in. Everyone was giving him a tough time, as most co-workers get when returning.

Semi said, "I'm sorry. This entrance is for employees only. Visitors must register at the front desk."

Winston saw Steve and said, "Sooo, they cleared you of that shooting incident, and you're no longer on paid leave?"

Walking into the building further, Steve saw Jessica. She asked, "I thought you quit to go work for the Russians. What happened, not smart enough?"

Steve just took it all in stride and smiled; for $30 million, he could take a lot of crap!

When he got to his desk, it was unrecognizable. Someone had taken their time to shrink wrap everything on his desk: phone, keyboard, mouse, each and every drawer was individually wrapped, and the monitors, too. He'd have to requisition a boxcutter from the Air Force One flight crew to resume work. As if this wasn't enough, all his handwritten messages were taped inside the shrink-wrapped blotter.

He set his computer down, and got a cup of coffee before getting his daily ass chewing from the Admiral. Moments later, he knocked on the Admiral's door, and muttered, "Let's do this!" He passed through the door, and closed it behind him quietly.

The Admiral asked him if he had a good month off.

Steve replied, "It was cool, Dude."

Obviously, the Admiral didn't like his sense of humor. He screamed, "Good! It's the last damn vacation your sorry ass is ever going to see again! If I had my way, I'd bring you up on charges, and throw you in the brig, myself! Whatever possessed you to install a trojan that wasn't even cleared yet on a law enforcement computer? You kids are going to be the death of me! I have a good mind to call the campus MP's, and have them drop your ass off in federal prison with the general population. You can wear a nametag that says Homeland Security jackass!"

Steve had had about enough of this. He got up, and opened the door shouting, "You know where I work and live, arrest me asshole!" The whole command center got silent enough to hear a pin drop.

The Admiral commanded, "Get back here, you little twit! I'm not even remotely close to being done with you!"

Steve turned around, and sat back down in the office chair, putting his feet on the desk. "So, talk, don't scream! I am your best coder and computer tech. You can't fire me or arrest me; you don't have that much clout! My contract states that no one less than the President himself can terminate me from this office!" There was an audible gasp from the command center peanut gallery.

Steve turned on the speaker phone, and dialed the direct line of POTUS. His assistant answered immediately and said, "Admiral, he's in a meeting right now. Can he call you back in three minutes?"

Steve said, "Hi, Marcia, that's fine. Thanks!" turning off the speaker phone.

The Admiral said, "Get your freaking feet off my desk, and shut up and listen! I don't care that you are in tight with Peggy or her father. The fact is that we have rules in place that must be adhered to at all times. That means, you don't *leave the reservation*, and do things your way, EVER! We have protocols in place that must be obeyed and respected. I don't ever want to cover for your filthy ass again. If something like this happens again, I'll personally take you out to an aircraft carrier in leg irons, stand you up in front of the blast shield, and launch a Tomcat. In other words, *I will kill you, Kid!*" The Admiral jumped out of his office, and said to the whole group, "Do You All Understand Me?! Every last one of you - I will own your ass, if you ever go off reservation again!"

Just then the Admiral's speaker phone rang. Steve put it on speaker, and cranked the volume up. "Admiral's office, Steve speaking..."

The Admiral just glared at Steve.

"Hi Steve, I got your message. What's up?" the President asked.

"I just wanted to express my thanks for that pardon. I think it just saved my job! Are we on for meatloaf at your place on Wednesday?"

The President just said, "I hope you're kidding. You can't be replaced! Yes, we are. Peter and Peggy can't wait to see you after a month's vacation. Later."

When the speaker phone was turned off, the Admiral said, "GET OUT! See Winston first, then go clean your desk off, and get back to work!"

Steve got up, and gave a mock salute, and said, "Aye! Captain Bly!" He strolled out of the office like he had just come back from a vacation!

The sixty or so people in the command center all looked at Steve, and then anywhere else. No one wanted to acknowledge his presence for fear of getting the Admiral mad at them. If the Admiral couldn't fire him, surely the Admiral's rage would fall somewhere close by...

When the Admiral had stopped by last week for the team meeting, he had told Steve they were going to have a showdown fight to cover both of them during the last month's vacation. He told him to bring his gloves, mouth guard, and dancing shoes! It would be just the two of them, but it was going to be noisy and ugly. Steve had thanked the Admiral for the heads up last week, and said he'd be prepared.

Chapter 55

Several of Angelina's crew were very creative. In Michigan, one went to Detroit, and found a small park outside a nuclear power plant. It was not a special packet, this one would take up to six months to activate.

It was taped under the seat of a steel picnic table, shielding it from the elements. Every time someone sat down, one of those tables wobbled because the scientist had used a set of pliers to remove the spacers on two legs diagonal from each other, making the table unsteady. Wind buffeting the table would make it rock side to side, by only a fraction of an inch, but the scientist knew it would be more than enough!

After the packet went active, it would irradiate the steel table and anyone who came into contact with it. If they found the money, it would be used. If not, it would still be deadly! A true Win, Win! Nobody in their right mind would be looking for radiation near a bench with the nuclear reactor within miles of the park. Again, the government would waste countless days and weeks trying to locate the radiation leaks of that reactor. The scientist emailed this idea to the group.

Angelina loved it! It was very close to her own safety deposit box idea she had done in California. An earthquake would shake the free-standing bills inside the box, irradiating the bank vault forever. Any person who entered the vault after an earthquake, would get a very lethal dose inside the vault. They would die 3-4 hours later, which was more than enough time to get them clear of the vault, and make it look like another unknown mysterious death.

Still others went early to rock concerts. Days before the event, they would deliver "very" special packet(s) in carefully crafted lead boxes with removable lead lids. This was like carrying a lit bundle of dynamite under your arm. These were active packets!

Dressed like Roadies, Angelina's crew would slip under center stage, and attach the box to the underside of the stage right below the center microphone position. Then, once they got out of the 20 ft. radius kill zone bubble, they would use a 100 ft. piece of 100-pound test fishing line to pull off the removable lead lid with one quick yank. The stage skirt would hide the lid and fishing line. Now, anyone who got on stage, walked by it, jumped on it, or climbed up to hug their favorite star, would "buy it"! Anyone who crossed that 20 ft. radius 3D bubble of death was a goner. Five to seven feet of that included the mosh pit area. The scientist who set up this dangerous application nicknamed it "Groupies Be Gone..." Too bad he couldn't patent it and sell it!

He still had 29 boxes inside his windowless van, and 29 items on his list of events. He planned on targeting 3-day weekend concerts that boasted 10+ acts or more during the festival days. It was Fall, but it was still great weather in the South for these concerts!

The final scientist who went to NYC had the most rewarding job. He would take tours of hundreds of sites. Three came to mind as no brainers. The first was to drop two normal loose packets in between the wall studs, one on either side of the entrance to the Statue of Liberty, so anyone coming through after the packet went active would get dosed. His second idea was to do the same with the USS Intrepid in the harbor. He would place a packet between the interior and exterior bulkheads. Over time, the rocking and winds of the harbor would be more than enough to cause the movements necessary to irradiate a substantial portion of the hull. Next, he went into the subway system after hours, and climbed down onto the tracks in multiple locations. Taking special "2 week" 100 bill packets, he wedged them securely under the rails of the subway track inside the dark tunnel areas. Between the track and ties, there was more than enough room to stack 100 bills high. He was able to hide them completely under the rails. By folding them, they were wedged there. This served two purposes. It would irradiate the rail, and the rail over time would irradiate the train wheels, which would kill people in the trains within several weeks.

Keep in mind that two bills rubbing each other had a kill zone bubble of about 3 ft., 5 bills about 6 ft., 10 bills about 12 ft., 100 bills about 75 ft.! Irradiating 75 ft. of rail in both directions was 150 ft. That much contact over 30 or 40 trips for the same section of track, meant many subway cars on many different lines would be affected, and many unknown deaths would occur in NYC long after they left the irradiated areas. Confusion would be King!

Angelina Gear and her team were indeed very talented and methodical in their roles as terrorists. When these seemingly random events of death occurred, the United States would be beyond terrified. Angelina's plan was becoming real. In another month, she would be known as Angel in a Rage!

Chapter 56

"Happy Monday, Johnny," Jack said, adjusting his office monitor which had been bumped by the cleaning staff over the weekend.

"Good morning," Johnny agreed. He continued, "I got a call from Winston earlier today, saying Steve Stevenson had returned, and cleaned up my laptop."

Jack said, "Let's go talk to him and pick it up."

Johnny said, "That's just the thing. Now that I know my laptop has been compromised, I don't trust it anymore. I'm thinking they can keep it forever. I have my new one, and I'm just not sure I want to risk it."

Jack said, "It's still a piece of evidence. We need to follow up on it, Agent Five."

Johnny agreed with that part of the argument, grabbed his keys, and said, "Let's ride together."

On the way, Jack stopped for coffee, and Johnny got a Dr. Pepper®. By the time they reached Homeland Security, they had finished their drinks. They went inside, and requested to see Winston. He met them in the lobby, and escorted them to his lab.

In the lab, Johnny expected beakers and chemistry items, but it wasn't that kind of lab. The dimly lit computer lab had all kinds of wires and electronic devices everywhere. He'd never seen an electronic playground such as this in his life!

Winston took them directly to Johnny's laptop. It looked just the same as when he had left it. He logged into it, and all his data was still intact. Johnny asked Winston, "Do you know how to remove the trojan now?"

Winston just smiled. He told Johnny there was a nice little removal tool that the original programmer made to recover the data it collected, and remove all traces at the same time. Very clever indeed.

Johnny demanded, "Show me which data

Homeland Security collected."

Winston had thought Johnny would probably want to see it. He tapped a few keys, and all the log files appeared.

Johnny said, "Gosh! You guys really know just what to take." He kept looking at the cache of data, and finally said, "The blown bust data from the mower scam raid isn't here."

Getting a hunch, Johnny asked Jack for his laptop. Jack's hair stood on end, "Why?!"

"We need to see if your laptop is infected."

"Johnny, we checked mine for your signature," Jack stated.

Winston piped up! "That's the beauty of this trojan! It creates a unique signature for every client, so that standard Antivirus and Malware scanners will fail to catch it every time!"

"Oh Crap!" Johnny screamed, realizing the amount of damage that this could cause if it got loose on the internet!

Winston had Jack log in. Jack then gave his laptop back to Winston, who ran the cache file collect and removal tool. Sure enough - pay dirt! Johnny and Jack looked over the data collected. The bust in Washington state was on the list of emails that had been redirected. Jack asked who got this information. Winston said it was sent via encrypted files to an encrypted destination. Now that the removal tool had removed the trojan, they'd never know. Even if they reinstalled the trojan, it would have a new signature file, and the encrypted data would be gibberish. Jack just slammed his fist on the desk in frustration.

It was time to get Steve and the Admiral in on this ASAP! Steve was in the top-secret lab, and only the Admiral could get him out. Winston wasn't even cleared for that area. Jack and Johnny were informed that the Admiral was on Capitol Hill in sequestered meetings for the rest of the week, and would return to the office next Monday. Jack just growled!

Winston took them out past Steve's desk,

and Jack noticed the shrink-wrapped items. Winston said, "Early this morning, Steve and the Admiral had it out in a very loud argument that the whole command center witnessed. At least 60 employees within the high security area heard an epic ass chewing of Steve, much to everyone's surprise. That Presidential pardon saved his filthy ass."

Winston described the epic throw-down, and Jack knew the Admiral had the right idea! He'd have to wait and talk to him next week. Steve may have won this round, but he sure wouldn't win the war - Jack never lost on his turf!

On the way out, Jack asked for Steve's home address, and was given it promptly. However, Jack didn't know Steve had moved from that address a month ago. He now lived just three blocks behind Jack, unbeknownst to Winston and everyone else.

Steve and the Admiral had slipped out for coffee and a quick meeting before the Admiral went to his meeting on the Hill.

Steve asked the Admiral if he was convincing enough for their charade.

"I believe we got their attention! I had several ranking captains come in to ask me if I needed a medic for a heart attack, or if they could perform a code red on my behalf on your ass. I'd say it was just what the doctor ordered. I suggest you lay low at vacation central for the next week. Just be available online to me. I'm sure the fallout over that trojan will not go away anytime soon, so we need you to play keep away from the Secret Service for a while. In the meantime, I suggest you bug both agents' homesteads toot sweet!"

Steve said, "That's where I am going now. My guess is, Winston will alert Jack that he may have been compromised when he returns Johnny's laptop. By the way, did you guys see the email I sent Saturday?"

Nodding, the Admiral asked, "Are you sure it was Angelina's kill? A random death of a young boy at a football game?"

"Sounds very promising. I hacked into the hospital database, and they still had it marked as an unknown death this morning. One of the notes in the autopsy stated that it may be radiation sickness, but they've never seen the onset symptoms like this before."

Chuckling, the Admiral said, "They won't have to wait too long for confirmation! Did they find the cash on him?"

"That's the really weird part. No, only fifty cents. I guess he gave it to someone else."

The Admiral just grinned, "The gift that just keeps giving! Angelina is indeed brilliant!"

Soon, the Admiral's Homeland Security budget would be whatever size he wanted it to be.

Chapter 57

Leaving the Admiral at the coffee shop, Steve drove to his vacation house and opened the garage. He ran inside, and started collecting electronic components from his work bench. He got back into his black SUV that belonged to Homeland Security, and drove to Jack's house where he picked the lock. Opening the door, he heard the beep, beep, beep of Jack's pre-alarm. He knew if he didn't key in the code within 30 seconds, Jack's phone would alert him, and the siren would alert the world! Steve typed in 08161958 (Jack's favorite rock star's birthday). A chime sounded, and a disembodied voice said, "Welcome home, Dear!"

"Some people...," Steve sneered.

Steve began working carefully, not to disturb anything. He set up a 360° downward looking camera and microphone in Jack's living room which was sensitive enough to hear Steve sneeze in his own house three blocks away. The camera covered the hall, living room, dining room, and kitchen easily. Performing several tests on his phone and laptop, Steve verified everything was crystal clear.

Next, he opened up Jack's wireless router, and connected a very small circuit board under the router's main board. This would give Steve access to anything that passed through Jack's router. This was better than his trojan, and Jack would never be able to detect it! Steve now could masquerade as Jack to access all information available to Jack as a Secret Service agent.

Upon completing his work, he cleaned up, making sure all the dusty areas were still dusty, and nothing was out of place. Steve reset the alarm on his way out, and the disembodied voice of Jack's favorite rock star said, "Come back in - I'll make it worth your while, Handsome!"

Steve just laughed! He locked the door with a pick on his way out, and drove to Johnny's apartment where he did the same process. Fortunately, Johnny's apartment didn't have an alarm to worry about yet.

After testing and cleaning up, Steve returned to his vacation house. He set up both, Jack and Johnny's, live video and audio feeds to record everything, and made the connections to both of their routers. As soon as one, or both of them, logged into their Wifi and connected to the Secret Service virtual private network (VPN), Steve would be masquerading as them! It would look like they had requested it, not someone like Steve with no access. Damn! Steve would be dangerous if he used his talents for evil purposes!

Ten minutes later, Steve sent a team email out stating that he now completely owned the Secret Service agents.

Chapter 58

Angelina's crew was still hard at work being creative. One of the scientists told himself he was an engineer in training. He borrowed a worker's outfit in a train yard, and left three special "2 week" packets under the inside of the control panel of the engine. These trains ran in the I-95 corridor, and many working professionals used them to commute into work. In about two weeks, the entire cab of the high-speed train would be contaminated, and hopefully would take out the crew and the train at the same time.

Next, he found several local rail systems in metropolitan areas, and did the same with those trains. Within a month, commuter trains of all types would be having issues which would lead to riders taking other forms of transportation, such as buses and ferries.

Trading his rail worker uniform for a bus uniform, he started working in the depots. The buses would come in to be cleaned, and he'd clean them, but he always left something provocative in two or three packets under the passenger seating, in each bus he cleaned. Over a four day stretch, he was able to dose 80 buses. Again, if someone found the money, they'd use it. Otherwise, it would just be one of 80 mobile radiation points in the big cities!

Yo had finished in Texas and Florida, and now he was in Vegas. Oh, the joy of Vegas! He decided that he would "borrow" a city worker's uniform and a city vehicle with an orange bubble on it for the worker's safety. Yo had 400 special "2 week" packets of 50 bills each. Using his special disguise, he stopped at every third streetlight on both sides of the strip. He unscrewed the base and secured the packet midway up, inside the pole. The swaying motion of the poles would do the rubbing. In two weeks or so, they would be poles of death.

On his way out of Vegas, at the airport, he tried something foolish and daring. He could have really screwed up big time, but the reward was just too much to pass up.

Yo distracted the information desk worker. She told him to wait there, and that she'd be back in five minutes.

When she was out of sight, he slipped behind the desk, and found a filing drawer that was way over packed. Yo slipped a special "2 week" packet of 100 bills in between the hanging folders, and laid it flat in the bottom of the drawer. Then, he shut the drawer, and walked back around the desk. No one seemed to notice.

The young lady came back with no further information on his request. He told her that he had managed to answer some passengers' questions for her while she was away.

She thanked him and said, "Have a momentous day, Sir!"

The kill zone bubble in that information desk would be about a 75 ft. radius bubble in the main path of the terminal and the food court. The safety of travelers within the United States of America would soon be at risk!

Chapter 59

Yo was always the last one off every airplane that he rode. This allowed him to have unrestricted access to the planes. Using special "2 week" loose bills, he placed five bills per seat. Folding them longitudinally in the center, the bills were then inserted into the top of the window shade. Once they were past the top edge, they would spring open, and get stuck in between the shell of the plane and the shade. He did this on both sides of the plane on the third row from the front, and the third row from the back. He made sure to keep away from the cockpit for fear of grounding the plane due to the radioactive sensitive instrumentation.

Back in Virginia, Steve had had a busy day, between the Admiral's showdown, showing Winston the removal tools, sneaking out for coffee with the Admiral, and bugging the homes of two agents. He went home, had a nice relaxed lunch, and then proceeded to go into a main branch bank. Steve knew the manager of that branch since Homeland Security did all its transactions there. This branch always carried a large amount of funds available for emergencies.

Steve walked in just after 2:30pm Monday. He found the bank manager, who greeted Steve like the old friend from college that he was. "How's the Homeland Security business?" Mark asked.

"Crazy-busy and expensive!" This was Steve's code phrase he had prearranged with Mark.

Mark showed him into the inner office, and shut the door.

Steve opened his soft side bag and said, "I need to exchange the old currency for the new currency."

Mark didn't know why, but he sensed that it was a requirement of an operation.

Steve answered Mark's next obvious question, "$500K in the new stuff."

Mark said, "That stuff is still pretty rare around here, but I'll get as much as I can."

He asked for a day to gather it.

Steve explained that it was time critical. If he needed authorization, he should call the White House at this number, and passed it over.

Mark replied, "That's not necessary." He promptly disappeared with the original old $500K.

Steve breathed a sigh of relief. He hadn't had time to brief the Admiral, and it would have been another cold call, not to mention, another ass chewing in public.

Mark returned smiling and said, "You're in luck. We had $20M!"

Steve said, "I'm sure there will be more requests coming soon. Did you put in dye packs?"

Mark replied, "No, would you like any?"

"Not this time. Please record the serial numbers under this, my cover name."

Mark looked down and saw, *Samuel Fixxen*, and said he'd do that.

Steve stood up, thanked Mark by giving him a firm handshake, grabbed his bag, and took his leave.

Mark typed in *Samuel Fixxen* on the computer form for the bank's records, and saved it. Then, sensing he had seen that name somewhere, he searched the internet. "Oh yeah! The little kid who died in California." Now, Mark figured it was a witness protection thing, and promptly dismissed the exchange, thinking there was a valid reason for it, just as Steve had planned.

Outside, Steve picked up his phone, opened the map option, and typed in Archie. In moments, *Bitching Betty* was directing him to the neon mobile. Six miles later, he drove up to the driver's door in traffic and honked.

Archie looked over, expecting to flip off an impatient cabbie and instantly thought, "How does he do that?!" Archie found a deserted strip mall, pulled in, and parked.

Steve pulled up, got out with the bag, and said, "It's time to set up your account."

Archie opened the back doors, and accessed the vault using his codes. Steve noticed that Archie had only $2,000 left on the i625 side. Business must be good. Archie stated, "I texted you 20 minutes ago, and didn't know how long it would take, but I figured hours, not minutes."

Steve just grinned and replied, "I'm just *THAT* good! You've got $500K. It should be gone five days from now."

Archie's mouth hit the ground. "How?!"

Steve mentioned that he was throttling back the search engine results. Once they opened the floodgates, Archie should see 150-200 addresses a day. "Let me know when you get below $100K to reorder."

Archie agreed. They talked for a bit, and then parted ways.

Samuel Fixxen's funeral was nationally televised, but his family didn't understand why. It was a closed casket ceremony, but there was no body in it. No one knew what had killed such a healthy kid, and the ongoing investigation required them to keep the body. Since the government wanted it to go away, they decided a quick funeral would get them off the hook for now.

Willie, Lisa, and their parents didn't know why they couldn't see Sam's body, even after talking to no less than ten high ranking officials in the state. Eventually, they accepted the conditions, but they never would forget Sam. The entire family had stopped living, and all were seeking counseling, but nothing could help.

Chapter 60

It was now Thursday, and the phone calls to Timmy's house had gone unanswered. The elementary school was not accustomed to having their inquires ignored, but it did happen from time to time. One school administrator looked at the contact records for Timmy, and discovered his single mother was a flight attendant. The school made a call to the employer to try to locate Timmy's mother. They finally got a message to her to call them.

When she called them back, she apologized profusely, explaining that she had changed phone providers and her number, since her ex-husband was harassing her. Once the administrator regained her attention, he asked her where Timmy was. He had not been in school for four days. Timmy's mother apologized, and said she would find out. Then, she hung up before the school could ask any more troubling questions.

Still stuck in Hawaii, after the volcanic eruption, Timmy's mom had tried to call him on the emergency cell phone, but it was not charged, so it was going straight to voicemail. They had moved into the area 18 months ago, but had no close neighbors that had a key. He was probably just playing hooky at the mall – she'd have to kill him when she got home.

He had never been a bad kid until he saw his father act up. Now, this sixth grader was beginning to get into more and more trouble, thinking it would impress his father, and he'd come back to live with his cool son. She called the airport to find the first flight home, and was again told Sunday morning was the best guess.

Three more days felt like an eternity, but Timmy was out having the time of his life, maybe even a party?! Oh great! If he was throwing a party, the house would be trashed. For the briefest of moments, she had the thought to call the police. Not knowing if leaving a kid unattended for 10 days was a crime, she decided against it. The last thing she wanted was custody trouble at her divorce. None of it would really matter now, anyway.

Timmy had been looking down at her, shaking his head side to side for six days now saying, "Wake Up, Stupid Mother!" At least his soul was at peace, knowing that she didn't have any more kids to put through this kind of living Hell she called an education of independence.

His family had recently returned from a six-month missionary assignment in the Philippines. Timmy had started going to missionary school immediately. He was given 20 pesos to get to school and back, each day. The routine was to hail a cab by himself from the apartment, ride five miles in the dark at 5:30am to a lone street corner, and wait for the school bus in Manila. Once on the bus, it took an hour to get to school.

The bullies at school tried to take the remains of Timmy's money. Hence, Timmy was always in trouble, both at home and school. The beatings at both locations became part of the routine. Then, he'd get on the bus for a 2-hour ride home, wait on the corner, and hail a cab back to the apartment complex.

If the bullies stole his money, Timmy would never get home. Would this have been a dreadful thing? He wondered! This arrangement sucked, but at least he didn't have a younger sister or brother to look after. All in all, his pathetic mother, who never wanted the responsibility of kids, was not going to endanger any other kids, ever again!

Timmy saw Sam Fixxen walking down the streets of gold, and apologized for being a bully at school. Sam was glad to see a friendly face. Neither one of them knew what had killed them in the real world, but they were going to find out!

Chapter 61

10am Friday, in DC at the BEP, Trent and Toby were very pleased with the new currency. They had been in production on Monday, Wednesday, and today. Nothing had cropped up in the printing runs, and everything was running as it should. Toby said he'd call Jack in a week for another full ink run to Inks4Life.net, and that should hold them until the first of the year.

Trent asked, "Toby, so, have you decided on how to spend the bonus money yet?"

Surprisingly, Toby said, "Yes, indeed I have. I'm going on a date!"

"A date?" Trent had never heard Toby mention a significant other ever since he'd known him.

Toby described the all-expenses paid vacation for two for a week in Hawaii.

Trent asked, "Isn't that a huge gamble?"

"Maybe," agreed Toby, "but we have stayed friends forever, and I am willing to see if it is fate, or just a lifelong friend."

"It sounds like an adventure of a lifetime. Go for it!" Trent cheered him on.

The next two fatalities were from a rib festival, 100 miles outside of Virginia. The married couple had been to one of these events 20 some odd years ago, and were wondering if it would rekindle some romance. It was a bring your own chair and blanket event, at what looked like an empty deserted lot with a huge stage up front. Admission was a can of soup or vegetables at the gate, so the price of romance was right on the button. Some 20 bands were scheduled to do concerts sponsored by a local radio station. Rib and BBQ vendors were everywhere. It smelled delightful! The couple said that they could die here, it smelled so good, but neither one of them really meant it.

The festivities had kicked off right at noon on Friday, and would go nonstop until Sunday at 6pm. You could get a hand stamp to leave and come back if you liked. The couple stayed until 7, when they left the festival grounds to go find a Mexican restaurant with a real bathroom to freshen up. At 10 pm, they returned to their blanket, enjoyed the music, and looked at the stars on this very clear night. Seeing stars and just talking like two best friends meant more to both of them than rekindling their romance, but that too was warming up.

Just then, the bands changed, and her favorite 1980's band took the stage. She talked him into going up to the mosh pit area to try to sing with them on stage. He was happy looking at the stars, but gave in.

Within thirty minutes, she had achieved her goal, and was singing on stage. Then, she invited her husband up, too. He was shocked when the stage bouncers approached him and said, "Your presence is required on center stage, Sir!" The security group showed him up the stairs where he joined his wife and her glam rock star who had also played in the soaps. This was definitely going to be a night to remember.

The band played one of her favorite songs, "Don't Talk to Strangers", and the three of them jumped up and down, totally oblivious to the diamondback rattlers performing at the exact same time under the stage!

After 40 minutes, they shook hands with the band, took photos, and got autographs. Then, they got sodas, went to their blanket to watch the stars, and take a well-deserved nap. It was the best night of their lives, except for getting married. Three hours later, they were talking to Sam and Timmy, wondering where all the people had gone.

Chapter 62

It was a bright and sunny Saturday afternoon at the rest area in central Florida where Jake and his hound dog, Pixie, were stretching their legs after driving from Miami. The previous three days had been nonstop thunder, rain, high winds, tornado warnings, and hail. Pixie was looking for a good spot to do her business, and Jake was leaning on the picnic table, enjoying the sunshine.

Suddenly, Pixie started pawing at a puddle. As Jake called her away, she obeyed, but Jake's attention was immediately drawn to a soaking wet envelope in the puddle. He walked over, kicked it out of the puddle, and then stepped on it with his shoe to dry it off on the grass. The paper envelope was past its point, and fell apart. Diamondback rattlers hissed their warning repeatedly, but when Jake saw five Franklins, he picked them up after rubbing them on the grass with his hand and shoes. They looked brand new.

Jake looked at Pixie, and said, "Good girl - steak tonight!" He knew a great little steakhouse just off Highway 92 named the Barn something. They even liked Pixie. Jake had a nice porter house, and ordered a filet for Pixie. Twenty minutes later, Pixie's was gone, but Jake got his other half wrapped to go.

Jake took Pixie for a walk, and started feeling strange. He didn't think it was food poisoning, so he shook it off. Pixie looked at him and barked, saying it's time to go. They got into the big rig, and he put the leftovers in his on-suite fridge and the leftover money in his hidey hole. They still had plenty of time to make it to Lake City tonight.

It was just getting dark, and he had made it through Tampa, when Jake saw a hill in the distance with brake lights on it that looked like a parking lot. He was going 75 MPH, but he was easily two miles away, and had plenty of time to slow down.

All of a sudden, Pixie howled in pain. At the same time, Jake felt a debilitating pain in his arm. His legs and arms refused to move. He uttered a prayer, and hoped some unseen force would stop his big rig from hurtling down the hill into that parking lot of people and cars. He tried to reach the air horn, but his muscles would not obey commands. He screamed for the people to move away from their vehicles, but it was no use.

Jake blacked out just 25 ft. from the last car. His semi was now doing 98 MPH, and he hit the parking lot of two lanes of traffic dead center. People were congregating outside of their cars like a tailgating party at a ball field. Some of them had been there for the whole four hours the road had been closed.

Jake's rig ripped through the first ten cars like your hand going through soap suds. Mercifully, the truck glanced off another big rig on the left side, but it didn't really help slow it down.

The people in front of the truck looked up, hearing the commotion. Shock filled their eyes, as they watched the truck hurtling out of control. It collided with a gasoline truck that had just refueled in Tampa. The explosion made Mount St. Helens look dim.

People everywhere took cover, if they could. Finally, Jake's rig and the gas truck punched through the metal guard rail, and hit several tall pine trees, igniting them into fiery kabob skewers which were going to fall back onto the parking lot, and crush several more vehicles.

All in all, there were 45 deaths, 137 injured, and $40 million in damages.
Unfortunately, Jake's hidey hole protected the money from burning, and it is still active.

Pixie was licking Sam's face as Jake walked up saying, "What happened? Thanks for taking care of Pixie for me."

Chapter 63

Timmy's mother had just landed Sunday night in California. Taking a cab home, she got to the house where she found the TV on downstairs and all the normal lights on. Nothing was out of place, except she noticed an odd odor. She called for Timmy, but got no response. She looked in the kitchen. It looked like no one had used it since she had cleaned it the Friday afternoon before she left.

Growing uneasy, she climbed the stairs, noticing that the smell was getting stronger, but not overpowering. She knocked on Timmy's door and tried to open it, but he had locked it. She ran into her bedroom and got the spare key. Opening the door, she saw him sleeping peacefully. Not wanting to disturb him, she just kissed him on the forehead, and pulled the covers over him gently. Then, closing the door behind her, she set out to find out what was making that strange smell.

Timmy was ticked off while watching from above. Sam made a face palm plant, and Pixie growled loudly, too. Jake just put his hand on Timmy's shoulder and said, "Don't worry, Kid. We've got your back now!"

The married couple from the concert couldn't believe what came the next morning.

Timmy's mother was shouting from the kitchen while making pancakes. "Timmy, shake a leg! It's time for school." What was it going to take to roust this kid out of bed? "Timmy, Now! Move it." Getting impatient, she walked to the stairs and shouted, "Don't make me come get you!" Frustrated, she opened the bedroom door, and ran over to pull the sheets off the bed. Timmy rolled to the floor without making a sound. She shook him, and screamed!

She called 911, and told the operator that she could not wake her son.

Chapter 64

The next set of fatalities happened in Florida at a water park. Jerry was walking his potbellied pig on a leash in a popular park in the gulf coast area. While he and Petunia were walking, he found a bank envelope with ten $20 bills in it. He looked around for a would-be owner, but the park was empty. Jerry took the envelope, and ran home with Petunia in tow.

Jerry and his youth group were planning to go to a water park tomorrow. Eleven hours of bliss in chlorinated water, slides, tubes, wave pools, and really expensive food, but so delicious! Jerry slept really well that night.

The next day rolled around, and Jerry was third to get on the youth group bus. He was the most popular guy in the group, and was friends with all the girls and the guys. Once his friends were on the bus, he announced that they were going to have a blast as he showed his prize to the group. When he said he found it in the park, four guys said, "Oh, that's where I lost my money!"

Jerry just put it in his swimming trunks, and said, "Dream on, folks."

The packet was a normal six-month release. Jerry was safe as long as no chlorine got on it.

Once they parked and paid, everyone hit the water, including Jerry and his ten bills. As soon as the bills got wet enough through the fabric, the cc625 melted away like butter in a hot frying pan.

All the kids were in the wave pool in a large group cluster having the time of their lives bobbing up and down with the rough waves. Like a washing machine on high agitate, the diamondback rattlers were making hideous noises, but they were drowned out by the fun everyone was having. At its highest peak of activity, Jerry and 12 of his youth group friends were exposed to the lethal dose within a 10 ft. radius. None of them felt anything.

Soon, they began to get tired of swimming

and bobbing, and the whole group moved to the concession stand. They passed the chaperones on the way, who were relaxing while enjoying the suntan opportunities. One of them reminded the kids to wait before going back into the pool after eating.

Jerry went up to the counter, and ordered 20 large sodas and 40 hotdogs. The gal at the counter was more than a little surprised when he handed over $180 out of his pocket. In her job, it was common to receive wet bills, but she still had not gotten used to it. As Jerry handed over the money, Becky recounted it, and the diamondback rattlers hissed their ominous warning that went carelessly unheeded.

The food and drinks were devoured in record time. Within seven minutes, the group was all climbing the tallest water slide in the park. As one calculus student in the group put it - *it approached infinity!*

Shortly after the youth group left for the water slide, Becky's manager came by with a cash bag for the park and counted her drawer down, removing $900. All of Jerry's money got turned in, and managed to stay together. Her manager then mentioned it was a slow day, and he needed a volunteer to go home early.

Becky had a term paper due on Tuesday, and this was just the break she was looking for to get caught up. As Becky left, she looked back at her manager, Egan, and said, "Thanks!"

Egan shook the bag and said, "Good luck with the paper." He didn't hear the rattlers either! He was slinging the bag back and forth briskly as he walked through the park to the next concession stand. He was glad to see the youth group kids having fun. He just wished he could attract more kids into his park easier, but the management always raised prices, and that made it harder to get more kids.

Once back in the office, Egan opened the safe, took out the nightly drop bag, and relocked the safe. He placed the fourteen additional money bags that he had just collected inside the drop bag.

Next, he put the night drop bag on a cart, and rolled it out to his car, like he did every other day. He opened his trunk, put the nightly drop bag inside, and closed his trunk. Looking around, no one seemed to notice or care. He had done this for several years routinely taking the drop to the bank in daylight hours, only today was different. When he had asked the park owner for his token 2% raise this year, the owner had told him that tonight would be his last night working there.

Egan was not going to take it sitting down! He had just closed on his house, cashed out all his accounts, and had bought a ticket to Jamaica to live the rest of his days in bliss. All told, he had $450K in his trunk, a large duffle bag, and now the nightly drop which was close to another $400K in cash. He had chartered a small private jet. He figured the $2,400 ticket was worth not dealing with TSA and customs. He was sooo right. He was just pulling up to the plane on the tarmac. In just over an hour, he'd be in Jamaica.

Chapter 65

When the paramedics arrived at Timmy's house, his mom had gone into shock, so they took her to the hospital. The paramedics called the police, and the police detective drove to the house. He looked at the scene, took pictures, and then released the boy's body to the paramedics. Their town did not have a coroner, so the hospital staff would perform that function, and report to the detective.

Detective John Graves had been with the force for nineteen long years, but had never seen anything close to this in his life. A healthy 12-year-old boy who died in his sleep? This was the second boy from the same school that had died in two weeks. Graves knew he was missing something huge, but what?! He'd have to see what the hospital had to say about the time of death and the circumstances. He went back to his car, and drove to the hospital to discuss it with the doctor, and find out when he could talk to Timmy's mom.

At the hospital, Detective Graves pulled the doctor aside after he finished examining Timmy's mom. The doctor had given her a sedative that would knock her out until tomorrow, and told him to come back then. They'd need at least that long to do the autopsy, and most likely much longer to get the results back.

While Graves was there, he asked if he could see the data on the Samuel Fixxen case.

"That belongs to the FBI now. They won't even talk to us about it," the doctor said. "Why, are these two cases related?!"

Graves explained that he wasn't sure, but they had come from the same school and the same class. The doctor changed his tone, and asked Graves to follow him. They walked into the morgue where the doctor pulled out the body of Timmy.

"Interesting, not good, still interesting," the doctor announced, ominously. "The Fixxen kid was DOA with no sign of foul

play. It was like his heart had just
disintegrated. Now, as I look closer at
Timmy here, he has been dead for 9+ days.
The two of them could have died within
hours of each other."

Graves thought that sounded crazy!
Timmy's mom would have noticed
something before today.

The doctor said, "Check with the school.
They may provide a clue."

He thanked the doctor for the extra look,
and asked to be alerted, day or night, when
Timmy's mom would be able to speak.

Graves turned on his lights, but not his
siren, and boogied to the school. The
principal greeted the detective. They went
to the same church. She asked him what
she could do for him.

Graves broke the news gently to the
administrator, who took it very hard. The
death of two of her students in two weeks
felt impossible. She thanked him for
notifying the school, and stood to show
him out. He motioned her to sit back

down. Not more sad news! He let her calm down, and then asked if Timmy had been in trouble recently.

She blinked as if a lightning bolt hit her. Timmy had been the class bully, and seen more of his share of time in her office. She also mentioned that he had been absent all last week, and she had to call his mother through her employer phone contact. Graves requested that contact, and she looked it up on her computer. She emailed that, and all of the boy's history, to Graves' email. Graves asked if he could do anything for her, specifically. She just requested that he find out what had killed both of "her" kids.

Chapter 66

Meanwhile, the sun was going down, and 13 of the 20 in the youth group were getting fatigued far earlier than the other seven. Finally, the park made the announcement that they would be closing in two hours, and the guests should begin to make those last-minute choices. The announcer also said that anyone who wanted to relax in a cabana could do so now, free of charge.

Jerry and his 12 friends liked that idea, and walked over to three cabanas next to each other. They shut the drapes to block out the sun, and then each chose lounge chairs or sofas, and laid down for a nap. Jerry thought this seemed strange, but was too fatigued to argue with himself. All the others immediately fell asleep, some even snored loudly, but all were too tired to care.

Time slipped away, and soon the chaperones were looking for the missing 13 kids. The park had made their closing announcement ten minutes ago, and they had sent the four fastest of the seven to round up the others. They came back empty handed, saying they had checked the locker rooms, parking lot, and game rooms.

The lifeguards had cleared all the water attractions. The youth group leader started muttering, "If this is the thanks I get, there will be no more trips ever!"

He was approached by the park owner who politely said, "We must close the park. Can you and your group leave?"

The youth leader informed the owner that he was missing 13 kids. They would not be able to comply until they were found.

The owner asked their approximate ages, and was shocked to learn they were all 14-17 years old. He went to the nearest phone, and made a park-wide announcement: "Attention! All of the youth group members, please meet at the entrance. Staff, please be kind enough to escort them to the gate."

In ten minutes, the phone at the gate rang, and the owner said, "This better be good."

The cabana attendant told him that she had 13 non-responsive kids in cabanas 55, 56, and 57. "Call 911, NOW!"

The owner's face went white. Calling 911, he reported 13 kids down, and gave the address and gate information that would get the rescuers there. He hung up, and redialed the paging system. "Code Red in Cabana 55, 56, and 57! This is not a Drill!"

The sleepy park came alive with activity! They had trained day and night to give the best medical care to any park guest, but thirteen?! *Holy Mother!*

The owner went to the youth leader, and asked him to leave the chaperones with the kids, and follow him. They ran through a back gate, through the parking lot, and to the back edge of the park. He unlocked the gate, and their eyes met Hell!

26 of his lifeguards were performing CPR on 13 teenagers. Four more lifeguards were calling the cadence for the others

performing rescues. The group leader fell to his knees and prayed.

30 seconds later, 15 ambulances, 10 paramedics, 9 police, 12 sheriff patrols, and three fire chiefs filled the parking lot in a haphazard conga line. If chaos caused chaos, this was it. Each paramedic took vitals, and then they traded off with the tired lifeguard teams. The owner found a phone, and had more lifeguards approach to relieve the paramedics and their own staff members.

Three minutes after the rescue workers arrived, the news choppers were hovering over the park like a swarm of angry bees disturbed by a bear.

Within the next four minutes, every one of the kids had been pronounced dead!

The owner was talking with police and fire officials, and trying to come up with a reason why 13 kids simultaneously died at his park. He called the office for a pH reading on every water attraction. They had all been computerized last year, and it was a Godsend to know the chlorine level any minute of the day. All the readings came back spot on, and there had been no leaks reported in the last four months.

Fire Chiefs were going through what could have caused the deaths. Chlorine and drowning topped the list, but neither had contributed here. Bleach was not even ordered for the park stores, in an effort to prevent such an accident.

Too many questions, not *any* answers!

The youth leader couldn't even stand, much less make a phone call. One of the police officers took the youth leader's phone, and called the pastor to ask how to reach the parents of the kids. The pastor explained that the kids had driven themselves to the church. When the officer heard this, he realized how difficult it was going to be to notify the next of kin. To further complicate the situation, the media had probably already broken the news. The officer cursed in disgust!

Chapter 67

Tired of working on her term paper, Becky saved her work on the computer, grabbed her cup, and walked downstairs to get some orange juice. While she was down there, her father was wondering what to do for dinner. Ever since her mom had left them six years ago for the Driver's Ed. teacher, it was just father and daughter. He asked her what sounded good for dinner.

Sloppy Joes was usually her default answer to the question, but this time she just said, "How about popcorn and junk food at a movie?"

He replied, "Sold! Got a movie in mind?"

She did; an action thriller where all the people died except for the hero and his true love. Becky said, "Give me three minutes, and we'll go. It starts in 45 minutes."

They got to the theater in record time. Becky said, "I'll take a large popcorn and

Hot Tamales®. It's good, if you mix them in." She disappeared to the restroom, leaving her father to purchase the goodies.

Becky was now a freshman in college, making great grades, and had her whole life in front of her. Her father smiled as he thought about the last six years, and how he and his daughter were so compatible. He cherished every day with her.

Using a tray to carry all the loot, he met her back at the door of their theater. "Hey Becky, you feel OK? You look a little pale."

"I had a long day at work, and my paper is getting on my nerves – I think, I'll live though."

They sat down, and what felt like five billion previews later, their movie started. By the end of the movie, Becky was crying because the hero and his true love survived a nuclear holocaust, but no one else did. They'd be able to hit big box and grocery stores until they died years later. It was sad, kind of! Most of all, she liked that every time she got scared, her father would put his arm around her, and remind her it was only a movie.

On the way home, she took the keys from him and said, "It's my turn to drive your Grand National."

He hesitated, but she deserved to have some fun. "Ok, but take the interstate where they won't notice you."

She grinned, and waiting for him to strap in, said, "Hold on!" In true fashion, she quietly and neatly made her way to the interstate.

Her father knew what was coming, so he told her to make sure it was clear, and hold tight to that wheel! "It's not anything like your Prius!"

She grinned, and turning left on the left arrow, accelerated on the ramp. Three seconds later, she had left so much of his tires on the on-ramp, he wondered if there was any rubber left! By the time they saw the main interstate, she was already at 90mph.

Nothing was in front of, or behind them, as

far as the eye could see. Out of nowhere, Becky saw a State Trooper with blue lights and a siren blaring next to her.

Her father muttered, "Of course!"

Becky wasn't going to get another chance anytime soon, so she just said, "Hang on!" taking it to wide-open throttle (WOT).

Her father said, "You'll probably lose your license for six months."

She just looked at him and smiled, "I've always wanted a chauffeur!"

Now the Trooper was on the PA system ordering them to stop, and was drifting further and further away in the mirror. She had achieved 160 mph, and the trooper just backed off and radioed ahead for a roadblock at the end of this 6-mile bridge.

Her father said, "Ok, time to slow down just a bit."

She nodded and said, "Do you think Tommy will really arrest me?"

Her father exclaimed, "You knew that was

Tommy?!"

"Duh! He brings that car to our house every other day!"

Her father said, "Ok! You got your old man. Now slow down, and let the car breathe regularly."

Becky was slowing to a nice 120mph when all of sudden, she blacked out and slumped at the wheel. At this speed, her father couldn't react fast enough. The car hit the metal railing, punched through, and raced into the water two stories below.

The impact only killed her father. She was already gone. Tommy came to a screeching halt, locking up his brakes at the point of impact, and called for rescue, but didn't hold out very much hope of survivors. What a waste of great people, and a great car! He would miss both of them dearly. On a somber note, they both had gone together, so they wouldn't be lonely! It was something, but not much.

Chapter 68

Steve was not getting anything from either Johnny or Jack's residences. They were both working out of the Secret Service offices, and doing routine items for now.

Steve had been watching the news feeds regularly, but didn't think there was much to report until today. Back at the outdoor festival, the concerts had stopped, the best BBQ award had been presented, and the crowd was breaking up slowly. By 5:45pm on Sunday, the organizers were getting everyone to leave the venue.

Several of the staff had commented that the couple under the orange blanket slept like the dead. "That first night of singing with the featured Rock Star from the 1980's must have worn them out."

Finally, the manager of the event said, "I'll wake them." He walked to the sound board, cranked the house volume, and said into the microphone, "Thanks for coming. See y'all next year!"

If a NASA shuttle had been taking off, the astronauts would have said, "Hey! Please turn it down!" from three states away.

The couple didn't move. The manager went over, and tapped the blanket saying, "Rise and shine!" Nothing. Next the manager pulled the blanket off, and tapped the man on the shoulder. "Come on buddy, wake up!" The manager had a sick feeling. He got his radio, and called for the paramedics.

As soon as the paramedics arrived, they saw the manager vomiting off to the side. He just pointed, and said that he'd be fine. Instantly the paramedics radioed for a coroner and police assistance. The police asked if there was any video footage that covered that area. The manager had no clue. He told them they could check with Security, but he doubted there were any cameras pointed this far back. There would surely be personal footage that may have captured something.

The police officer asked if they kept records of the tourists that went up on stage.

He responded, "No."

"Any idea what killed them?" the officer asked. They weren't stabbed, beaten, or drowned in a field of 20,000 people. It was a mystery.

Steve was now compiling the news feeds for the team.

So far to date:

TX - Ted & Wife, 70+, traffic accident, heart attack?
TX - Evangelist, 45, traffic accident, mysterious
CA - Samuel Fixxen, 12, football game, mysterious
CA - Timmy, 12, Sam's schoolmate, mysterious
FL - Jake, 58, trucker, road accident, mysterious
FL - Pixie died with trucker
FL - 45 Deaths, 137 injured, $40 million in damages
FL - Freak accident with above trucker
NC - Married Couple, 50+, BBQ Concert, mysterious
FL - Youth Group, 13 DOA, water park, mysterious
FL - Becky & Father, bridge accident, mysterious

Angelina clicked on each link, and read with interest. She knew each one could be hers, *or not*. But she liked to think they were all due to her product. They were!

Back in Jamaica, the water park concession manager had flown in, and arrived at the beach vacation house of his dreams. This place was a paradise compared to his Florida shoebox apartment. He had beach access, a huge covered patio, a swimming pool, two bedrooms, and a kitchen furnished with new appliances that was fully stocked with the special party deluxe package. This package was "hot" at Spring Break time, but now in November, the host included it at half price to encourage more rental traffic. Liquor, groceries, and the rental for three weeks had only cost $1,200 for everything!

Egan was indeed happy with his choice to leave Florida. He changed into his bathing suit, and blew up an air chair. After doing that, he got a cold beer from the massive fridge, and sat down in the air chair in the pool. He took a swig of beer, placed the can in the chair's cup holder, laid back, and drifted off to sleep. He never awoke again.

A couple of days after he died, there was a rough thunderstorm that rumbled through. Two days later, Kelly, the pool boy /

housekeeper, came by to check if the rental guests required any service, grocery refills, or help of any kind. Kelly noticed the house was still as immaculate as he left it, except the back-patio door was open. He stepped outside, and saw Egan floating on his back in the unmoving pool. He said out loud, "Damn! I wish I could relax like that, Dude."

Egan didn't respond. Kelly shrugged it off and said, "Enjoy," and took his leave. On his paperwork, he checked off that the kitchen was filled to capacity, and the guest was happy and content with the premises.

On Kelly's next visit, four days later, he found the house in the same shape. This time, he heard a buzzing sound coming from the kitchen, and went to investigate. Actually, the sound was coming from the patio. Just as he got to the door, he noticed a swarm of flies over the pool. Covering his nose and mouth, he shut the door, and ran in to the bathroom where he promptly lost his breakfast.

Once Kelly had recovered, he picked up his mobile and dialed his boss who called the local police. When the police arrived, Kelly was sitting out front waiting for them.

Sergeant Montgomery said, "Did you touch anything?"

Kelly said, "Yes, four days ago I cleaned, and thought he was sleeping on his back in the pool. Today the flies told me I was mistaken."

The officer looked through the rental carefully, noticing the unpacked bags thrown on the bed, and that not much else was disturbed in the rental. Then, he got to the back-patio door and exclaimed, "Holy Cow! The kid wasn't exaggerating! What a scene." Montgomery went outside, and calmly talked to Kelly as they waited for the coroner to come inspect and retrieve the body. He took Kelly's information and released him.

Once the coroner had arrived, and retrieved the body from the water, he made a very startling announcement. "Montgomery, this man didn't drown!"

"Ok, so what was the cause?"

"There's no foul play, and no markings. I see no evidence of drug use. This man shouldn't be dead! Maybe there's something inside that will explain it."

Montgomery went straight into the bedroom, and took pictures of the scene. Then, he carefully emptied the big army duffle bag onto the bed. "Amazing!" He called the coroner into the room, and they both stared at the contents. They saw two pairs of every kind of clothing for a man, about a million dollars in bills, and the empty duffle.

The coroner said, "If it were foul play, they would have taken the money. Why not take it, counterfeit?" Both of them looked at it, and judged it was the real stuff. The coroner looked at Montgomery and asked, "Do you have kids in college, Sergeant?"

Montgomery did, but he wasn't going to pay for it this way. "Yes, but No. I'm a career man."

The coroner knew Montgomery very well

and said, "It's a pity we're both honest men."

"It's not the first time I've passed on living happily ever after!" They locked up, and both left together.

Chapter 69

Back at the water park in Florida, the news headlines said it all:

Mysterious Deaths of 13 Healthy Teenagers!

The media was already profiling all 13 teenagers as wholesome, church going kids, with few wants or needs in a well to do community. Drugs, though prevalent in the area, had not been part of this church community. All the kids seemed to have good records at the local high school. Some were promising sports stars, and were going to be on the football team next year. All five of the girls were honor students, and were in band or orchestra.

Counselors were on hand for the remaining students at the high school. Thirteen deaths was a surreal number of students for this small town high school of about 800. No one could fathom the horror that the parents and church leaders were going through. Many of the *Living Seven*, as they were called by the media, questioned God, and continually asked him why they were allowed to live. Some even wanted off this earth more desperately now, than before.

The coroner and county medical services had called in the CDC for help with diagnosing the cause of death. Local officials had theories, but no hard proof to base them on. Again, it looked like their hearts had just disintegrated, but there was no cause for it. No other organs showed any stress or dysfunction. Nobody had a clue of what could attack the heart so fast and brutally without affecting other organs. It acted like cancer, but at a lightning speed. This would be like going to your doctor, and hearing him say, "You're dead, and you have cancer." In that order!

Chapter 70

Jack and Johnny were in DC, and still nowhere close to discovering where Archie was hiding the $2.6M Suburban. Johnny had some feelers out, and one of them just had called on his phone with a tip. The caller had said, "You never heard it from me, but checkout Paint Central A to Z on a custom paint job," and hung up. Johnny checked out the website. They claimed to do all kinds of vehicle wraps for anything you needed.

Johnny told Jack about the tip, and Jack grabbed his coat and said, "Let's Ride!"

Within moments, they were in a very industrial part of Virginia, looking for the address. Once located, they went inside as a team. Jack let Johnny take the lead on the interview, for practice.

Johnny introduced himself to Daniel, the owner of the paint shop, and asked if they had ever painted an armored Suburban.

Daniel's face lit up! "I've got just one that I've done, but it's my best work yet. The lady who wanted it done, didn't care how much it cost. She just needed it the next day. Business is good I guess, although I still couldn't figure out why she used an armored vehicle."

Johnny and Jack glanced meaningfully at each other. It was the question of the day.

Daniel pulled up the job, and presented the agents with his fabulous resume, showcasing Archie's vehicle. Johnny was stunned! That's how Archie had left the hotel. He drove right by Johnny in broad daylight. Johnny and Jack thanked Daniel for his time and got back into their vehicle.

Johnny was doing something on his phone.

Jack asked, "What are you up to?"

Johnny told Jack that he was investigating a hunch. He typed the message PROMO to SEEDC, and instantly got a text response back. "Well, I'll be damned!!" It looked and felt exactly like the mower scam in

Oregon. Johnny looked through his notes, and then texted IWANTTOWORKWITHYOU to SEEDC. Immediately, he was sent latitude and longitude coordinates. Johnny typed them into his smartphone, and noticed the location was about ten minutes away.

Jack turned on the *excuse me* blue light on the top of his vehicle, and they were off in a flash! As they drove, Jack asked, "What makes you think this is Archie?"

"I read the paint job that Daniel did for them. If the same people who set up the mower scam server set up and sold one to Archie, it stands to reason they may have similar codes. I just tried the one I used to get David Jones' location."

"Damn! Johnny, when I grow up I want to be as lucky as you!" Jack grinned. Within seven minutes, they had arrived at the coordinates, but nothing was there, just a busy intersection.

Not giving up, Johnny re-sent his text, and got different coordinates. Then, he had a thought - *Archie was driving, not stationary!*

"Wow, Kid!" Jack said. "If you're right, this business is brilliant!"

Johnny entered two new coordinates, and they drove to them. It was a gas station. Johnny grabbed Jack's arm and pointed. 1/8 mile away was the greenest looking Suburban they had ever witnessed! Jack pulled quietly behind it, and followed expertly, after turning off the blue lights.

Archie's finely tuned senses did not notice the car behind him because he was looking for a mailbox. He pulled into a post office lot, went to the back of the vehicle, and did something.

Jack popped the trunk, and told Johnny to get the mic and binoculars. Johnny returned in a moment, giving the binoculars to Jack.

Jack said, "It looks like he's stuffing envelopes. He's putting $500 in each one, sealing them, and getting back into his vehicle."

Archie drove up to the mailbox, deposited

what looked like 30 envelopes, and drove off.

"If those have counterfeit bills in them, we've got his ass!" Jack pulled up to the post office, and went in with Johnny.

They were Secret Service, and they didn't require a warrant to search for counterfeit bills. They got a postal official to open the mailbox, and pull 2 envelopes out. They took them inside and inspected them, photographing them first, then carefully opening them.

Sure enough, $500 cash! "Who sends cash?!" Jack asked.

Johnny and Jack looked at the bills, and noticed they looked brand new. Johnny, on another hunch, called Toby and gave him the serial numbers. "They are real! Just printed this month."

"Tear proof!" Jack said in disgust! "What the Hell?!"

Upon finding the bills to be legitimate currency, the postal officials demanded they reseal the envelopes, and let the mail go to its final destination in Alabama as addressed. Johnny and Jack were thoroughly confused, but there was nothing illegal about sending real money to strangers! *Weird*, yes!

Thanking the postal officials, they quietly went back to their office. Jack couldn't let it go. "What was their motive?!"

Chapter 71

Back in Jamaica, Sergeant Montgomery returned to the rental property with a crime lab tech named Leesa. To collect evidence, they took pictures of items laid out on the bed, and both counted the money to confirm the amount and number of bills. Neither one of them heard the diamondback rattlers spitting their deadly message to them.

Leesa suggested that they separate the new and old bills of the American dollars, just to be thorough. There were only nine new bills total. After they had finished, they loaded Montgomery's vehicle, and returned to the station to lock up the evidence. The money was signed into the evidence locker, and by some wondrous act of mercy, it did not contaminate any other officers on duty.

Montgomery and Leesa took a short trip over to the coroner's office to see if any progress had been made. After they were admitted to the morgue, the examiner took out Egan's body. He asked if they had discovered his identity, or if he was still a John Doe.

"Still John Doe, so run the prints." Montgomery answered.

Looking at the body, the examiner pointed out how the victim's heart was mutilated, and there was literally nothing left of it.

Montgomery asked, "What on earth could do that, and leave most other organs untouched?"

The examiner replied that he had never seen anything like it in his 21+ years of service.

Leesa spoke up, "Is it an accelerated form of cancer?"

The examiner shuddered and said, "If so, the population of the world is at considerable risk!" He had never seen cancer work this fast, maybe four hours from start to finish! That's hardly enough time to visit a doctor, much less diagnose it, and be told you're going to die in two hours.

They all stood there in a long-stunned silence. Finally, Montgomery asked if the examiner had called the Center for Disease Control (CDC) in the United States yet?

"Nope, but that will be my next conference call."

"Do you need us there for anything?" Leesa asked, hopefully.

"No, I expect not. You may return to your usual routine."

Leesa could not contain her disappointment. She was hoping to learn something important today. Unbeknownst to her, she would be able to help the CDC, but not until she died!

Montgomery and Leesa drove to an early dinner. Neither one had anyone waiting for them at home, so they took their time, and talked about the case and their lives. Before long, they realized that it was approaching 9pm, and they had been at dinner for almost four hours; a record for Leesa, whose longest conversation was maybe 45 minutes.

Montgomery respected the young crime tech, and was greatly enjoying her company. He said, "I'd better get you home before my car turns into a pumpkin." They both laughed, and left.

Montgomery drove her home, and he walked her to the door. There they kissed forever, smiled, and gave one more kiss good night. Montgomery left saying, "I'll pick you up tomorrow. Sweet Dreams!"

Chapter 72

Dr. Erika Stone of the CDC and the medical examiner of Jamaica were having a video conference call to discuss the mysterious heart mutilation of John Doe. Dr. Stone had heard of this before, but it had demolished the entire body, all organs were affected, and there was usually a nerve agent or poison responsible for the deaths.

Stone Cold, as her colleagues had nicknamed her, wanted to see the body in the lab, and would be on the first plane out. If this was something new, they needed to get a handle on it before it spread.

Six hours later, Dr. Stone had arrived at the city morgue in Jamaica, and she and the medical examiner were looking over the body. She couldn't believe that the patient's heart was obliterated, but all the other organs were untouched. She suggested that she cut into the lungs, and look inside them to see if John Doe had inhaled a substance. But again, nothing was there. Everything was intact and working as it should be, if only he was alive! The two of them examined other parts for another two hours, and then called it a night.

Back at her hotel, Dr. Stone called a colleague at their lab, and asked him to research anything that consumed the heart.

He asked, "What's going on?"

She told him that within four hours, this John Doe's heart had been obliterated as if someone had rigged it with C4, and detonated it.

"Wow! Something new for our staff to look into?"

Dr. Stone said, "Yes! Definitely, but I can't find a reason for it at all. The medical examiner suggested a new deadly strain of cancer, but I've never heard of a four-hour cancer that only attacks the heart."

He was silent at the description, and then said, "Holy Shit!" once it had sunk in.

Dr. Stone agreed. She said that she would bring the body back with her, and they could test to their heart's content!

Montgomery got home, and feeling tired, he got ready for bed. He took his nightly medication before nodding off. He never moved again.

Leesa was reading in bed, and thinking about the conversation she and Montgomery had. It was the nicest time she could recall since her high school days, ten years ago. She was young next to Montgomery, but she didn't think it mattered, as long as they both were happy. Who cares what other people thought? If it became an issue, she'd leave the force in Jamaica to keep this soul mate she had just found. Drifting off to sleep with a huge smile on her face, she never awoke, either.

The following day, neither Montgomery, nor Leesa showed up at the station. The Captain called both their residences and their mobiles. Finally, he sent men to their homes to find out what was wrong. In ten minutes, the first officer reported that Leesa was dead in her bed. Eight minutes later, the same report on Montgomery was given to the Captain. He called the medical examiner, and told him that he had two dead officers, and needed answers *now!*

The examiner asked, "Who?" Then, he called the airport to stop Dr. Stone; just catching her before she boarded the plane.

He explained the problem, and that these were the two that were working on the John Doe case. She told him to wait for her! Twelve minutes later, she met him at the morgue. They travelled to Leesa's house first - it was closer.

Chapter 73

The water park in Florida had been closed indefinitely. The owner was trying to remain calm, but he was defeated as well. His whole life's business was in jeopardy of closing down.

He had called a lawyer almost immediately. His lawyer had recommended a high-profile group that could actually help him more than he could.

Insurance companies were calling, and his bond was at risk. If any of this was proven to be his fault, he would be bankrupt and imprisoned for many years. He couldn't believe his park was responsible, but what else was left? Thirteen kids between the ages of 14 to 17 years old were dead. What could have caused their deaths so quickly? Why was it only these kids?

The owner had not noticed that the bank drop had not been credited yet to his account, nor did he realize that Egan was missing, as was Becky.

The local police and coroner were working with the CDC, but not with Dr. Stone. The CDC representative called the lab tech that Dr. Stone had called, and asked if they had any unsolved cases involving healthy kids and mass suicide. The tech looked up the cases, and read them over the phone, but nothing jumped out to either of them.

Finally, the tech mentioned that their colleague was investigating a John Doe who was otherwise healthy, but his heart was gone. That was enough for Jackson Smithe to get a hunch.

He had the medical examiner do a chest X-ray to see what their victims' hearts looked like. To his amazement, nothing showed up. "For crying out loud! What is this about?"

Next, Jackson Smithe called Dr. Stone in Jamaica. She answered saying, "Hi Jackson, I'm too busy to chat about dinner plans for Saturday."

He said, "STOP! We're on the same case!"

She almost dropped her phone. "You're

kidding me, right!?"

"Nope." Jackson said that he had 13 dead teenagers who looked like they had died from natural causes, but there was nothing natural about exploding heart tissue, was there?!

Quickly, Erika explained that she had three bodies in Jamaica, and what they had to go on, which wasn't very damned much! They were still waiting on fingerprints, but they weren't hopeful at this point.

Jackson said, "Ok. Raincheck on dinner for now, but come see me as soon as you can break away. I could use an extra set of talented hands here in Florida."

They said goodbye, and ended the call.

Dr. Stone called her boss, and explained the small epidemic that Florida and Jamaica were seeing. She requested additional resources for Jackson in Florida. Her boss told her to ship those Jamaicans to the CDC Lab, and go join Jackson immediately! He would call all the US agencies, and get more details on any other mysterious deaths in the country.

Within 23 minutes, the head of the CDC was on a video conference with 15 different agencies and the Presidential cabinet and staff. He began with, "We have no idea what we're dealing with, except it's a really quick killer." He briefed all of them on the conditions they had seen in Florida and Jamaica with the obliterated hearts. "Right now, there seems to be a 4-hour window or so, to isolate the problem before the victim expires."

There was an overlapping response to this unwelcome news! Everyone seemed to talk at once.

Finally, order was restored to the conference, and the President of the United States asked, "Do we have any idea how it is being passed from victim to victim? Is this a weapon, or a virus?"

Next, he asked his Generals if this could be a weapon that they were developing that somehow got out into the wild.

Many of the Generals wished that was the

issue, but replied, "No, Sir. It is not from within."

Lost for ideas, his cabinet took over the meeting. "Dr. Stone has the most up to date information. Can we conference her in now?"

"No, Sir. She is in flight to Florida as we speak. May I suggest we conference in the lab tech who spoke to both doctors?"

Seconds later, Skeeter Williams was on the conference call, and muttered, "What the Hell?!"

The cabinet speaker said, "Mr. Williams, sorry for the surprise call, but we need answers, and you are the one who has talked to both Dr. Smithe and Dr. Stone."

Skeeter swallowed hard, and began like the retired college professor he wasn't. "To date, Dr. Stone had three victims in Jamaica who had obliterated hearts. Dr. Smithe is investigating 13 kids from the water park with identical symptoms. They found no external trauma, punctures, drugs, bruising, contusions, or sense of foul play, such as poison. But, obviously something killed every one of them within about four hours, with respect to size. The bigger people lived 20 to 60 minutes longer.

"We are currently scouring the crime records for unsolved or mysterious cases, but cannot find matching symptoms. I did notice there were several traffic incidents that may have been caused by the sudden onset of this epidemic, but since they were classified as traffic accidents, there was no follow up on the deaths. Most notably, a 45-victim pile up in Florida looks suspicious to me. Also, there was that Sam Fixxen kid that made the national news. If we could look at those incidents, we might see a pattern."

The President came online and told Skeeter, "You have the power of the President of the United States behind you. Make it happen! Get to work. Thank you for your candid ideas."

Within three minutes, the director of the CDC was standing in the lab congratulating the young lab tech who had just been promoted by himself and the President.

Skeeter asked, "Do we have Sam Fixxen's body?"

The director nodded and said, "In Lab 49, drawer 12."

Skeeter jumped up, and ran to the lab. Getting help, he got the X-ray machine and looked. Sure enough, nothing resembled a heart!

The director hadn't run, but just entered the lab. He said, "Well?"

"Confirmed cases exist in California, Jamaica, and Florida now."

The CDC director said, "Ouch! That's gonna leave a mark on our country! You're flying to Florida, Skeeter."

Skeeter refused! He said that he could confirm information over the phone, and not waste valuable time like that.

The director just smiled, knowing he had

hired the best and smartest staff, even if they disregarded him at times.

Skeeter went back to the lab, and called the medical examiners in Florida. He told them what he was looking for, and to his surprise, they asked, "The dog, too?!"

"What?"

"The trucker always traveled with his dog. He had a will stating that he and Pixie would be buried together forever."

Skeeter said, "Yes, please!" He insisted on waiting on the line. In 3.5 minutes, both hearts were confirmed gone. "Shit! Thanks guys, we'll be in touch."

Chapter 74

Johnny and Jack were at the Secret Service office in DC, brainstorming why Archie would be giving away $500 cash to strangers on a mailing list.

Johnny suggested, "Maybe they really did get something out of it."

Jack gave him a sideways look and said, "Yeah, maybe...!"

Neither of them could think of one logical reason why Archie, or Angelina, for that matter, would want to give away real money to complete strangers.

Two days ago, when they found Archie and the neon Suburban, Johnny had signed up for the SEEDC offer using his cover address. Their administrative assistant had just delivered today's mail. Johnny held up the envelope, and waved it in front of Jack. "Finally!"

They took it to the lab to have it dusted for prints, but found nothing significant or useful, not even a partial.

"Blast!" Johnny said.

"Easy, Johnny," Jack cautioned. "It's only another piece of the puzzle."

Inside, they saw a nicely printed flier suggesting hotels, restaurants, local attractions, national parks, and historic sites to visit. Johnny suggested that maybe Angelina and Archie had made deals with the business owners to get a cut of the profits for sending people their way. Jack hoped Johnny wasn't seriously entertaining these ideas, but had to agree with him that it may be a possibility, if Archie was really legit. But, NO! Archie was up to something. Jack would stake his career on that!

Dr. Stone had just rejoined Jackson Smithe in Florida, and was beginning the task of investigating to determine if other organs had been damaged besides the victims' hearts.

Jackson and Erika were discussing what had killed the kids in loose terms, and how it looked over time. Erika asked Jackson what the injuries looked like to him. He suggested cancer, if only it would be allowed to incubate for years after the patient would have normally died. Erika agreed that if a patient with the worst stage of cancer was kept on life support for five more years, it may look like these kids, but that was silly! No one had ever seen a fast-acting cancer that matured in only four hours!

"Oh, My Goodness! Someone has found a way to weaponize a lightning fast strain of cancer!"

Jackson breathed, "Oh Shit! You're right. This is bad... Very, very bad! What caused the cancer to start with? We need to find the cause, and how it found our victims. Then, eradicate it from the environment so nobody else gets infected."

"What caused only these people to get it?" Erika wondered.

They brainstormed causes of cancer:

Smoking
Asbestos
DNA / Hereditary / Gene Pool
UV Rays / The Sun / Nuclear Radiation
Alcohol Abuse
Chemical Contamination

Chapter 75

Back at the CDC, Skeeter and the director were on a video call with Erika and Jackson. Erika and Jackson explained their premise, and broke the shocking news to the director. "Holy Cow! I'm going to send you folks a whole lot of people to sweep that water park."

They disconnected, and the director asked Skeeter to join him in the technology command center. The two of them called the POTUS and his cabinet to discuss the data. The President was appalled with the thought of a weaponized cancer strain loose in his country. He tasked his military minds to gather intelligence on which state actors had the capability to weaponize cancer, and told them to find them YESTERDAY! He thanked the director and Skeeter for their prompt support, and asked them to continue feeding ideas to him.

Within minutes, all law enforcement agencies had classified instructions to be aware of any mysterious events that may look like a heart attack, or unexplained death. All hospitals were issued statements to check hearts in patients who died mysteriously, or quickly for no reason, and to call the CDC with any unsettling discoveries.

So far, the media was not in the loop, and all the agencies involved were thankful for every waking minute that was true. They didn't need panic in the mix. They didn't know yet what was causing the deaths, how to stop them, or how to prevent them. Four hours was not enough time to diagnose the cause, much less, treat it, or postpone it.

Chapter 76

Steve was reading the Homeland Security alerts online, and emailed the team immediately. "They have discovered a weaponized form of cancer, but don't understand how it is spread or manifests itself in the victim!"

Angelina read the email, loving every minute of the confusion. They would be years figuring out the cause at this rate! Her plan was turning out far better than she could have planned.

Jack and Johnny were in Jack's office, when Jack saw the bulletin on the weaponized cancer. Jack said, "Oh my!"

Johnny looked at the alert, and said, "You've got to be kidding me! What enemy has that kind of weapon, and the technology to make such a weapon?"

Chapter 77

Within four hours of the CDC video call, Dr. Erika Stone and Dr. Jackson Smithe were swarmed with 200 FBI, CDC, RN's, Paramedics, and military reserve forces scouring the park. They had all kinds of test equipment to look for chemicals and radio signals which might have manifested themselves into a cancerous source. No one knew what they were looking for, including the water park owner. Yes, he had loads of chemicals for water and cleaning, but he couldn't imagine 13 teenagers getting into them and no other guests being affected.

The workers looked at everything. Video arcade machines were disassembled, computers, video kiosks, the public address system, music amplifiers, speaker systems, electrical transformers on the ground and on poles, cash registers, lighting, TV's, freezers, concession appliances, wireless systems, pumps, parking lot tram engines... You name it, they checked it, powered on, or off.

Manual water tests were collected and analyzed in mobile labs. After 72 straight hours of investigating the water park, they had found a slightly elevated level of butter on the popcorn machines, but that was it!

Frustrated beyond belief, the CDC doctors concluded the cause was not the water park, or its systems. The park owner was thankful to be legally cleared, but they left his park in shambles, and he would be closing a month ahead of time. He wondered how much insurance would cover. He prayed again for the kids, and his park.

He started reviewing the bank records for the day of the tragedy. He called his bank, and said that he was missing a full day's receipts, totaling $460,047.32. The manager of the account at the bank checked and double checked, and confirmed that no deposit had been made that day, or since.

Now, recalling he had told the concession's manager, Egan, that his last day was going to be the night of the tragedy, he almost fell over. Immediately, he called Dr. Stone's mobile number, and informed her about the missing money and manager. A disgruntled employee may be the explanation for a terrorist act such as this, but wouldn't there be a clue left over that they would have detected? Dr. Stone wondered.

Dr. Stone put out a broadcast for Egan. Everything was used in their arsenal. Silver Alerts were splashed on interstate signage to encourage people to report his vehicle. A nation-wide manhunt began for the missing man.

Unbeknownst to all the agencies in Florida, Egan had been planning his escape far before his manager told of the water park's discussion to let him go. He had planned well in advance by getting a fake ID, and by taking a chartered flight. Security didn't even blink at the fake ID.

Before leaving the water park, he had disabled the cameras that had any view of the parking lot. When the security team reviewed the footage for that day, they saw him leave the park through the turnstiles, and that was the last image they had of him!

Egan had walked directly to his car, put the nightly drop in his trunk, and used a screwdriver to remove his license plate. Then, he had gone for a short walk. Looking for the same make and model as his, he had found six cars to choose from. What luck! The owner of this car must live close to him, since the plate was almost identical. Then he realized that they had both used the same used car dealer. It was the biggest one in the city. Egan's tag was XTU-582, and the other car's was XTV-382. Quickly removing it, he replaced the stolen tag with his own. He then put the stolen tag on his car.

Now, if law enforcement checked, the officer would have to inspect the VIN of the car. He figured this was safe enough. Besides, people rarely look at their plate, since the electronic key unlocks the doors and flashes the lights. Also, being at the waterpark tends to take a toll on kids and their parents. Most parents are ready to drop their kids at the local orphanage, and go back to being empty nesters, following a day at the park.

After a lengthy man hunt, the FBI, Homeland Security, and many other agencies were scratching their heads as to where this Egan guy could have gone. He was a loner, and had no living relatives or friends. His neighbors recognized him, but no one had seen him in weeks.

They searched his apartment, but it looked like a motel room; no personal effects, except for toiletries and some rotten milk. There were no notepads, or anything that amounted to a plan. They did notice he had a cable connection, so they subpoenaed his provider, but he didn't have activity through them. Another dead end.

Where was this guy hiding? He definitely had planned this out well in his mind.

Finally, law enforcement subpoenaed his mobile phone provider, and found he had made zero calls from his mobile. Egan had received several calls from the waterpark asking him to come in on his days off for the past five months. Blast it all, didn't this guy communicate with the outside world?

Dr. Stone finally got a call from Drew Hampton, the lead investigator of the FBI, stating they were still looking for Egan after four days of searching. They talked for a bit on the phone, and then Erika asked him if they had reviewed the water park phone logs. He stated that they had checked his office phone log.

Erika rephrased it, "No! I mean did you review all the calls? They must have 500 phones out there."

Drew told her that he'd check into it, and call her back.

Twenty minutes later, Drew called Erika back, and said, "Your hunch paid off. Someone called and arranged an air taxi service for a Jamaica ride."

Erika dropped the phone! "Shit!" Finding her phone, she asked, "Can you send me a picture of Egan with no hair?"

"Sure, but why?"

"The Jamaican morgue team shaved a John Doe clean while looking for skin punctures as a sign of foul play. Some of the gangs down there have killed people with overdoses by injecting them under the hairline."

"Crap!" Drew said, "Scary shit down there, huh?!"

Within seconds, she had her John Doe identified. She relayed the story of the three dead in Jamaica to Drew. He thanked her, and said he'd have a team go to the CDC and check for themselves.

Next, Drew Hampton got on the phone with the Jamaican Police chief. Drew said he was sorry for the chief's loss, and asked to have the evidence that Montgomery and Leesa had collected sent to FBI headquarters in DC. The chief took down the address, and assured Drew that it would be there in the morning.

Then, the chief called Lieutenant Dokit in. He told Dokit that he would be taking a trip to DC with evidence. Dokit would leave tonight, and stay in DC until the FBI found out what had killed Montgomery and Leesa. Dokit agreed.

Dokit walked down to the evidence locker where his longtime friend, Freddie, was manning the desk. He requested the evidence.

Freddie said, "I sure hope you find out what killed them. The whole department thinks it was an act of Black Magic."

Dokit assured Freddie it was most likely man-made, based on the weaponized cancer reports he had read.

Freddie excused himself to go collect the evidence, and returned with a bag of clothes and three large bags of money. Checking the computer logs in the evidence locker, Freddie told Dokit, "That's all of it! You're gonna need an armed guard with you to carry all that cash."

Dokit just slapped his Desert Eagle on his belt, and said, "I've got it covered."

Unbeknownst to Freddie or Dokit, the

officer on duty the night of the tragedy had missed recording a small nine bill bag. He had only recorded three bags of cash, but locked up four. Lucky for everyone there, the nine bill bag was left untouched in the vault in Jamaica.

Chapter 78

In NYC, the Wednesday night before Black Friday, Angelina's scientist was preparing for the worst. He had gotten a job with a parade organizer in the city, two weeks ago.

He had glued a secret compartment inside each of the seven most popular balloons. Then, he had placed a special "2 week" 100 bill packet into the inside of the balloons. Using the same material on top of the existing material, it looked like a patch made by the balloon manufacturers. The outside of the balloon looked perfect, as always. The only way anyone would notice anything out of place would be if they walked inside the balloon as it was filling up, and ripped the patch open to discover the bills freely bouncing around in the oversized patch.

It was Wednesday night about 11pm, and the weather forecast was looking like a full balloon parade tomorrow starting at 9am.

The scientist had rented an apartment a

month before to serve as base of his operations. It overlooked the balloon filling site. He was well over ten times away from the maximum range of a lethal dose, but close enough to use binoculars to watch *his investment*, as he called it. So far, he had not seen anyone give the inside of the balloons a second glance. He had seen several people watching as the balloons were filled earlier that evening. Most of these people would go home, and die in their sleep.

Hungry, he had called for Chinese, and they had just delivered to his 26th floor apartment. He had more than enough groceries to last until Cyber Monday, if need be. He would then be flying out to Hawaii for a surfing contest, and some much needed fresh air.

Chapter 79

Lieutenant Dokit arrived in DC at 10pm, and was greeted by Drew Hampton, personally. Drew thanked him for the prompt delivery of the evidence, and said he was free to go back to Jamaica.

Lieutenant Dokit said, "No, Sir. My chief wants me here, to oversee what killed his people, and I would like to be part of your task force."

Drew was pleased, and eager to accept any help given to him on this most baffling of cases. Drew asked Dokit, "Do you have any valuable experience on task forces?"

Dokit gave him a two minute summary, most notably several kidnapping cases and gang murders.

Drew replied, "I'm sure we can find something for you to cut your teeth on." He pointed to Lieutenant Dokit's weapon, and told him to keep it in the holster unless his life depended on it.

Nodding, Lieutenant Dokit agreed.

Drew dropped him off at the FBI's chosen hotel with instructions to tell the front desk clerk that all charges would be paid by the "Hoover building account". He then gave him an 8-digit code. "I'll have a pass at the main FBI desk tomorrow by 10am for you. See you then, good night."

Lieutenant Dokit was amazed at the accommodations afforded by the FBI. He was given a premium suite on the eighth floor which overlooked DC. Though tired, Dokit wanted to walk for a bit. It was a perfect fall night for stargazing. Even though it was almost midnight, there seemed to be a lot of people out. He walked for about two miles, and returned to his hotel after finding a local beer.

By the time he got back to the room, it was almost 2am. Turning on the 24-hour news channel, he realized that the media had discovered Drew's worst-case nightmare. All the channels were covering the Florida water park tragedy, and some were reporting unconfirmed sources in Jamaica.

How the Hell did they know about Jamaica?

Lieutenant Dokit called the police station in Jamaica. Freddie was on duty covering the phones. "Hey, Lieutenant. You're up late! What's up?"

Dokit said that there had been a news leak in the US about the Jamaican connection. He instructed Freddie to pass the word that no one was to confirm the story at the station.

Freddie understood, and screamed, "Holy Crap!" with his internal voice. Externally, he said, "10-4, Lieutenant."

Freddie had taken a late dinner with a reporter friend, and had discussed the case. He had casually mentioned that a Lieutenant on the force had told him that it wasn't Black Magic, but a new threat on the terrorism board.

Freddie didn't think his friend would ever use him like that! Wasn't that a kick in the teeth! Hopefully, they'd never find out, or Freddie's career would be over.

Dokit went to bed and woke by 8am. He got ready, found breakfast, and watched as the 24-hour news channel pumped up ratings for the tragedy in Florida.

Chapter 80

Toby called Jack at his office, and requested another ink refill trip from Inks4Life.net. This one should be enough to cover December and January for the BEP. Jack said that he would make the arrangements as before, and they could expect the shipment during the week of Cyber Monday. Toby told Jack that it would be perfect timing, as always.

Jack asked Toby, "On a side note, hypothetically speaking, can you think of any reason why someone would want to give away money to strangers?"

Toby asked what this was about.

Jack just answered that this was his latest puzzle at the Secret Service. A perp was mailing cash out to strangers, and Jack explained that he couldn't figure out why anyone would do that.

Toby said that a payoff would be his first guess, or a repayment of a long-standing debt.

Jack thanked Toby for his time, and said, "My thoughts exactly!"

Johnny walked into Jack's office and said, "What's new, Boss?"

Jack just shook his head, and said that he still couldn't figure out why Archie was giving money to complete strangers.

On another note, Johnny asked if they were supposed to get involved with the Weaponized Cancer Threat.

"Only if it involves the BEP or POTUS, otherwise the other agencies will chase it down."

Johnny understood.

Angelina Gear was back in the shelter after a long week of visiting different banks in California, and delivering more *Packets of Death*, as she was calling them. Her team would be returning shortly to the shelter, and they would be getting another ink shipment ready.

Yo, she noticed, was back in his office already coordinating the shipment

arrangements with Jack from DC.

Chapter 81

Angelina and her staff hated America for killing the village in her parents' homeland 30+ years ago. One of Angelina's scientists was interested in robotics and drones in a very big way. On Saturday afternoon, he realized that he could have some fun at the Michigan State game, and at the same time strike a hard blow to those Americans.

He created a drone with a remote control robotic arm. Using the drone, he had it pick up a Packet of Death (100 bills). Then, he flew the drone just above the swimming pool, submerging the packet for a full minute, essentially melting the cc625 off the bills in the chlorinated water. Next, he directed the drone to fly over the packed stadium about 6 ft. over the heads of the audience. Some thought it was a game, and tried to catch the packet, thinking a prize was inside. Others ignored it. Still others just posed for a picture, hoping they'd be famous on some website.

He did this section by section. Each time his battery was getting low, he'd let the packet of death drop to some lucky victim, and have the drone return to the parking lot. There, he'd change the batteries, and repeat the process. He had 20 sets of batteries. He was getting much faster, and more adept at flying. By halftime, he had flown over everyone twice, and he had only used nine sets of batteries so far! He recalled the drone, and went back to his hotel.

About 8pm, he heard sirens all over the campus, growing louder and more numerous than he thought he'd hear. He turned on his police scanner, and discovered that several thousand people in Michigan were dying mysteriously!

By 11pm, the nation knew about the victims in Michigan, but just like in Florida, they had no idea what had caused the illness to spread so rapidly, or why anyone would want to wipe out a whole college town.

Steve Stevenson promptly assembled the

story highlights, and sent them to the team. Angelina congratulated the team member for his creativity and initiative.

It was now less than a week until Thanksgiving.

What would the future hold?

Chapter 82

At 8am on the Thursday before Black Friday, Angelina's scientist was safely watching all the activities below, from his apartment window. He wasn't sure how many people had *bought it* last night, but he was sure about 4,000 people were currently exposed. He wished he could find out how many of the seven packets were active, but they would be able to estimate it by next week.

Annually, this holiday parade drew 2-4 million people into the city each year to brave the elements and watch the show.

The parade started right on time at 9am. All the balloons were out flying high, and kids of all ages were cheering on their favorite rock stars, balloon mascots, and marching bands. The sheer amount of people in attendance was staggering!

By 11:30am, Santa was passing by the window perch of the scientist, and several hundred thousand people started walking behind the sleigh.

Everyone would be going home soon to have dinner, and some would be making plans for Christmas shopping. Some sales would be starting as early as 4pm this afternoon. The day after Thanksgiving is known as the busiest shopping day of the year, and referred to as *Black Friday*.

This year would be the *Blackest Friday* of them all!

The scientist had his computer tied into the cable network, and was set to record multiple local and network stations for the next 96 hours.

It didn't take long! By 5pm, the NYC local news desks were reporting several hundred people feeling like they had just had a heart attack. The City's 911 operations were getting upwards of 50,000 calls a minute. People were dying by the hundreds per second by 8pm. This was by far the worst terrorist attack anyone had ever seen on American soil!

There was nothing anyone could do, but wait and see. It was horrific! By the time someone felt the effects of the radiation, they had, at most, 15 minutes to react. No doctor or health professional in the city could have even thought to diagnose this illness.

By 10pm, there was chaos everywhere in NYC. People who didn't go to the parade were having heart attacks themselves, out of fear of those dying around them.

By Friday at 1am, people had forgotten all about the wonderful meal of turkey, leftovers, and holiday shopping. It was estimated that one in every household in NYC was dead. Estimates were wildly out of control!

The National Guard was called in by the Governor of New York. The rest of the country was watching the news unfold, but many were still sleeping.

By 9am on Black Friday, almost everyone was watching NYC. Angelina had a video conference planned for 10am EST with her team. Everyone except the NYC scientist was able to connect, since all communication and network services in the NYC area were snarled with traffic, panic, and fear!

Angelina asked Steve if he could prioritize the network traffic for her favorite scientist. Steve told her that he could, but they'd be able to trace the signal, and it might jeopardize plans later. They decided they could do without him on the video call.

Angelina congratulated her team, and instructed them to meet back at the shelter within a week. All agreed, and said they were finishing up now. One scientist mentioned that this day would now be renamed to the Blackest Friday. Everyone agreed.

Archie seemed aloof and uncaring. He asked Steve for more new currency, and Steve told him that he would see him on Cyber Monday.

At the end of the call, Angelina reminded her people to stay smart, and not to accept any new bills.

Back in NYC, people were trying to leave the "City of Death" as fast as they could.

Traffic just stopped. Gridlock was everywhere. The banking system was on the verge of failure due to people making runs on banks looking to get money to escape by rail, boat, plane, or bicycle. Using any mode of transportation, people were trying to leave.

The Governor and the President together made the next gut wrenching decision. They closed the entire area! Tunnels, airports, ferry stations, rail systems… everything was halted and closed, and secured by armed National Guard troops.

Some people who didn't know what was going on, tried to make a break for it. They overtook the National Guard platoon on the city side of the tunnel. By the time the crowd had walked to the other side of the New Jersey tunnel, armed reinforcements had arrived. They posted signs and barriers a half mile inside the tunnel, trying to warn the civilians that they meant business. Still, the crowd raced on, trying to leave the "City of Death" behind. They were unsuccessful.

Many heard automatic gunfire, but didn't care. The massacre was brutal! The National Guard troops had orders to defend NJ at all costs. No one was to leave that tunnel alive! All told, about 50,000 lives were lost, until a human barricade blocked the NJ side of the tunnel.

The country was horrified by the news coverage inside NYC and outside the NJ border!

By noon on Friday, it was estimated 2,750,000 were dead in NYC.

The President of the United States addressed the nation saying, "We are praying with the rest of the world to find out what is causing the deaths, and how to stop them." He urged people not to panic, but everyone saw panic in his eyes, too! It was the Blackest Friday in our history.

He then announced, "Until further notice, NYC will be totally isolated until it is clear what we are up against. No traffic will be allowed out. Traffic will only be allowed in by ferries, and will be available to first responders only."

He and the Governor stood shoulder to shoulder, not wavering an inch. This was Serious! A Military State was declared inside NYC.

POTUS told the people of the "City of Death", that he did not know what they were dealing with, and to be patient and calm. If this was an airborne virus, it would likely get worse. If it were a local attack, it would get better, and then they could open the borders and get help. If it were a biological weapon, he said he'd pray for their souls!

He ended with, "May God bless the people of NYC, and the United States of America."

Shelters were opened which would be free of dead bodies, and have supplies. This worked for about two hours, and then the shelters got overrun by fear, panic, and dread. Within four hours, all the city services were overrun and obliterated, unless there was an armed platoon at that site. It was evident to the Governor that they would have to ride out the worst without city services running. The people would just have to take their chances during the first and second stages of this crisis!

Chapter 83

Cyber Monday rolled around, and the BEP trucks arrived at Yo's Inks4Life.net. Yo and his skeleton staff loaded the trucks with each of the inks. When they were finished, one of the Secret Service drivers mentioned the NYC attack. He said he was glad to be in California, away from what was happening on the east coast. Yo and the driver agreed about how crazy the world seems today, and that terrorist acts are exploding out of nowhere.

Yo asked the driver if anyone had found the cause yet.

The driver explained that even though they had looked at everything, they still had not found a cause. He continued, "Those poor people who are alive in the city are now trapped with all the dead ones. I sure hope they open the city up soon. I have family up there."

Yo asked if he'd been in contact with them.

"Yes, I got one text message through that

got answered. They're all fine for now, but will be running out of food in a week."

"Wow, I never thought about running out of food in that giant city," Yo said. He shuddered at the thought of another month in the city without food. Another 4+ million would die easily! This really was going to leave a mark! Yo snapped out of his daze, and said, "I hope your family survives this!" He slapped the truck door and said, "You're good to go!"

When the convoy was gone, Yo called Jack and told him the trucks were loaded and on their way. Jack thanked him, saying that he and his office were going to be busy for a few weeks with this NYC attack. Yo wished him well.

Yo went back to the shelter and found Angelina. She was watching the news networks to figure out how so many people had died so quickly in NYC. Yo mentioned that the agent was concerned about them running out of food in the next few days. Angelina had not thought of this, either. With all the trucks and shipments restricted from entering, there was indeed a good chance that these one to two-day shoppers would be out of groceries very soon. People and first responders would be looking for safe food and water, with the food riots, services not running, and hospitals overworked. Her scientists were the best! Damn! If they could only do a few more parades they could really wipe out America. She would have to get a list of large parades, so she could continue on this path of destruction.

It was time to call Steve, and get an update on Cyber Monday. Steve answered the phone and asked, "So, are you ready to kick some Cyber Monday butt?!"

Angelina answered, "You must be reading my mind."

He continued, "Now that the banking system thinks their new 10X system is secure, it's time to show them our *real* power!"

When the credit card system got hacked, the first thing that had happened was that the Admiral had called the banking commission to ask if they needed help from Homeland Security with protecting the new network. Of course, they begged for help, immediately.

The Admiral, Peter, Peggy, and Steve had pre-assembled the code before the first attack. The Admiral was more than happy to provide this code to the commission. By using this code, the transactions through the banking systems would now be more vulnerable than before, although they were portrayed as being ten times safer!

Basically, they had installed Steve's trojan into the base system, so now any computer network that collected data and transactions would be accessible by Angelina's team.

This trojan not only affected the banking network, but also big box stores, US government, major corporations, TV networks, automobile manufacturers, US Military, insurance companies, drug companies, and anywhere you could make a credit card transaction. Once this software was installed into a network, it proliferated itself to all the networked devices with onboard memory, such as: computers, laptops, mobile devices, printers, copiers, cars, planes, and game systems.

Angelina said, "Set it for one hour, let's do it!" What she meant was, kill it for one hour, and then re-enable it after that. All computers in the affected systems would be "bricked" for one hour, and magically be restored to working functionality after that.

Steve counted down, "In 10,9,8,7,6,5,4,3,2,1..."

Chapter 84

It was _AWESOME!_ Angelina was watching six different news channels, internet sites, and listening to radio frequencies for local fire and police stations.

All of it just STOPPED!!

There were an estimated 5.6 million auto accidents during this time when all the lights went out in the cities. Power grids across the country: Broadway, theme parks, subways, hospitals, and airports went dark. Nothing was on!

There was complete CHAOS!!!

Like when your parents came in and turned off the TV, only this was an _Adult Timeout_.

Somehow, all the nuclear facilities were able to shut down safely. Angelina had instructed Steve to make sure the nuclear plants were not bricked. She didn't want to destroy America, just the people living in it. She still wanted to be able to repopulate it later, with her choice of people.

After one hour, the computers all rebooted automatically, and started up correctly. It took the power grids about five hours to come back online again safely.

Many IT professionals just up and left for the day; it was 5 o'clock somewhere! Others were there when the systems came back online. Both sets of IT were perplexed by the ability of the trojan to brick the machine, and then unbrick it at someone's will, not their own.

Then, the real horror set in amongst the IT world. If the IT staff detected this trojan, and tried to remove it, the machine would be permanently bricked! The owner would have to purchase a new computer that had never been turned on. The only problem was that every other device on the network would reinfect the new computer with the trojan that just been removed. Many IT professionals knew it had to be a government that was responsible. They just didn't think it could be coming from their own!

Steve called Angelina back after the hour had passed. He told her that 7-8% of the users had attempted to repair their systems during the outage, resulting in permanent bricking of their machines. He read off the list of top hits from this collection:

White House
Army
Navy
Air Force
Marines
Nuclear Commission
LAX
Reagan National
Homeland Security
DEA
CIA
FBI
NSA
Computer Chip Manufacturers
Antivirus Companies
Operating System Companies
Mobile Device Providers

Soon, it would be common knowledge that if you tried to remove the trojan, your machine would be useless. This was one step past ransomware, since you could just re-image that computer with the backed up data, and start over. With Steve's trojan bricking the computer, you couldn't use it again, ever! You would have to purchase a new computer, and then restore the data to it, if you had a copy!

Steve and his team had thought outside the box on this, too. They had contacted the chip manufacturers, and embedded the trojan on the latest chipsets. Many of the new computers that people were going to buy to correct the bricking problem, would never display the trojan in software code again. Damn, he was good!

Steve sent out an email asking if anyone on Angelina's team was affected by the "Adult Timeout", as he put it. None of them had seen any sign of it on their computers, but they had seen it in network outages. Steve could live with that answer.

Chapter 85

Shortly after the "Adult Timeout", the President addressed the nation. He began with reminding everyone to remain calm, and not to panic. This was much easier said, than done.

Everyone who had a smartphone, laptop, desktop, tablet, cloud services, new cars, internet access, or used power had been affected by the "Adult Timeout". You name it, it had stopped working for one hour at the least, or eight hours at most. Hospitals had lost power, and their backup generators had failed to start, due to the computer components in them. Airports went dark, runway lights had failed, and communications systems had just stopped functioning. The White House had lost power, computers, surveillance, and security checkpoints. If someone had wanted to gain access to the White House, it would have been the perfect opportunity! But that was not Angelina's plan, yet.

The President continued to say that

Homeland Security and the other agencies were looking into the "Adult Timeout", but they would need time to gather information on the details of the attack. Many of the White House Press staff asked how the Encryption Hackers attack, the NYC attack, and the "Adult Timeout" were related. The President had no answers, and said that he didn't think one had anything to do with the others. He was dead wrong!

Angelina just smirked her Cheshire grin, and thought to herself, "This will do...!"

During the Presidential address, Steve called Angelina, who glowed over the video call with him. She was amazed at the scope of his code, and its absolutely wondrous results! Steve pointed out that three quarters of Europe and Australia were both inundated with power and network outages during the same time. Wall Street had stopped all trading at once, and didn't know if they'd be able to open Tuesday. All of Wall Street's redundant systems, like most power grids and airports, had failed to recover the lost data in the channel at the time of the "Adult

Timeout". There were going to be a lot of unhappy traders who lost a lot of revenue over that missing hour plus of stoppage.

Ending his address, the President reminded everyone to be aware of their surroundings, and to be patient with the recovery efforts. After the President left the podium, the White House aides took over the question and answer session.

First and foremost, on all the reporters' minds, was the question of when New York City would be reopened for people and supplies. The aides dodged this question repeatedly, and gave no indication as to when the city would be reopened, if ever!

Someone asked how the White House systems were affected during the "Adult Timeout". The aides just said that the White House operations were classified. Next, the press asked how many people were affected by the Timeout. Much to everyone's surprise, the aides responded with approximately 1.4 billion, worldwide. The aides ended the Q&A session, thinking they had given out too much data, which

they had!

Steve and Angelina were thrilled with anything over 500 million! Steve had earned his bonus today! Angelina told him to have another beer, on her, and winked over the video conference.

Chapter 86

Back in NYC, during Steve's "Adult Timeout", many people were still trying to clean up the corpses. Several thousand had heart attacks during that hour while they were evacuating dead bodies in elevators. The power outage had left those people in a dark elevator with one or more dead bodies. Since they didn't know if the bodies were contagious, fear and distress immediately entered their minds. Soon, their brains took over, and thought too hard about the effects of being stuck in a small area with dead people. Human psychology took care of the rest. Whether they were heart or panic attacks, both had a similar effect on them.

With all services being turned off in NYC, raw sewage began flowing places it shouldn't. This caused more health problems that just added up to more chaos. The subway trains, that had been running, trapped people in dark foreboding tunnels, and again, many people panicked. Few stayed on the train. Many evacuated to the tunnels looking for emergency exits, but with no lights or flashlights from their smartphones, people were completely in the dark, both physically and figuratively.

For some people, this time was a dream come true. These people believed that you could improve your life by looting businesses for food, clothing, jewelry, new electronics, computers, and alcohol. Since there was no power, all of the burglar alarms and camera systems were offline. Some even tried to rob banks, but most just ended up getting shot, or becoming trapped in a vault.

There were some that just travelled by truck, from site to site, looking for people that were dead, but physically fit. They would toss them in the back of the refrigerated truck, and store them to sell their body parts on the black market. As soon as the crisis had hit NYC, most of the organ donor sites had gone crazy looking for corpses to harvest organs. Providing body parts would be a great service to those needing lungs, kidneys, or even joints. It was a grizzly job, but there were worse jobs coming!

During the power outage, there were issues at several prisons and jails around the country. Some prisoners were just waiting for the opportunity to riot. When the power was lost, and all the computers were "bricked" for an hour, the convicts took their chances and proceeded. Several prison personnel lost their lives in the ensuing conflicts. Many maximum security facilities were obviously caught off guard, by having absolutely no communications, or computers to direct the operations.

Many facilities and businesses had gone to Voice over Internet Protocol (VoIP) solutions to save money. They believed the computer networks were completely reliable. If they went down, the backup systems would be triggered by the computers, and the startup sequence for the generators would begin instantly. Steve's trojan took these systems offline, too. There were no instructions given by any computer to start the generators.

Prisons, hospitals, businesses, and power plants all were dead. Yes, people could have started their generators by hand, if they had even known which room it was located in, and if they had committed the startup sequence to memory. But no one had done that. Everyone just hoped someone else could restore power for them. After all, it wasn't their responsibility to bring everything back on, right?!

Meanwhile, on every street corner, there were many religious nuts, preaching about the end of the world. Many just pointed to stacks of corpses in the alleys, and said, "*You* could be next - are *you* right with God?" This made sense to a lot of people who didn't know what was in store for them after death. Suddenly, they had several hundred followers with them on the street corners. Some of them bought into religion. Others just thought there was safety in numbers.

After four days in NYC, small, armed teams of people known as public gangs formed a group and travelled together to protect one another from real street gangs that endangered public safety. Since the police presence was nonexistent, the people formed these public gangs as a service to whichever condo or section of the city they represented.

There were groups of lawyers, doctors, hospital workers, and even a Central Park condo association group. Many of these groups fought anyone standing in their way. Police, rescue workers, and the Red Cross all threatened these groups with restrictions on rationing food items. These groups would not let any legitimate resource limit their rights.

Many of these groups turned into vigilantes, and were classified by the police as unwanted groups, roaming the streets. Soon, some of the street gangs started talking with the leaders of the groups, forming alliances with them to make more troops with weapons and drugs. These drugs could be used by the groups for makeshift medicines, in some cases, which they couldn't obtain unless they looted drug stores.

This left one group of people to still cover, the survivalists. These people had been training for years: stockpiling food, weapons, water, money, and other necessities to survive in a harsh environment. Many considered themselves and their families as the only thing worth protecting. One of these was the scientist who was the one responsible for all the deaths in the city. He was high enough above the city to watch the chaos unfold. He had secured four floors of his building with provisions and weapons to keep him and his floors secure. The top floor had a helipad on it, and if things got bad he'd call for a pick up from Angelina.

All in all, NYC was quickly becoming a cesspool, all over again. It had only been a couple of days. What would it be like in a month or two — COMPLETE CHAOS!!

Chapter 87

On Cyber Monday, after the Adult Timeout in DC, Steve had gone to the bank to get some more new cash. When he got there, he asked the manager if they had been affected by the blackout.

"Lord Almighty, Yes! It was scary! All the systems went out, and even the computer generated backup systems failed. Luckily, no one was in the vault, because when we lost power, the magnetic locks on the door of the vault slid closed. It didn't lock, but it's a very heavy door. Now that everything's back to normal, what can I get you?"

"I need one million dollars in new currency," Steve stated.

Disappearing and returning within 20 seconds, the branch manager handed over the currency, which he had pulled and completed the paperwork for ahead of time. Steve walked out of the bank with one million dollars in new currency, and a big smile on his face.

Archie was in a small suburb of DC. Steve drove out to meet him, finding him looking at imports at a high end auto dealer. Steve honked, and a startled Archie looked up, and smiled. They found a quiet place to do the refill.

While they were filling up the neon Suburban, Steve asked, "Hey Archie, what do you think about the recent activities?"

Archie secured the lead plate, locked the safe, and then sat down in the back of the trunk's floor area. "I was truly shocked by the magnitude of the NYC operation. *Truly horrifying* comes to mind, and now I'm a little scared that if they find us, we will not survive! When the 'Adult Timeout' hit, I was astonished again! How did you manage to infect all those devices without anyone, or better yet, any virus detection software detecting the hacks?"

Steve just laughed out loud, "Tricks of the trade. Actually, Homeland Security has several government contracts with all the major security providers. These anti-malware and virus protection companies give us keys that we include on the computer systems to allow us to mute alerts. Some call it a whitelist. Either way, we can put whatever we want on a system, so long as the registry keys are turned on. Once the keys are activated, the third-party applications will ignore all attempts of intrusion.

"The government wants to be able to access anyone's machine covertly. This includes: computers, tablets, laptops, mobile devices, game systems, smart TV's, and other network technologies in data centers. By utilizing these keys, we, at Homeland Security, can bypass any added security the people put on their systems.

"Every United States agency has a set of these keys, unique to themselves, so we know who put the spy software on the machines. However, since Homeland Security assigns the key sets to each agency, we know all of them. So, this will look like another agency is responsible for the infected code."

"Wow!" Archie knew it was clever, but he

didn't think it was a government conspiracy, until now. "So, between the Adult Timeout and the NYC Blackest Friday event, you and your people expect to have a budget to combat these attacks in the future?!" Archie queried.

"Now you're catching on, Archie. Once the people of America figure out how desperately they are tied to technology, we'll be able to prove beyond a shadow of a doubt, that a budget as small as we currently have is not sufficient to protect them and their country."

Archie asked, "But what about the nuclear money?"

Steve said, "Angelina and Yo have a way to stop that from being a problem, only when the American people see the errors of their ways."

"But how? Most radioactivity lasts for hundreds of years."

Steve said, "If you need more details, talk with Angelina." He jumped down off the Suburban, and said he had to get back to the vacation house.

Archie said, "Ok. I'll stop by later tomorrow to relax a bit."

Chapter 88

Johnny Five could not believe his luck! He had been lucky enough to be in his car when he texted the IWANTTOWORKWITHYOU to SEEDC, and it gave him a latitude and longitude about four minutes away. When he got close, he pulled into a convenience store parking lot.

He saw the neon beast, with a black SUV next to it. Both vehicles were facing him. Johnny saw people loading the neon Suburban with something. He decided to wait and see who it was. Getting out his binoculars, he trained them on the Suburban and the SUV. Neither had a visible front plate. Nothing was easy!

He got out the parabolic microphone, and turned it on. Listening intently, he heard Archie's voice and someone else he didn't recognize. Then, someone stood up, got into the SUV, and drove off. Johnny stayed with Archie. Johnny didn't know who the other driver was, but then it hit him. "You'll get that little red dress yet!" The guy from the gym! What was he doing with Archie?!

Now watching Archie making a phone call on his mobile, Johnny turned on the tape recorder. He picked up the phone, and texted Jack, "Can you meet me?"

Jack called him back, and said, "What's up?"

"I found Archie making a pickup, and the guy from the gym was with him. I'm on Archie now." Johnny described hearing that Archie was going to meet the guy tomorrow at the vacation house.

Jack said, "I'm tied up here with NYC. They still don't have a clue what's killing the people, if it is contagious, or what the source might be. The CDC knows it's a weaponized form of cancer, but they can't locate the source in the city. You stick to Archie like glue, and find out what you can. Hopefully the meeting tomorrow with Archie and the guy from the gym will help."

Johnny ended the call by saying, "I'll keep in touch."

Archie was completely aware of Johnny's presence; his eyesight was better than 20/20. He noticed the binoculars Johnny was holding. He also knew that Steve had no idea what Angelina's true motivation was. It was not to get more money for Homeland Security, that was for damn sure!

Archie started his mailing activities with Johnny in tow. Johnny couldn't believe how much business had picked up for Archie. He did the math! Archie mailed 70 envelopes. That's $35,000! "Shit!" Then, on a hunch, Johnny called information on his notes from the other week. He asked for the Alabama phone number for the address. He dialed it, and a housewife with a baby in the background answered.

"Hi, I'm Johnny. I'm just calling to find out if you received your SEEDC package from us."

Jenny was super excited, and said, "YES! Thank you so much! The information was of immense help, and we like that you sent cash and not coupons, like so many others do. We told all our friends about you, too. They are thrilled!"

Johnny asked, "Do you know when you'll be arriving?"

Jenny replied, "Well, we just had this baby girl, so we're not planning a trip just yet, but we will definitely keep DC on the list now. Thanks," and she hung up.

Johnny reviewed the call, "So, Archie's envelopes did get sent to the real people listed. They weren't intercepted in the mail. Hmmm! Again? Why give money to complete strangers?!"

Johnny saw Archie get back into his Suburban, and drive off. It was almost 6pm, and Archie would probably be heading home, so he'd watch where he went. Johnny saw him drive into a large parking garage, and thought to himself, "So, this is where he lives?" Johnny parked on the road, got out of his car, and walked toward the expensive condo that owned the garage.

Johnny was 400 ft. from his car, and 1,200 ft. from the opposite end of the street when he heard a horn honk behind him. Then, he heard Archie shout, "Good night, Agent Five!"

"Shit!" Johnny turned around, and started running for his car. He ran to the street, but Archie was long gone! "Damn, he's good!" Johnny just swore over and over all the way home! As he was pulling into his condo's parking lot, he received a call from an unknown caller.

Johnny answered the phone, and said, "Johnny Five."

"Hello, Johnny. Sorry, but my home is my castle. I just like my privacy. Please forgive me."

Johnny recognized Archie's voice, and asked, "How long had you known I was there?"

Archie replied, "You were quite obvious in the parking lot with binoculars."

Johnny just gritted his teeth in anger. "What can I do for you, Archie?"

"It is what I can do for you, Agent Five. When the time is right, we will talk again. Good night."

Chapter 89

Erika Stone and Jackson Smithe were both in NYC investigating the bodies of all the people who had died earlier last weekend. They and their team were trying to piece together what had happened. Still, they had no clue what was going on, except they were armed with portable x-ray units that looked like large smartphones. These were being used to confirm how the patients had died, without having to perform surgical procedures.

Teams of Police and Firemen were going door to door, searching for survivors among the people who died. The question was always the same: *What had they done last week?* Since most of the families had attended the parade together, there were no witnesses left alive to tell the first responders where they might have picked up the weaponized cancer. The teams collected food and water samples at each house and apartment, but the lab results would be weeks or months out, because all the labs were busy testing human remains.

Erika and Jackson were brainstorming and wondering, "If it was the parade, how did it infect so many people?" Jackson took a break to use the restroom.

Erika jumped up, and said, "That's it! Maybe someone infected the portalets! Thousands of people at the parade probably had to use the toilet."

Soon, NYC was conducting the world's largest portable potty investigation known to mankind. It was a dirty job, but somebody had to do it! After sampling and testing some 1,500 potties, they found all kinds of contaminants, but nothing that would cause cancer for at least another 50 years! Giving up on that theory, they decided to look elsewhere.

Erika explained that they had just learned one more way that it was not possible. They would just have to keep looking. She sounded just like another scientist earlier on the project.

Jackson and Erika kept at it. No one had found any parts of the parade, floats, or people that could have been responsible for the contamination. Erika was thinking water could have been contaminated, but there were millions that brought their own, or didn't have any water at all.

Soon, they started examining the things found on the victims of the devastating event. Some of these items included: wallets, keys, purses, makeup, food, and drinks.

One of the victims was a radiology tech, who looked like she was on her way to work. She was wearing a dosimeter on her uniform. A dosimeter records the amount of radiation that a person has been in close proximity to. They sent it to a lab immediately, and continued looking through the thousands of items on the victims. Still, nothing jumped up, and said, "Look at me."

About 10 hours later, a lab technician opened up the envelope with the dosimeter inside. He proceeded to measure the amount of radiation it had tracked. "Oh Crap!" It was off the charts! It was likely this was the issue. He called Erika's mobile.

Erika was trying to get some rest, and she was groggy. Answering the phone, she mumbled, "Heeeelllooo."

The tech said, "I found the cause of the epidemic, Ma'am!"

Instantly, she was awake. She told the tech that she was in the building, and she'd be down in three minutes. She pounded on Jackson's door and said, "They found it!"

Jackson was out the door before he was fully dressed.

By the time they got to the lab, it was standing room only. They were introduced to the Lab Tech, Harvey Walbanger, and asked him to show them what he had found. Harvey held up the dosimeter, and said, "This is the reason why 3.75M people died this past week. The tests on this device show that this person was standing 1,000 feet away from the SUN!"

Chapter 90

Erika and Jackson did a double take, "Did you say 1,000 feet from the *sun?!*"

Harvey said, "Yes! This is what killed all those people. They were standing 49 trillion times closer to the sun than normal! Radiation is what killed them within four hours after they were exposed. That much radiation *should* be able to be found very easily. If *you* stumbled over it, you'd die just as quickly. I suggest Geiger counters for all search personnel. Anything that resembles a hot spot, let a qualified Hazmat team member check out. Again, this should be a no brainer to find, but 50,000 first responders have yet to stumble onto it!"

Erika and Jackson excused themselves to make a video call to the CDC and the Presidential committee on the disaster. They broke the news that radiation was indeed the culprit. They told the group that the dose of radiation could be compared to standing 49 trillion times closer to the sun than normal. Death would be achieved about four hours after exposure.

Next, Erika and Jackson asked if there were any classified weapons that had this signature. The committee members did exactly what Jackson said they would do. They stalled, and said that they'd have to check on it.

Erika said, "If there is such a weapon, we need to know before more people get killed."

The committee said they would take it under advisement, and disconnected from the call. They didn't even say goodbye, those bastards!

The Director of the CDC said he'd check with his sources. In the meantime, he told his people to go slow and methodically while hunting for this blasted stuff. He didn't need to add their names to the casualty lists.

Erika and Jackson agreed, and said good night. They'd been up for some 98+ hours, and were going to bed. They'd let Hazmat look for the items on the parade route and throughout the city.

Chapter 91

Michigan State had almost an 80% absentee rate on the Monday, Tuesday, and Wednesday before Thanksgiving! Many kids had missed exams on Tuesday, and this was a most disturbing phenomenon.

On Friday, the staff made a horrifying discovery in several of the dorms, both on and off campus. Of the 75,000 people at the game on the previous Saturday, at least 60,000 had died in the dorms and surrounding areas. No one had noticed because everyone at the dorms had either gone to the game, or home early for the holidays. Only the handful of people that came back on Friday had noticed something weird, and notified the police.

The Blackest Friday was not just happening in NYC. It was now confirmed in Michigan, too! Panic was slowly creeping into the northeastern corner of the United States.

When the Presidential committee found

out, they tried to cover it up. NYC was big news, but up to 60,000 people should be easy to cover up. Anything to give them a little time to figure out what to do.

On Cyber Monday, the cabinet thought the President had arranged a diversion with the Adult Timeout. They congratulated him on his fast thinking! But, when they learned it was not his doing, they all panicked!

Someone was seriously playing with the United States of America. Everyone saw it was not a game to lose. Depending on whatever these people had in mind, this could easily be the end of America. No one had a clue who, or what nation, was behind the attacks. America could retaliate by launching missiles, but they could not just randomly pick a target, and hope they were correct.

"Blast it to Hell, and back!" The President slammed his hand on the table in front of his cabinet, and commanded, "Find out who's responsible, *Yesterday!*"

They all scurried from the room, trying to

get intel for their boss.

Chapter 92

By Tuesday afternoon, there was chaos everywhere! People who were expecting their kids to return after performing in the Thanksgiving parade never saw them again. Most tried consoling themselves with the hope that their families were only detained due to the closures in NYC. Still others had no hope, and knew something was terribly wrong.

Some of the kids and family members that had taken trips into NYC to perform in the parade were OK, and just caught inside the biggest quarantine known to mankind! Others who were vacationing, were not prepared for what lay in front of them. Between the street gangs and the public groups forming in the city, any visitor was basically in no man's land! Everyone in NYC was too worried about their own ass to worry about kids that didn't belong there.

Then, there were those dedicated parents that vowed to find their kids at any cost, both inside and outside the cities. Armed to the teeth, these savages basically didn't care who was in their way. No one would keep them from their kids, or other family members. Period!

This turned out badly for the savage parents, mostly because the National Guard had orders to keep NYC quarantined at all times. Scores of dedicated parents died as they stormed the National Guard, just like the mass exodus that failed when NYC occupants tried to break out. Some over achievers tried some movie type rescues to get into NYC using high speed boats that would put a Florida drug dealer's cigarette boat to shame. But, even at those speeds, the coast guard just shot them to pieces. It's hard to negotiate peace at 120 knots!

Some parents tried to parachute in, only to be shot at by the people of the city, or gangs fearing an invasion. Others that landed safely were just mugged, and left to die, since people thought they had supplies or money on them.

Between the Encryption Hackers, the deaths in NYC and Michigan, and the Adult Timeout on Cyber Monday, cash was in high demand in America. Most people had used what money they had on hand for gas, food, medicine, and whatever else they needed. Yes, they may have had some in their bank accounts, but the banks weren't allowing anyone to make withdrawals until new funds arrived in cash at that location, if at all!

This was bad. The President knew it, the people knew it, and Angelina was eating it up!

Meanwhile, as all this chaos was going on, Trent Lester was getting an earful on his end, on how to speed up production in the BEP to get cash out to the banks sooner, rather than later. Trent suggested bringing the new money online in Texas. Within seconds, Toby was calling Yo and Jack to set up a delivery to Texas, one month ahead of time. Yo assured both men that they had product waiting to be shipped. Jack set up the routes, and sent the trucks to California.

Yo called Angelina, who was thrilled to death that they were expediting the schedule for Texas, and asked if she was ready for another business trip. Reluctantly, she said she'd go with him, if for no other reason than to see another city that would soon be destroyed by her further plans of destruction!

Chapter 93

Angelina had a whole new plan, but she'd need to explain it to her best scientist. She rushed to his office to see if it were possible.

He was in the midst of making plans to ship the ink, but upon seeing her, he immediately stopped, and asked how he could help her. She explained her concept in detail. It wasn't going to be easy, but what in life ever was! He said he would make up a special three-day packet, or two, using 100 bills each. Her suggestion had merit, but it would be very complicated if he didn't get the job first. He described what he needed from her to ensure that he got the job.

Angelina left first thing in the morning to prepare for the charade. When Angelina landed at DFW, she found a local pet store, and purchased a cute little puppy. It had no self-control, and didn't pay attention to Angelina at all.

A brief time later, the scientist emailed the

requested information to Angelina. This information consisted of a photo and a surveillance package on the cattle yard veterinarian's preferences and dislikes. Angelina was glad that she wouldn't have to dye her hair for this assignment.

The following day, she found the man on the grounds of the Fort Worth cattle yard. She walked slowly past him to make sure she caught his attention. Almost immediately, it was apparent that he was not afraid to look at, or touch, anything. He introduced himself as Harmon. Harmon scratched Scruffy behind the ears. Angelina introduced Scruffy, and then herself.

As if on cue, Scruffy jumped from her new owner's hands, and ran at breakneck speed into the ring of bulls. The little dog was ferocious, but didn't know what those bulls were capable of doing. Just then, one of them had enough. As Harmon walked over to pick up Scruffy, one of the bulls kicked him to the side. Scruffy yelped, and Angelina swooned longingly after her new dog.

Harmon took pity on the young dog, and said, "Come with me. We'll patch him up, good as new." It took just a few minutes. Harmon sedated the dog and checked his ribs. None were broken, but Scruffy wouldn't be running for a few days. He told Angelina that their vet's office was first-rate, and suggested that they keep Scruffy for a couple of days until he was ready to move on.

Angelina offered to pay him, but he refused. Instead, he offered to take her to dinner after they enjoyed some wine at his place. Angelina was ready for this, too. It was time to let off a little steam. They left at 5pm to go to his place, have some wine, and then a nice dinner. Angelina would never see Scruffy again.

Once she and Harmon got comfortable, he got up to get some wine. Angelina said that she wanted to freshen up, first. Harmon went into the kitchen, and found a nice red wine and some cheese and crackers. Angelina watched silently from five feet away, as Harmon slipped two small caplets into the glass with the red ring on the base.

Angelina hurried back quietly, making her entrance now with her blouse loosely covering her. Harmon saw her, and smiled broadly.

He said, "I was hoping you'd forget all about Scruffy tonight."

She smiled and said, "Who's Scruffy, I'm here for you!" Then, she kissed him.

It was now his turn to freshen up. He excused himself, and said that he'd be back in a few minutes.

Angelina immediately grabbed both glasses and dumped his down the sink, pouring her drink into his glass. Then, she rinsed hers out, and poured herself a fresh glass.

She returned to the great room, and started asking where he was from. He appeared behind her, and said that he was from a small town, not too far from here.

Startled, she turned around, and said, "You clean up good!"

He smiled and asked, "What should we drink to?"

She answered, "To sex."

He smiled and agreed.

Without hesitation, she drank three quarters of her wine, which made him smile with delight.

He took his drink, and up ended it, saying, "That's a fine red. Would you like more?"

She said, "No, we've got work to do."

He looked at her puzzled, and said, "We sure do, and pulled out a gun and handcuffs."

Angelina asked coyly, "For me? You really shouldn't have!" Then, she noticed him waffle. A moment later, the gun dropped to the floor.

She asked, "Would you like a little more wine?" She dumped the remaining pills, all 48 of them, into the bottle, swished it a few times, opened his unresisting lips, and poured it slowly down.

He didn't seem to fight it.

She cleaned up the room and the kitchen, making sure she left nothing behind. One pleasant thing about this guy's pad was it was so far off the road, they'd never know who he was with.

Unbeknownst to Angelina, this was not Harmon's first rodeo! He had cameras all over the house, and thousands of films of his other conquests. He was constantly bragging to the cowhands that he got a new one every night, but they never believed him. Soon, they'd be believers!

Angelina checked once again to make sure she had left nothing. Then, she got in her car and drove to a rundown hotel where she changed out of her disguise, removing her wig and makeup. She peeled a transparent set of skin tight gloves off. She liked using these gloves in the lab, since you couldn't tell anyone was wearing them, even if you shook hands. Very useful indeed! She placed the evidence in a bag, drove to an undisclosed location to dump it, and then checked into her luxurious hotel room.

Three days later, there were two stories on the local news channel. First, the BEP of Texas was starting to print new money to help the United States take back their country after the attack by the Encryption Hackers on the credit card systems of the world. Second, the longtime veterinarian who ran the Fort Worth Cattle Yard had died while trying to seduce an unknown lady.

Angelina screamed, "Damn It! Damn Cowboy!" Even though she didn't need to wear a wig, she was really glad she had. It was nowhere close to her own hair style, and didn't look anything like her. She'd skate free again, but *Damn that Cowboy!*

Thank goodness, she had worn a wig, makeup, and gloves! The gloves would soon throw the police completely off the trail, since the fingerprints on them were Marilyn Monroe's!

Chapter 94

It had now been a week since Cyber Monday, and the Adult Timeout. Everyone was waiting for the other shoe to drop. No one had been able to crack the "bricking" of the devices infected with the Adult Timeout code embedded in them. This was the big one! This was the one where most high-tech techies just gave up, and said they'd have to wait until the Homeland Security, or the Antivirus people came up with a workable solution... until then, pray!

Some network administrators convinced their clients the best thing to do was to "Kill the Hostage". This meant take the network and all devices out of service, and not give the hackers the use of their data. Many large corporations tried the approach after learning that the new machines they'd bought were becoming infected just as soon as they were imaged. At this point, carbon paper and typewriters were now being sold by online vendors for tens of thousands of dollars! Who knew those old electronic typewriters would ever be valuable again?

Many people were afraid to use airplanes for transportation. They worried that if the power grid went down for longer than four hours, planes would start falling out of the sky. Especially at night!

There were abundant theories and plots as to what was going on, but none of them were even close to the *real truth!* The closest people to the truth knew far too much to even breathe about it, let alone go to the press with a story! Several papers were offering insane amounts of money to anyone who would reveal secrets of any kind that shed light on the events of the past months.

As things were starting once again to fall into a routine, both Johnny and Jack decided to go *old school*. They checked into a hotel, and did not use any technology while they were there.

To Steve Stevenson, it looked like they had fallen off the planet. He knew they were close, but they had given up their plush homes for somewhere off his grid. Steve guessed that this meant either his gear had been compromised, or they were just staying closer to their office. He hoped it was the latter, but his gut knew it wasn't!

Chapter 95

Angelina's scientist just happened to be in the right place on the day of Harmon's burial. He was wandering around the cattle yard, looking for the guy in charge, when he finally found someone who gave him a mobile number. He called it, and asked if they were hiring any animal techs or veterinarians. He provided them with his impeccable credentials - fake, but first class, as everything is that Angelina does.

They immediately asked him to come by the office to sign the paperwork. They were in dire need of a chief vet to take Harmon's place, but the closest possible replacement had a sexual harassment case pending against the now deceased Harmon.

Zack, Angelina's scientist, was a hands-on type. He wasn't shy about diving in to save *or* kill, if that's what was going to be required in his new position. Most of his duties were to walk around and inspect livestock to be bought, or sold, in the upcoming auctions.

Tomorrow, one of the highest priced bulls was going up for auction. His owner insisted that his bull be kept with the others because he was moody and uncooperative when he got lonely.

Zack needed three hours alone with this prize bull. That night, he said to the staff, "Here's $1,000 - beer's on me! I want to celebrate, but I need to drop by one last call. By then, the party should be underway."

No one argued. They left for the bar at 10pm.

Once he was alone, he quickly began. Zack hit the bull with a tranquilizer that would have knocked over an elephant! Then, he severed the huge horn on the beast. Lord all mighty, this guy stunk! He drilled a two inch hole into the center of both sides of the horn. Inside the holes that he drilled, he then fitted a stainless steel pipe, cementing it into place on the loose piece of the horn. He placed the 3-day money packet into the pipe, staggering the bills so that they could move freely.

Next came the dangerous part! He tilted the bull's head, so he could pour salt water into the still attached portion of horn. Then, he smeared the end of the pipe with cement. After lining up the pencil marks that he had made on the horns, he mated the two pieces. Last, he painted them to conceal the crack.

The operation was completed by midnight, and Zack was in the bar by 12:15am. He told his staff that he forgot, and left the prize bull in his pen at the office. He asked them to let him out at 6am. After Zack downed his second beer, he left for the airport to fly back to California.

At 10am, there would be an auction and several deaths - both man and beast would be affected. Zack estimated that the featured sale of that bull, and the photos afterwards, and grazing time before and after, would dose 10,000 people and 40,000 head of cattle. This would show the world that livestock could be susceptible, too. He knew this bull would last much longer than an average man - how long, he was not sure, but maybe by 2pm, the shit would hit the fan. With any luck at all, the bull would be going home by that time.

Zack was also sporting the skin tight gloves. Hopefully, the police detective that handled the case, would be amused that Gene Autry was back for one last performance.

Chapter 96

People felt defeated, and were disgusted with the United States government. They were no closer to finding answers to the Michigan, NYC, and Fort Worth cattle yard disasters.

The most recent one, in Texas, had killed 40,000 people in the stands and 50,000 head of cattle. This was almost double what Zack had predicted. The owners that had purchased the prize bull wanted the crowd in attendance to be able to pose in a shot with the bull. So, for one hour after the 10am sale, there was a huge photo opportunity with the now world-famous bull!

Just as Angelina had predicted, they performed an autopsy on the bull, but never glanced once at the horns. Later, the horns were boxed and sent to the next of kin, which happened to be the owner's great grandson that was born one day after the Texas disaster.

The baby's family had all died that day.

When the coroner had found the 17-year-old granddaughter was pregnant, they had delivered her baby at the hospital, after she had been placed in the morgue waiting room. It was a miracle the child had survived, but the team had chalked it up to the chilly temperatures. Cold tends to pause *this* radiation. Maybe in forty years, when the child grows up, *he* can have revenge on the country that killed *his* family, too!

Over the next three weeks, every agency in NYC, Michigan, and Texas tore cities and towns apart looking for the deadly radiation that was 49 trillion times closer than the sun. It continually stumped and baffled the agencies of the entire government.

Newspapers were constantly poking fun at, and insulting Homeland Security, the FBI, and many other agencies for their inability to solve these tragedies. This made them even more determined to hunt down whoever was responsible, and to kill them one little piece at a time.

Meanwhile, it was now one week before Christmas, and everyone was stressing about what was in store for this most special holiday. Although some people tried to carry on a normal lifestyle, and enjoy the holidays, everyone was guarded and waiting for the next disaster to unfold. It made for a horribly tense holiday season.

By this time, both BEP offices were running at full capacity to try to get the new cash delivered and passed out at Federal Reserve Banks just as fast as possible.

Shortly after New Year's Day, there was an earthquake in California. Anywhere west of Las Vegas felt it, and it was recorded at 4.9. The seven aftershocks were almost as strong as the earthquake itself. All eight of the seismic events lasted only a total of 70 seconds.

The shaking time that the scientists had found necessary for a lethal dose on metal surfaces was 30 seconds. This was more than double the time to irradiate the bank vaults where Angelina had stored her cash.

Yes, Angelina had used her real first name to rent the boxes from the bank, but she had always used fake middle and last names. She had also worked out a schedule with Steve Stevenson to mask the bank cameras every time she had walked in. Each time she had rented a box at the banks in California, she had always used the same gloves. Papa don't preach!

San Francisco seemed to be the first set of banks that gained the most attention. Apparently, one specific bank had mysteriously lost upwards of 750 employees among its 25 branches throughout the city. Most had been on the way home, stuck in traffic, or out with friends and family when they just fell over.

The CDC had sent Erika Stone and Jackson Smithe to San Francisco to investigate. As soon as all of the victims had been identified as employees, SWAT teams cleared all 25 locations.

Interviews took another ten days to locate

the source of the problem. Erika discovered that one self-service bank did not have specific vault personnel. The tellers actually went into the vault with each client, similar to having an individual waitress at a diner. Every one of these tellers had turned up dead, as well as their clients. The only people that had survived working in this bank were the people who had never entered the vaults.

Erika and Jackson revealed their findings with the Hazmat teams, and encouraged them to handle the bank with extreme caution. Several Hazmat cowboys *bought the ranch* on their first day. Again, this was very powerful stuff, and a simple radiation suit was not enough to protect the person wearing it.

After losing four Hazmat specialists, the SWAT team sent in their robot. Its Geiger counter registered two orders of magnitude higher than those found on the NYC dosimeter! No wonder tellers were dying! Radiation measured 4,900 trillion times closer to the sun *inside* the bank vaults!!!

Erika had no idea how to get close enough to the bank vault to see what was causing the radiation. She and Jackson contacted the military to try to locate something that would protect them from this danger. The military's best minds said to *encase it in lead, and walk away!* Come back in 200+ years!

Erica and Jackson were flown to the nearest naval base to discuss their theories with the best nuclear minds in the country. They all said the same thing! *Pour lead on it, and walk away!!*

Finally, the President of the United States asked for volunteers! He knew what he was asking, but the world needed to know what was responsible for this deadly radiation! This was not what he signed up for when he wanted to be Commander in Chief of the world's best military.

Fifteen sailors signed up for the hazardous duty. There was a quick, but sincere moment with their families. Then, they were flown to San Francisco for training on the tools they would be using to break into the safety deposit boxes. One at a time, the men were sent in, just as another one was coming out. The four hour window was much shorter now that the radiation was concentrated!

Each man was lucky if he had ten minutes before his heart gave out. The twelfth man was the one who finally got the box opened and emptied onto the floor. By the time the money settled on the floor, it had stopped moving. The Geiger counter just registered 0 Rads. The metal frame and box, however, registered off the charts.

He finally said, "It's in the steel of the vault!" He still didn't know what the problem was, but what he did next helped more than he could have ever realized. He picked up the money from the safety deposit box, and placed it back inside. The diamondback rattlers hissed and shrieked their warnings. Even they knew this guy was "*Done*". He placed the whole deposit box inside a lead lined box, and secured the lid. Then, he put that box inside another lead lined box, and set them both on the trolley. The powers that be pulled him and the boxes out.

There was a flurry of activity from then on. The sailors were rushed to the hospital, but none survived that had entered the vault. The two lead boxes were delivered to a secure lab at the far end of the naval base. They were handled as if they had killed over 4.5 million people.

Many tests were run on the lead boxes, but since they were encased inside another lead box, the bills were completely stable and nonreactive. This made the military that much more frustrated, along with the rest of world.

Why did those sailors have to die?! They learned nothing new! They should have listened to the military, and just covered the bank in lead, and let those boys live.

Erika and Jackson were just as distressed as everyone else. There had to be a clue, but what was it, and why was someone killing non-combatants?! Maybe the victims would tell a story. Erika left her assigned room, and knocked on Jackson's door.

He looked at her, and said, "You can't sleep either?"

"I feel like we are missing something right in front of us!"

Jackson said, "Let's take a walk."

The Naval base was a beehive of activity, even though it was 3:45am on a Saturday. He and Erika walked for what felt like five miles, but this took two hours, so they were mostly relaxed. They found themselves at the morgue of the naval base.

They both dressed and scrubbed, and went into the main center where they saw four doctors checking out the 12 sailors who had given their lives for their country. The doctors all looked at them, and then realized who they were. All four doctors tried to console the CDC doctors, but somehow felt their pain, too.

Erika was the first to speak. "Damn it! We are missing something!"

Jackson put a hand on her shoulder. They all agreed that they were missing something. The four naval doctors waved them over to look at one of the sailors. His heart was missing, just like all the others in NYC, Michigan, and Texas.

One of the doctors noted that the banks had all been working smoothly for four months prior to the terrorist actions. What had changed?!

To everyone on the team, this was the question of the month!

One of the Navy doctors said, "There was an earthquake two weeks ago. Could a crack in the earth be radioactive, and then reseal itself on an aftershock?" It was a suggestion. They could check it out, but none of them felt like it was the right direction.

What could kill so many people: in NYC, at a stadium, at a rodeo, and in 25 banks? Erika added her three in Jamaica, and the 13 kids in Florida.

Then, Erika had an idea. She called

Lieutenant Dokit.

Groggy at 7am on the east coast, he said, "Yes, Doctor, how may I help you?"

She asked him what kind of evidence he had brought from Jamaica.

Lieutenant Dokit said, "Clothes of the dead man, and about $1 million cash."

She asked if there were any metal items in the evidence.

"No, just a plastic zipper."

"What about the other two Jamaican officers?"

"Yes, they had guns and cuffs."

"Could you get the locals to wand them with a Geiger counter?"

"Sure, but why?" Dokit asked.

"If I'm right, they'll know."

Dokit said he'd call her back in a few minutes. Then, he called Jamaica, and made the request.

The Chief dispatched two squads each, and he personally called Dokit back. "That CDC lady is one smart cookie!"

Dokit asked the chief to hold, while he got the other doctors on the line.

After brief introductions were made, the Chief said, "Montgomery and Leesa were both buried in full dress. When my officers wanded the grave site, the Rads were off the chart! It's amazing they didn't kill anyone who buried them." The Chief mentioned that he had checked, and found that they had used a backhoe to fill in the plots. That alone probably had saved 30 people.

They talked for a little while longer, and said goodbye after about 30 minutes. They were still no closer, but had found another piece of the puzzle. Erika was on the right track, but where would it take her?

Chapter 97

It was almost February 1st, and Toby Lipton called Jack and Yo, saying that he needed two double orders of ink. He estimated the BEP would be out of ink by February 15th, so this would keep them printing through April 10th. Yo said the inks would be ready by the time the trucks arrived in California. Jack thanked Yo, and said he'd email the schedule as soon as he had the drivers.

The CDC and other first responders still had not discovered the source of the Blackest Friday of NYC, the Michigan stadium deaths, the Texas cattle yard disaster, and the California bank vault deaths. They had lots of evidence, but no clues as to what had caused the initial radiation. They looked at everything: water, weather conditions, ground samples, sunspots, radon gas, and ore deposits underground. Nothing was ever found near all these fatalities.

Money was always near the attacks, but

everyone was looking for metal or radio waves near the fatalities, not paper money. Since the money was always static in the investigation phase, it never gave off any radioactive signature by design.

Angelina's team had indeed created the most devastating weapon of the 21st Century! She wondered what those scared Generals in her country were thinking now! But, she still couldn't contact them, since any ties to them would lead to World War III. That just wouldn't do. Her revenge only worked if she and her country got away with it!

Angelina called a meeting with her team to discuss the unexplained deaths that had occurred thus far. They summarized all the Radical Payments!

- ❖ Ted and his wife – Died while giving their all at church.

- ❖ The Bankrupt TV Evangelist – Too greedy for his own good; Traffic accident in Lubbock killing several others.

- ❖ Sam Fixxen – Died at his brother's football game; He either spent the money, or gave it to someone else.

- ❖ Timmy – Stole Sam's money; Died while playing the role of a Las Vegas dealer in his bedroom.

- ❖ Jake and Pixie – Found wet money at a rest area on Interstate 4; Had a heart attack and their truck barreled into traffic jam on Interstate 75. Death toll 45 people.

- ❖ A married couple – Died near 1980's Groupies. 50,000 people saw the concert; No one saw anything happen to the couple. They died of exhaustion right in front of them.

- ❖ Upon further review, there were several other unknown deaths at that time; No law enforcement agency tied the questionable deaths together.

- ❖ Blackest Friday in NYC – 3.75 million people dead. The balloons were put away and carefully saved in storage crates for next year's performance. Crates were wanded by first responders. Then sent off site for storage at a data storage facility buried in a mountain.

- ❖ Michigan stadium game – 60,000 people dead also found on Blackest Friday; Officials tried to hide the attack, but failed, losing valuable time and evidence. No one to this day understands what happened to those people, except those people reading this account.

- ❖ Texas Cattle Yard Disaster – 40,000 people / 50,000 head of cattle, all died under unknown circumstances; Radiation killed all of them, but again, no one found out what horned into the party. Horns were removed from the steer, and boxed up for the great grandson's 18th birthday surprise...

The gift that keeps on giving!

- ❖ California Bank Vault Deaths – 750 bank tellers, 12 sailors on hazardous duty pay, four SWAT specialists, and one robotic investigator died; Vaults will be radioactive for 150+ years. The money was dumped into a lead lined box inside another lead lined box. Investigators still have no clues what infected the 25 bank vaults in San Francisco.

- ❖ Now they have discovered 37 other cities in California that have multiple bank vaults that have been tampered with in the same exact way; They still have no clue which boxes were affected because the vaults are so "HOT", no one can even sample them yet!

Angelina concluded the meeting, saying, "Keep the games going. You're doing great!"

The radiation source could not be found in NYC, so on February 4th, they reopened NYC to all traffic once again. The world was shocked at what the city looked like after only 12 very long weeks. NYC looked like a war zone. Barricades were everywhere; vandalism happened in some of the strangest places.

It was amazing what scared and hungry people would do to access food for their loved ones and themselves. Every food or restaurant establishment that wasn't fortified like Fort Knox had not survived the last 12 weeks. The same was true for grocery stores and convenience marts. If they had food or drinks inside, that establishment was now trashed, and would need to be rebuilt from scratch. Many of the stores and restaurants had no insurance, and would just go away altogether; A moment in time, gone forever!

Some mom and pop restaurants tried to avoid vandalism by opening to feed the neighborhood. It sounded like a Win, Win for anyone there in that situation. But, as rescue workers would discover, after they ran out of food, the Mom and Pop were killed in the ensuing riots due to people thinking that they were holding out on them.

Meanwhile, Jake, Pixie, Sam, Timmy, and the couple from the concert were watching all this unfold from above. They couldn't believe what humanity had come to in such an abbreviated time. It had been only four months since Angelina's campaign had started. Their civilized country and its government were obviously not prepared for the end of the world. They all wondered what they could have done to make the world a better place, if only they all had more time. None of them had realized they would never get that chance again.

Would you change if you could? Do you want to change? It's that easy. *You just have to want to change!*

Chapter 98

When the NYC subway re-opened on February 4th, more deaths started appearing in the city. One of Angelina's scientists had set up a 100-bill packet on one of the busiest subway routes. Several hundred trains passed over this spot every day. With packed train cars of 600 to 800 people per train, that added up quickly. The 100-bill packet of money irradiated the train cars within a 150 ft. diameter. This included some people standing on the end of the platform by the mouth of the tunnel.

Over the next four weeks, 30,000 new people were reported dying every day, with no idea how they were getting dosed. The problem was that they would die away from the location where it happened, and the responders had to try to piece their lives back together without their help. Most people who knew the victims were too concerned about themselves expiring, so they rushed to the hospitals to get checked out, just to find out they were fine. Again, several of them had heart, or panic attacks, that were just as dangerous as getting dosed. This had the same effect on the people and resources of the city.

By March, the BEP was mass producing the new money in both locations at an astounding rate of $30 billion per month. They had shifted into high gear. They were printing around the clock at both locations – Hell would be here before they knew it! Angelina was now thinking maybe she should taunt the government with a message from *"Angel in a Rage"*, but decided to wait a little longer.

Now, trivial things had started popping up all over the United States. People traveling on the airplanes where Yo had placed money inside the windows, for the *Window Treatments*, got to their destination, and died.

The first responders were getting closer to discovering some of the hiding places of the money, but they were still only looking at the metal and radio waves. They were completely clueless as to how up to 16 people on a flight found death, but the other 160 survived just fine. They searched food, water, inflight phones, and sound systems. When those panned out to be safe, they looked in the aviation systems area. Again, they found nothing. Maybe, if they had the plane turned on and rolling, they might have detected the source, but no. The plane was at a dead stop, and all systems were off. Lastly, they checked the cargo hold, but that revealed nothing. Damn! It was so Frustrating! Grrrrrrrrr!

Each time they put the plane back into service, more dead people showed up. With about 50 planes infected with "Window Treatments", approximately 800 random people a day were dying in the United States.

Could *YOU* be next??!!

Archie was down to his last $50K of the new money, and called Steve for a delivery. Steve said he had just picked it up yesterday, and he could deliver it any time. Archie proposed the spot, and Steve agreed. Steve pulled up about 40 minutes later, and they transferred the money into the neon Suburban.

"Business must be pretty good, if you keep running low," Steve said.

Archie asked, "Can I get more ink, labels, and envelopes on my next money refill?"

Steve looked at Archie, and told him there wouldn't be another refill of money. "Angelina is recalling everyone home to California in two weeks. If you run out before that time, head to the shelter address."

Archie said, "I'll probably be out in 2-3 weeks."

Steve said, "I will be staying here working for Homeland Security making sure no one gets wise to the real project."

Archie asked, "Are the Admiral and kids going to be at the shelter, too?"

"The kids, yes. The Admiral will most likely be sequestered with me at Homeland Security."

Archie inquired, "Has anyone suggested putting packets in the other agency offices?"

Steve showed an evil grin, and said, "No. Would you like to try?"

Archie replied, "Yeah, I can do that!"

Steve wondered how he'd pull it off, but he could try! Angelina was right. This guy *was* a great asset to her team.

Archie had a brilliant idea! It was amazingly simplistic in its cleverness. He had gotten together with the DC parking authority. He was working with another one of his Israeli agents, who had the contract with the city parking structures for replacing all of the wooden barricade arms with new fiberglass ones. Archie had found out that the new arms were hollow inside. He asked his buddy if he could seal them for him. His buddy jumped at the offer.

Archie went to the storage unit where over 2,000 barricade arms of various lengths were being stored. He took 20 individual bills, and pushed them all the way down into the arm. This would have a kill radius of about 15 ft. Then, taking an insert pre-filled with salt water, he stuffed it into the end, blocking the end of the barricade arm shut. The end nearest the bills was salt water soluble. The outside edge was fused to the fiberglass as soon as Archie inserted it into the barricade arm.

The salt water would eat through the insert, injecting salt water into the money pit in about four days. The key was to stack them in such a way that the salt water was against the fiberglass end. Archie had nice little arrow stickers on the barricade arms that read, this end up. The rails were already sorted by size. It took him about four hours of work to accomplish his task. The fact that it would take four days for the salt water to eat through the end of the insert meant that the workers delivering and installing the arms would not be dosed.

Again, Archie was not going to be out done by Angelina's scientists. _He came to play!_

Archie called his friend, and informed him that they were ready to deliver.

"Great news! Thanks, Archie! We just got an order to replace all the barricades at the Secret Service, FBI, NSA, White House, and CIA. All of these places have steel pole and concrete placements, but once a year, they replace the arms like clockwork."

Archie just smiled and said, "Gee, no kidding. That sounds like a really expensive idea."

His buddy chuckled, "They don't call it wasteful government spending for nothing!"

Archie said, "Well, glad I could help all these agencies out."

They both laughed evilly, and said, "Goodbye!"

Chapter 99

Archie's Israeli friend got right to work, putting in work orders for the guard shacks, entry, and exit points for each agency that had requested the barricade arms to be replaced. Multiple crews went to work installing the "Deadly Barricades".

The American people would be astonished at how fast this task got accomplished in DC. No one had to get a bill passed in Congress to get it done, so all the agencies had the Deadly Barricades in place within three days! This was a near world record for Congress and the other agencies that protected them. Within a week, all types of Maryland, DC, and Virginia employees would start dying off for no reason at all.

Archie knew this would cut the staff of these agencies down quickly and most effectively, causing not only death, but confusion. A vast number of highly trained specialists, in any number of high tech fields, would quickly deplete these agencies by a loss of resources. With any luck at all, the vehicles would be irradiated as well, causing the agents' loved ones to become contaminated and die.

Again, Archie, came to play. His family in Israel had been killed, as American troops sat by watching. Instead of protecting them, the troops had laughed when his family died. Never did the US troops step in to help the Israelis when the circumstances dictated it. Archie harbored almost as much animosity toward America as Angelina and her team.

Chapter 100

Just as Archie predicted, the Deadly Barricades were having a dramatic and adverse effect on the people of Maryland, DC, and Virginia. Two weeks after they had been installed, Archie had contacted his Israeli friend. He was told that all 2,000+ barricade arms had been deployed at all the key agencies in the Maryland, DC, and Virginia area.

The leftovers were randomly placed in parking garages all around DC.

Archie flipped out on his longtime friend! "We discussed this earlier. Nothing should have been deployed anywhere except for the government agencies!"

Archie's friend said, "The crews ran out of normal barricades, and started using yours. Why, what's wrong?! Why are you sooo upset, Archie?"

Archie just said, "Bah," and hung up! "Amateurs!" Archie never did tell his friend the whole story because he didn't want it to get back to Israeli Intelligence.

Archie had to call this in to Steve, so he could warn the Admiral and the other members of the team. His next thoughts were, "How could he get out of the city without being dosed by his own scheme. His friend had really screwed the pooch on this task! Grrrrrrrrr! He truly hated incompetent people, especially the ones in his agency!"

He called Angelina next. She was amazed at his creativity, and insisted he drop all his activities, and come to the shelter at once.

She also reminded him that the neon mobile protects the POTUS from a nuclear blast, so he should be safe!

Archie thanked her for reminding him, and said, "I'll get a list of all the sites where my friend had barricades installed." He ended the phone call stating that he'd see them in a week at the shelter.

When he got off the phone, he emailed his friend, and apologized for losing his temper. He asked for a list of venues where his barricades had been installed.

Moments later, Archie received this list of offices in Maryland, DC, and Virginia:

- White House
- Secret Service
- CIA
- DEA
- FBI
- NSA
- NASA
- DC Parking Authority
- Congressional offices
- Senate offices
- Library of Congress
- ATF
- Airports
- Weigh Stations
- Toll Booths
- Draw Bridges
- HOV Ramp Lanes

Chapter 101

After Archie had left DC, the shit really did hit the fan! As predicted, Archie's "Deadly Barricades" took center stage on all the news feeds. Americans soon learned that many agencies in Maryland, DC, and Virginia were under attack. The people in power didn't know where to start looking. Devastatingly effective, these barricades had been killing off people going to, and leaving work. Most of the people were random high level executives for the President's cabinet and all the supporting agencies. Most notably, was Trent Lester. He went to his monthly meeting, and got dosed right after leaving those offices.

The next high profile case was the Vice President's wife. When she decided to go shopping, her detail refused to move the vehicle. Being the one in charge, she said that she'd walk, if necessary. Getting out of the armored limo, she asked the guard to raise the gate. She walked right under the arm, getting a full, lethal dose right outside the White House.

Her detail was there to protect her, not cater to her whims. Many high level people forget that their security details really do their jobs quite well. All they need to do is listen to their advice.

By the time Archie crossed the Tennessee border, he turned on the radio, scanning for news updates. It was noon, and there should be a lot going on in DC by now. The barricades had been active for eight days at the various locations. Each and every guard shack with one of these arms in place, was far enough away from the packet inside so that the guards would not get dosed – as long as they stayed away from the end of the barricade itself.

This was another lucky break for Archie and Angelina, since the guards and toll attendants would have been the first victims. This fact alone would rule out the toll plaza and guard shack as the crime scene!

Just then, Archie found a news network reporting that 25 to 40 percent of the Maryland, DC, and Virginia government agency offices had been hit hard with unexplained deaths similar to those that had hit: NYC, Michigan, Texas, Florida, California, and Jamaica! At this rate, DC would be out of resources, and calling Israeli Intelligence by the end of next week, if they hadn't already.

Archie stopped at a pay phone, and called his handler from Israeli Intelligence. "Agent Archie, technology section, random, sixteen, and flower. I have contacted those responsible, please advise." Archie nodded, and said, "Yeah, I can do that." He ended the call.

Archie's handler told him to remain in place, keep in contact, and continue collecting intelligence for the time being. When the timing was right, they would be contacting him.

By the time Archie had made his way out of Tennessee, he had heard on the news that they were evacuating the White House until further notice.

If they ever found out who the notorious villains were that had concocted this evil plan, they would surely kill them all, one painful piece at a time. Archie hoped this shelter was all that Angelina and Yo had said it was. They would need some serious defenses to hold off the troops.

Right at that moment, in the California shelter, Angelina was popping popcorn, and getting a red wine to watch the evening news. She had heard rumors of the evacuation of the White House, and wanted to see all the news feeds. Archie's "Deadly Barricades" was going to leave a high tech mark on the DC metro area. With luck, they would never find the issue, and would have to look for another United States Capitol City!

Wouldn't that be a Hellish task!? To move 1.4 million people to another workplace, and keep the country up and running. Just imagine all the chaos and confusion it would bring into the mix. Millions of people all over the United States would be affected by mailing address changes, and missing, incorrect data. It was the petty things that Angelina truly enjoyed in this project!

She wondered for a moment what the country would look like in: 12, 24, 36, 48, 60, and 120 months from now! Yes, she had run sample data of her project over the past year, but none of her sample runs looked anything near like the numbers she was currently seeing!

If Steve and the Admiral's data was accurate, they were now seeing some six million dead, and it was only March! Her sample data runs had predicted six million by 24 months! She was 18 months ahead of schedule! Damn! She and her people were the best!

The money they had printed in November would just now be going live all over the country, maybe the world! By June, two months, this number would grow by an order of magnitude to 60 million people! Two months after that, another magnitude, 600M people dead. Shit! That would be the current population of the United States of America. These were scary numbers, even to her!

Back at the CDC in Atlanta, all the doctors

and scientists were having a meeting to discuss all the mounds of evidence without a smoking gun! Everyone knew that the radiation of the material was extremely powerful, and yet so elusive. They started looking for things found in nature, or man-made, that had this kind of radioactivity. They only found two: raw weapons grade plutonium, or a break in the earth's crust. OK, so it was obvious that NYC did not suffer a crust breach, so it must be man-made weapons grade plutonium.

No one had ever seen anything this powerful, and lived to tell about it. Who were the first people to stumble onto this substance, and where were they from? One scientist said that he had a comrade in China that had described a form of radiation too powerful to handle. What if they had found a way to stabilize it?

The Director of the CDC contacted the President's cabinet on board Air Force One. He explained the "rumored" radiation signature, and asked if his Generals and Admirals had knowledge of this. The director of the CIA muted the video call, and said, "Mr. President, this is very high level classified intel."

The President blew up! "We have six million dead in this country! Come clean now, or I will throw your ass into Leavenworth myself!"

The CIA director only had rumors - no hard intel on China as the perpetrator of the attacks. He quickly continued, "According to our sources, the new isotope they found was so unstable, it killed 80,000 soldiers, as well as the highly skilled scientists trying to handle it during tests. They mothballed 200 tons of it! Since then, it's been buried under a high security mountain bunker."

The President's color started coming slowly back to his face. He said, "So we don't know if the 200 tons are still there?!"

"That is correct."

The President looked around the table and said, "Gentlemen, this is your task: *Find out before breakfast tomorrow!*"

The President said, "Go live in 3, 2, 1... Director, thank you for holding, and bringing this detail to us. We are currently looking into this allegation, and will be getting back to you by this time tomorrow, if not sooner. My staff will need to communicate with the diplomatic staff, and hopefully we can see if this rumor has merit. Thank you. Please keep working on this with the utmost urgency!"

The Director disconnected and addressed the meeting moderator, saying, "The President and his cabinet are considering this rumor. He instructed us to continue as if it were true! Since we do have six million dead, someone has made this into a weapon! Our task is to figure out how they weaponized it, and how they transported it without killing themselves."

Chapter 102

By the next day, Archie had almost reached California.

He turned on the news in the Suburban, and heard that the White House had been evacuated, and the main players were all on Air Force One. He called Angelina, and told her he would be coming in soon. He was about two hours out.

She smiled her grin and said, "Excellent!"

He asked if they needed any groceries.

She just laughed, and said, "You'll see when you get here!"

Archie shrugged, and said, "Ok."

Upon Archie's arrival, he parked next to the Inks4Life.net building, got out, stretched, and rang the bell. Yo answered on the intercom, saying, "May I help you, Archie?"

Archie replied with the phrase, "Have you inked the deal yet?"

Yo buzzed Archie in, and told him to give them a few minutes to get there.

Archie looked at the size of the small building, and thought he could make it from end to end in ten seconds. This was by no means a shelter capable of supporting life for years to come. He was getting verrrrry concerned with his life being in their hands. Nevertheless, he'd reserve judgement for now.

Archie opened the door, and looked inside at the small office lobby. "Good Lord!" It was worse than he first thought! He tried to get out, but the war door was quite secure. So, there he sat, waiting.

After about a minute, the other war door swung silently open, and Yo and Angelina both stood there. In unison they said, "What do you think of our five year shelter?"

Archie almost attacked them, and then noticed them grinning from ear to ear. "Ok, funny joke Americans play on Archie."

Angelina stayed in character, but Yo smiled and said, "Come on, I'll give you the tour."

Yo gave Archie his ID card, and showed him the bollard to swipe it on to access the ramp. Silently, as if it were a Swiss watch, the ramp appeared.

Archie's jaw just bounced off the floor. "You've got to be kidding me!"

Yo grinned appreciatively, knowing that Archie never gave away his thoughts. Inside the tunnel, Yo explained the ruse of the ink factory, and that if the front door opens, the ramp closes automatically as a safety precaution. Archie was impressed. All this steel and concrete moving silently, making no noise, was inconceivable! If the government raided this ink factory, they would find a dead end!

Yo asked, "Are you ready to see our little shelter yet?"

Archie was now very curious, and Yo pointed to the card reader. Archie swiped his card. Again, silent as death in space, he saw a crack of light open into a warehouse space. Archie walked slowly up the ramp, and said, "My Lord! How did you create..." and trailed off into a state of AWE!

It took him a full minute to compose himself to speak again. His eyes took in every detail as a trained spy would: wireless, networks, servers, trucks, four elevators that carried trucks, mixing stations, filling machines, palletizers, vacuum systems, and high-tech gadgets of all types! Archie then noticed the walls of the shelter and screamed, "Shit! Nuclear walls! What in the name of Hell are you people preparing for?!"

Yo turned to Archie, slapped him on the back, and said, "I think we will all be safe in this edifice!"

Archie just whistled. He knew most facilities only looked impressive on the inside, and did not reveal the secrets so easily, so there must be more than what he was seeing. He took a deep breath, and said, "Please continue the tour."

Next, Yo took him into the offices and living quarters, where he was assigned one of each. Yo showed him the voice stress analyzer, and how it worked. It was true magic! Israeli Intelligence had nothing on this technology, and they'd most likely kill for it!

Proceeding, Yo showed Archie the lobby which was a prison in disguise, just like the one he had entered through at the Inks4Life.net building. Then, Yo showed him the offloading system that the government had set up for the rail cars, and how to access any truck or trailer in the shelter.

Archie again stood there in utter amazement. He asked, "Your government installed this to sweeten the deal?! I'm lucky if I get a coffee service from mine."

Lastly, Yo asked, "Are you hungry?" They walked into an elevator. Yo explained that it worked just like elevators at a hotel, but was for trucks. They got off on level two, and walked into the cafeteria.

Angelina was there, with a nice red wine,

some grilled scallops, and a salad. Archie looked at the automated kitchen and said, "No staff cooks here? It's all computerized?"

"Delicious! All of it!" said Angelina; meaning the whole operation, not just the kitchen.

Archie got it! While Yo and Angelina got back to work, Archie looked through the stores of available food, drinks, bar, and supplies. Anything he could think of, they had it. Archie asked, "How do you locate items? From memory?"

Yo laughed, and said, "All throughout the facility there are these yellow buttons, like on a video game cabinet. Press one, and follow the prompts and lights."

Archie did so, and a disembodied voice of Nurse Chapel said, "I am always available, Archie. How may I assist you?"

"Beer," he said.

"We have 69 distinct types of beer available. Please specify, or say, let me choose."

"Let me choose." The floor lit up, and showed the pathway into a huge walk-in cooler, highlighting a fridge door, then blinking three shelves.

Archie grabbed a great international one, and said, "Thanks."

Next, the computer asked him if he would like to customize the voice to his personal choice.

He laughed, and said, "Later!"

Rejoining Yo and Angelina, he said, "You folks get high marks for technology around here."

Yo replied, "The computer will help with any question, in or out of the facility. For example," Yo tapped the yellow button, and said, "What's the status of Air Force One, and where is it exactly?"

The voice of Buck Rogers came over the speaker, and said, "Flying a holding pattern over DC to Chicago, approximately 138 souls on board, currently passing latitude and longitude at 34,000 ft."

Yo then explained, "Since the President's computer, as well as most of his staff's computers, have been breached, our computer has data that is not available to the public!"

Archie responded, "Oh My Lord! You folks are scary SOBs!"

Angelina and Yo both said, "Thank you for the kind words," and winked!

Chapter 103

While Archie was taking his ultimate tour of the shelter, the President was screaming at his people, demanding answers. The diplomatic corps had yet to get an answer from China that confirmed whether or not they were involved. Military leaders were working on plans to devastate China, if they were involved, but couldn't proceed until they had rock solid proof - which they would never receive. Several of the Seals and other special forces teams were trying to assess the feasibility of a recon strike on *The Nuclear Mountain,* as the Generals called it. It was highly fortified, and well into China's territory, which made it next to impossible to get people in and out. Correction, to get people out!

They could parachute in at night and recon the target, but getting out would be the definite problem. After the 12 sailors gave their lives at the San Francisco bank, the President wasn't going on a hunch. He needed undeniable proof before proceeding with a nuclear nation.

In Atlanta, the CDC meeting was on its second day of a four day session. The main topic was how to make radiation stable enough to plant it in public, and get away safely while making it reactive. Everyone in the room was thinking of current technologies around radioactive components. At this rate, it would take them five years to come up with a solution.

Everyone knew the only safe way to transport this material was within lead lined containers, but how could you make those containers open when you were away? One CDC member suggested a removable lid with an explosive cover, but it was shot down because no smoke or explosions had happened on any of the sites.

These people could not think outside the box. They just kept thinking on how to build a better box.

Finally, the moderator suggested that they create the world's first radioactive material that could be turned on! Their minds instantly "clicked".

A member stood up, and said, "We would need to make a substance that had all the material needed for the radiation, plus an inhibitor that would prevent the activity." He called it meltable lead. He suggested a dissolvable lead that melted away after some amount of time.

All at once, the naysayers said, "That's impossible," but the moderator stepped in and said, "Let him finish. We haven't heard of anything that's even close to this yet!"

The member thanked the chair, and continued. "The meltable lead would have to be soluble in open air, or maybe water. I don't know how to make it, but whoever did, is using it as a weapon of mass destruction."

A different member took it from there, and said, "Why not just separate the components that make the radiation, and then combine them with a pill coating instead of lead." Everyone was silent, imagining if that were possible, what horrific problems they would have!

Another member shot up out of his seat, and shouted, "We *have* created it! Bring up the lists of evidence collected at the crime scenes. Let's see what was recovered from the events."

He suggested the bank vaults, since they were the most secure facilities they had to work with. The banks were in California, and had been contaminated by radioactive activity that had made the bank vaults *HOT*. "What residue was found in the boxes and vault?"

Erika added, "They found nothing, but money in them."

"That's exactly what one should find in a vault, so we can rule it out! We need to find the safety deposit box, and have it analyzed for trace residue. Once we see what trace evidence is in that box, we can narrow the field further," the member summarized.

Dr. Erika Stone called the doctors at the naval base, and asked if they had found trace evidence in the box at the bank.

They all agreed that it had been empty; just money was in it, and that wasn't radioactive either.

Erika asked, "What about at the microscopic level?"

The doctors agreed that no one had tested for that, but they did have the equipment to examine it safely. They'd call back in a few hours...

Erika rejoined the CDC conference, and said, "Keep working on thoughts. The Navy doctors are examining the safety deposit box for trace evidence."

About three hours later, the Navy doctors called Erika back, and said, "We only found one solution that we can identify. It's the new clear coat on the money."

Erika asked, "Why do they need a clear coat on money?"

They responded, "To make the eco-green inks seal properly, and to make the money strong like Tyvek®."

"Wow, I had no idea money was that strong!"

"Only the new stuff, according to our data. The old money tears really easily compared to the new."

Erika said, "Nothing else?"

"Actually, there was something else, but we're scratching our heads on it, too. We found marks in the safety deposit box on a microscopic level that look like the steel had melted! These boxes don't melt unless it hits 2,100°F. Before you tell us it was caused by the torch, we confirmed it was the inside edge of the box nearest the concrete wall!!!"

"So," Erika recapped, "we have a safety deposit box that was 24 inches away from the torch. It melted on the inside where the money was stored, and left only trace amounts of a clear coat residue."

"Yes! You got it."

"Just more puzzle pieces," Erika sighed!

Chapter 104

Back in Maryland, DC, and Virginia, the Deadly Barricades were still destroying the multiple agencies where they had been installed. All the agencies were working with skeleton crews at all facilities, except for Homeland Security, where only three percent were affected. All the agencies were wondering why Homeland Security was not being killed off. Currently, roughly 74% of the staff of the White House, FBI, CIA, NSA, DEA, ATF, and Secret Service were dead.

Soon, there would be Peace on Earth!

With so many unexplained fatalities, many people started evacuating the Maryland, DC, and Virginia areas to avoid death. This only compounded the problem, since many toll booths in the areas were using the deadly barricades! People were panicking, and making it worse for themselves and their families. As a rule, running only works if the runner knows where the danger is going; otherwise it is possible to run straight into death!

The President's diplomatic corps finally came back with an absolute denial of involvement by China on this crime against America.

Back in California, all five scientists, Angelina, Yo, and Archie were finishing up the mixing of the four orders of inks, when a phone call came in to Yo. "Hey Toby, how's life in Texas?"

Dejectedly, Toby said, "Life here is good, but I need to inform you that Trent died two nights ago. He's part of the casualties of the DC office of the BEP."

Yo said, "Dude, we are so sorry to hear that. Are there any leads on the deaths?"

"None, except Homeland Security doesn't seem to be affected at all. All other agencies are near 80% dead. They are currently evacuating Maryland, DC, and the Virginia suburbs in attempts to save the resources, but it doesn't make any sense to run, without knowing where it is safe. I will be here in Texas for now. Trent's service is postponed until the city is safe again. I'm calling to see how the ink shipments are coming."

Yo said, "We just sealed the last crate for shipping. The trucks should be here in three days, according to Johnny and Jack. So far, none of the Secret Service drivers have met with any of the deaths."

"Great!" Toby said, "We desperately need all the cash to help with the run on the banks, since the credit card and bank failures."

Yo agreed, "Those Encryption Hackers did an enormous number on the financial systems of this country, and should be put to death when they are found!"

Toby agreed.

Yo concluded, "If there's anything we can do for you, or your team, please don't hesitate to call."

"Thanks, Yo!"

Chapter 105

Erika Stone initiated a video call with the naval base doctors and the CDC members at the meeting, and brought everyone up to speed.

The Navy doctors were astounded by the thoughts of the CDC members. They said, "The facts of the case match your description, but all we found was money and the clear coat traces."

One member said, "What if the clear coat is the inhibitor?! The *money* could be the nuclear source!"

Now, all the people said, "It's not metal, there's no way it could be reactive."

The Navy doctors injected, "Wait! Not all sources are metal!" One doctor said, "Hold please, I'll wand it." He took a Geiger counter into the lab, suited up, opened the box, and wanded the bills. Nothing! Luckily, he walked to the back of the lead box, and wanded it there. Nada! Blast! He started walking past the cart, and bumped into it, knocking it four inches.

"Oh My God!" The diamondback rattlers spit their evil warning, and the Geiger counter shot to the moon and back! Instead of clicks, he heard a solid tone! "Shit!" He closed the lid, went into the decontamination room, and hit the alarm.

The whole lab went into lockdown mode, and 20 Navy personnel were onsite within 45 seconds!

The other doctors on the video conference call said, "Shit! We found it! Gotta go!"

Shouts occurred all over the room. All in attendance were both, awestruck and thunderstruck, by the news. They would all have to wait until tomorrow for answers.

The Navy doctors were on the intercom with the doctor who was being decontaminated and treated for radiation poisoning as a precaution, in case it got through his superhero suit.

"*MOVEMENT* is the key!" He was talking so fast, the other doctors just recorded what he was babbling, not knowing how badly he had been dosed.

"Money needs to be moving to give off radiation! Geiger counter - No clicks, just one Damn, Solid Tone! If money's static - ZERO Rads! If money is moving / rubbing 100+ million Rads! *Extreme Danger!!!*"

Without another word, the Navy doctor grabbed his arm, and died right in front of them. They passed a portable X-ray unit through the airlock, and said, "Check his heart!"

The tech's face told them what they needed to know! There was none!

The three remaining Navy doctors called the President and the director of the CDC. "We found the source of the deadly radiation! It's the new money."

The President said to his staff, "Can money be radioactive?"

His staff asked, "Coins or bills?"

The doctors emphasized, "*Bills*, specifically the *new* money!"

Someone in the cabinet picked up the phone, and called Trent Lester of the BEP, just to discover he was confirmed dead two days ago. "Who's next in command? I need his mobile number now!" He was connected to Toby Lipton, and he demanded, "We have reason to believe your new bills are the reason everyone is dying. Please *STOP* all production immediately! Please contact your Secret Service liaison."

"Shit!" Toby said. "Let me make some calls! Damn! What the Hell!" Toby picked up the phone and called Jack's mobile.

When Jack picked up the call, Toby said, "I am calling in a **_Broken Press Plate_**."

Jack knew this code phrase, and put the call on speaker, telling Johnny to listen! "What's up Toby?"

"The President just called me, and said that our new money is the reason why all those people are dying. I need details! I was told to contact you. You should have something coming to you through official channels."

Jack just groaned, and said, "10-4. We'll be in touch in two hours - max."

Toby responded, "I am shutting down and evacuating both plants now. I'm in Texas, and operating from here. Stay safe!"

They disconnected, and Jack snapped his fingers! "That's why they were mailing cash out - *THEY KNEW IT WOULD KILL!!!*"

"Oh, No!" Johnny saw it, too! "Angelina and her team could be a rogue element, but who are they working with?!?"

Jack just lifted his hands, and said, "Who's left in our chain of command who isn't dead yet?"

Johnny looked up the site, and said, "Oh, My God! POTUS! All other members have died as of today!"

Jack said, "Sure, why not throw another log on the fire, Johnny?" Jack dialed the White House switchboard. He looked up the correct keyword coding, and requested, "Mr. Samuel Perkins, Jr., please."

The phone line started the beep recording, and someone said, "Perkins here. What's the issue?"

Jack replied, "Seven Swans a Swimming."

"Your name, please?"

"Jack B. Quick, for POTUS."

"Hold, please."

The cabinet answered, and said, "Thanks for getting back so quickly, Jack. It's been a long time since we have spoken."

Jack quickly explained that he was talking to his new bosses now, since his people had died as of today. He called it a bad field promotion!

The cabinet members agreed, and wished for better circumstances, but welcomed Jack to his new high-ranking staff position!

Jack introduced Johnny Five on the call, and said, "This is the information we have on the perps." Jack gave the military leaders all the data verbally over the phone, since he believed all his devices had been hacked by the same Encryption Hackers that had hit the banking system.

Next, Jack suggested they all check their systems for the same code.

The President scoffed, "That would be a huge feat!"

Jack said, "I believe a high-ranking Homeland Security techie is behind this! I would put nothing past him."

The President asked, "Do you have a name?"

"Steve Stevenson."

"I personally know Steve, and he loves this country."

"Please!" Jack begged. "Check your system now, Sir!"

POTUS waved over an IT techie on Air Force One, and requested he look at his system.

"Shit!" was the first thing out of his mouth after looking for two minutes! "Sir! Yes,

Sir! You are bugged! It says an FBI code, but Jack is right. Homeland Security passes out the codes, so they have all the codes necessary to plant evidence that it was, supposedly, the FBI."

The cabinet and the President's faces went white. If it was passed by email, the cabinet and Generals' data may well have been breached! "Good Lord, All Mighty!" the President shuddered.

The IT techie looked at the Army General's computer, and again said, "Shit!" He dialed his staff. They swarmed the conference room. Within two minutes all laptops on Air Force One had been terminated and taken offline.

About that time, Yo's phone chirped, and alerted Steve and Yo that the President's cabinet just went dark. Yo paged Angelina, and conferenced Steve in online.

Angelina began, "What's up?"

Yo said, "Air Force One just went dark."

"I think it is time," Steve said. "I just got a ping from Toby that he called Jack. He reported a *Broken Press Plate* which is an *Oh, Shit!* code for the BEP. I'd say it's time to expect company."

Angelina said, "Ok, don't panic. It will still take them days, or weeks to find it all! Steve, can you still do that thing we discussed?"

"Sure, no problem!"

"Do it! No one survives!"

Steve said, "Peter and Peggy will be pissed!"

Angelina replied, "So will 300 million other people."

"You're So Right! In 5, 4, 3, 2, 1...!"

Without warning, all of Air Force One systems BRICKED!!!

Nothing had power. All backups of backups failed, and the doors were locked. The Secret Service agents tried to override the emergency door operations, but nothing functioned. The controls in the cockpit failed, and were set on a vertical dive before they froze. Everyone on board Air Force One was pointing downward to the earth from 34,000 ft., traveling close to Mach I, straight down! They had maybe 90 seconds to do what?! Anything!

Most chose to pray, others screamed, or cried! Some just tried to figure out how to fly a plane. Nothing helped. Steve's code was brutally efficient, especially the part about pointing it nose first at the ground, increasing the speed to max, and then bricking the controls.

The pilots realized that they were just, DONE!

Moments later, the controls came back online 500 feet above the ground! This would make it look like a freak accident, not sabotage or mass murder of the government of the United States!! If you had been looking at the crash, moments before the impact, it would have looked like a lawn dart going into someone's yard!

Angelina asked, "So, who takes over the nation now?... Uncle Buck, a Former President, a Military Personality, the

Designated Survivor, a Movie Star, or Jack B. Quick?!"

Chapter 106

Once the Navy doctors had evidence that the money was the culprit of the deaths, things started moving rapidly. Several public service announcements (PSA) went on television, radio, and internet news feeds everywhere. These PSA were instructing anyone that had new money, to get rid of it. The problem was how to make people believe this was life and death related, and not just another scam to get people to hand over their cash! It also, was an issue of how to take said money to a recycling center that was equipped to handle substantial amounts of radiation. To tell people to take the money to a bank or hospital, risked death to most of them, immediately. Dropping it into a well, or sewer, would risk other calamities downstream from there.

The Navy doctors called on the last day of the CDC conference and shared their results with the horrified members. Almost anyone who would encounter the money was a goner! Navy personnel were still testing the money to see if quantities mattered. At first glance, they all agreed that it did. The more you had, the bigger the sphere of death! Their labs were testing two to ten notes, and found a range of radiation between one to five meters. They would continue testing, but they had to collect more of the worn new money.

The CDC members were now extending their conference to come up with some guidelines and useful tips on dealing with the new currency. They still did not know how devastating their enemies were at playing this game!

Erika had called Jackson, and informed him of the findings. He suggested they go back to all the known cases, and see if they could find new money in the evidence collected. She didn't recall any in NYC, the Florida water park case, Michigan State case, or the Stock Yard case in Texas.

Erika called the Michigan investigators, and quickly brought them up to speed. One snapped his fingers, and pulled up the TV footage from the sports network that covered the stadium. He fast forwarded the tape until he saw the footage in question. Someone was illegally flying a drone over the people of the stadium. Upon closer review, they saw people trying to throw stuff at it to get it down. They zoomed in, and saw to their horror, about $10,000 of cash in a claw-like grip. They estimated 100 x $100 bills!

Erika put them on hold, and called the Navy doctors. She told them what the Michigan investigators had told her.

The Navy doctors said, "Shit! 100 bills at 10 ft. above their heads would be a kill zone of nearly 150 ft.! They could mow the lawn of people, and cover the stadium in about 45 minutes. All of them would die. Damn! Someone is playing for keeps!

"They could have done that at NYC, and anywhere else, and it would be just as effective. People are going to panic, and not know where it is safe. Have we seen any evidence outside the United States?"

Erika just said, "Jamaica is all we know of…"

"The President needs to notify all the other nations - NOW!"

Erika thanked the Navy doctors, and took the Michigan people off hold. "I have really shocking news," she said. "The kill zone has a 150 ft. diameter."

"That's what we were thinking, too. Thanks for the assist," and they ended the call.

Erika went into the director's office, and broke the news to her boss, who initiated a video call with the President, but it just rang and rang; no one answered it! They both asked, in unison, "Is the network down?!"

Skeeter just then flew through the door, and said, "Quick! Turn on the news. *NOW!*"

The director fumbled with the remote, but finally got it to work.

Breaking News was on every single channel! The caption on the screen was beyond anything they would have guessed.

AIR FORCE ONE is DOWN:
all 138 Confirmed Dead!

Holy Mother of God! No one spoke.

They couldn't believe it! Erika had just spoken to them two hours ago. It seemed so surreal! So many people dead, so fast. Was this an accident, or another mass murder? Nobody had answers, just a whole lot of questions.

The main question was: Who's running the country now?

This breaking news had Americans wondering: How will we recover from this? First there was the radiation threat, and now most of the existing government has died. Who could be responsible?

By this time, Jack and Johnny had heard a commotion in the hotel, and opened the door to find mass hysteria. People in the lobby were awestruck by the events unfolding. Jack just stood still, reading the headlines, and said, "Shit!" He was not ready to be Commander in Chief yet... Not this way.

Johnny said, "Jack, let's go back to the room and figure this out."

Jack agreed, but still didn't move.

Johnny pulled at his arm, and said, "Come on, Dude."

When they got back to the room, Johnny poured both of them a stiff drink. "Here's to finding those bastards, and burying them under their own money!" They both drank, and cussed for a while.

Johnny stopped, and said, "Do we truly believe that Angelina Gear, Eduardo Yo, and Archie really did this by themselves?! I'm thinking they had help, but from whom?!"

Jack just stared at Johnny, and said, "Motive?"

"Didn't you say Angelina's family died, and Yo knew about it?"

Jack nodded, but was silent.

"How many died?"

Jack picked up his phone, and logged into his Secret Service database. It was too late to worry about data breaches now - he needed information fast! He typed the town location into the database, and pulled up a classified account from 42 years ago.

Jack read aloud, "Towns X, Y, and Z were first thought of as helping Radical Terrorists develop a nuclear weapons lab deep in the heart of China. After the nuclear strikes in Japan, China vowed never to be a victim of such a weapon, and told the President of the United States that they were working on a nuclear deterrent.

"It scared the US government so badly, they ordered the special forces to destroy any such lab, and the people associated with it. During the campaign, it was found that the three towns in question were all linked together through underground tunnels, similar to those in Vietnam. These tunnels were boobytrapped and intertwined with the three towns.

"Population of the towns were roughly 35,000 people each. The special forces teams leveled everything: men, women, children, livestock, insects, and buildings. Nothing was left of those places, but scorched earth! Then, the special forces went on a hunt to look for any remaining family members to ensure China would never think of trying this again. The only living relative of this disaster was a young orphan, by the name of Angelina Gear, in the United States."

"Shit!" Johnny breathed.

"Yes, Johnny, I think she had help, but I think *she* is in charge of the project, solely! When I got the field promotion today, my clearance level increased four levels higher than I had yesterday. Yesterday, I had no way to review these files. Now, we both know the truth, so I am not breaking any laws by reading you into this. You are now promoted to second in command."

"Thanks, Boss, but I would have liked to earn it a different way."

"I hear you loud and clear, Director Five!"

"Any idea where they are hiding?"

"None, Johnny. That is your new assignment!"

"Thanks!" Johnny grinned lopsidedly. He took out his phone, and texted IWANTOWORKWITHYOU to SEEDC, and moments later he got a set of Latitude and Longitude coordinates.

"Christ, Johnny! You think they'd leave that on?" Jack moaned.

Johnny got the coordinates, and typed them into his smart phone. "Archie's in California, at the Inks4Life.net building. Correction! The neon Suburban is!"

"Johnny, if I ever try to stop you, just give me five 5's! Go get 'em, Director Five! Keep me posted."

"Can you get a warrant for me?"

"At this point, I'll wire you some blank ones!" Jack winked!

Chapter 107

The new money was deadly! It was plastered from coast to coast in the United States. The Stock Exchange was taking a gargantuan hit. Trading stopped and resumed six times before Wall Street pulled the plug, and shut down for the day, maybe days! Overnight, banks shut their doors, and allowed only electronic payments through debit cards and online transactions. Then, it happened!

Steve initiated another data breach on the banking system, and published everyone's data to the website where all the other data was posted. If you didn't know someone's password, social security, or PIN number, all you had to do was search their name on this website. Overnight, there were 150 million cases of identity fraud. Banks and creditors locked down accounts worldwide.

This made the first Encryption Hackers' attack look like two ants fighting over a piece of cheese, compared to an all-out ant colony war. This was considered to be the World War III of the financial world. Nothing could have been worse for that moment in time.

So far, Angelina's plan has resulted in: killing the President and leaders on Air Force One, unexplained deaths continue daily in NYC and across America, radioactive money is killing millions, Americans' financial data has been released publicly, and Adult Timeouts can remove technology at will.

Her master plan continues to march forward! Angelina has the capability to completely destroy America. When will it end, if it ends, and will it ever be enough for her?

Radical Payment, indeed!!

Jack and Johnny will have their work cut out for them, as they attempt to rebuild America's government from the ground up, and catch Angelina and her team along the way. When can they help America start the much needed rebuilding process, and will other nations assist, or help destroy America? Angelina has had her Radical Payment, but will she be stopped, *Ever?!*

By the way...

Did you happen to notice that the cover of this book is covered in green and black ink? Yes, *THAT* Ink!! I wonder how long it has been...?

...Sweet Dreams!

Angelina Gear

Angelina Gear
a.k.a. Angel in a Rage

Are you wondering what will happen next?

- Who will lead America out of this Chaos?
- How do you get "ALL" of the poisoned money?
- What do you replace it with? It was legitimate, printed US Currency, after all…
- Can the money be destroyed without the radiation going airborne?
- Will those responsible be found, and punished or destroyed?
- How will America look years from now?
- Will Wall Street recover?
- What happens to the infected banks and monuments?
- How long will this radiation last?
- How many deaths are acceptable?
- Can we prevent it from happening again?
- Can we retrain people to get along?
- Can we all live in Peace and Harmony?

Come back and read –

Radical Reconstruction

by Mike Parry

Acknowledgements

I would like to say Thanks to numerous people for their support.

Beth,
Without you there would be no book.
Thank you for your patience, guidance, and support!

I love you!

My Steering Committee:
Carole M, Heidi B, Richard W, Bunny C, Norman H, Scott W, Wayne B, Anne K, and Norman S

My Publisher:
Wayne D and The Creative Short Book Writers Project

Stars and Personalities mentioned but not associated with this book:

"Papa Don't Preach" by Madonna
"Money" by Pink Floyd
"Don't Talk to Strangers" by Rick Springfield
Gene Autry
Marilyn Monroe
Nurse Chapel
Buck Rogers

Tyvek®
Dr. Pepper®
Jolt Cola®
Hot Tamales®
BMW®
Buick® – Grand National®
Chevrolet® – Suburban®
Toyota® – Prius®
Ford® – Mustang®
Vogue®
Cosmopolitan®
Grand Hyatt®

MTA New York City Transit
Statue of Liberty

AOL®
Gmail®
Yahoo®
Hotmail®
Facebook®
Twitter®
LinkedIn®
Dropbox®
Cloud services®

White House
Army – Delta
Navy – USS Intrepid, Seals
Air Force
Marines
Coast Guard
Nuclear Commission
LAX
Reagan National
Homeland Security
DEA
CIA
FBI
NSA
NASA
Antivirus Companies

Photo Credits

Front Cover modified from:
© www.istock.com/MrPants
"Deceased Person Laying on Table with Toe Tag Attached"

Back Cover modified from:
© www.istock.com/OSTILL
"Sexy woman holding gun silhouette"
Stock Photo: Posed by Model

Title Page modified from:
© www.istock.com/PandaVector
"Corpse icon in black style isolated on white background"

American Humane Association®
http://www.petliferadio.com/petdocep160.html

About the Author

Mike Parry is a resident of North Carolina, where he resides with his wife and their four-legged children. He has been in the Information and Engineering Technology fields for the past 30 years. His insight within these technologies brings a new level of compelling drama to his writing. Using current and future technologies for good and evil plot lines, he tells his stories in ways that will capture your imagination. You will be able to see the plots unfold in front of you, as well as, the Oh Shit! moments that follow. This makes his stories both believable and intriguing.

Follow us on:

Facebook.com – Radical Payment

www.inks4life.net

email us at: yoe@inks4life.net

Made in the USA
Columbia, SC
08 April 2018